A VERY ROYAL ROOMMATE

AN ENEMIES TO LOVERS SECOND CHANCE ROMANTIC COMEDY

CIDER COVE SWEET SOUTHERN ROMCOMS
BOOK 6

ELANA JOHNSON

ISBN-13: 978-1638764540

CHAPTER ONE

TAHLIA

I look in the mirror in my master suite, feeling very much like that teenage girl who finds out she's a princess. "This is as good as it gets."

The first weekend of June means freedom for me. Three glorious months of it, though I still feel the bone-weary tiredness of the end of the school year.

My hair is freshly blonde, where I've put in accents just to give my already pale hair more color and texture. Curls bob around my chin, but I won't look elegant the way Lizzie will, or stunning the way Em will.

They're getting married today. Yes, together. A joint ceremony at the Dorothy, one of Charleston's premier hotels. The past few months have been wild with ups and downs and twists and turns and changes.

I suppose that's life, but it's been crazy here at the Big House.

And it's about not to be.

Emma's already moved out, and Lizzie has most of her things packed and boxed and waiting on the back porch.

Matt's chemistry buddies, who are also Lizzie's former co-workers, are going to come move them into his townhome while they're on their honeymoon.

I leave my reflection in the mirror and flow out of the master suite in my deep blue gown, exiting to the foyer and pausing as I look through the high arches and into the living room. In my mind, I see Emma weeping there as she tells us that Aaron's grandfather's backyard—where he lives and has been renovating the house for the past many months—has to be dug up.

"New—pipes," she says with a hiccup. "There's no way we can get married there next month."

Hillary had sat on one side of her with her arm around her, and Lizzie moved from where she'd been standing on the other side of the coffee table. She smashed herself in between Ryanne and Emma—much to Ry's displeasure—and hugged her tightly too.

"What do you need?" she'd asked.

I see myself reach out and pat Emma's leg, my voice almost a ghost as I say, "Whatever we can do, we will."

"We have the orchards," Hillary says.

"*You* got married in those orchards." Emma gives Hillary a grateful look, but shakes her head. "Everything is booked. You have to book the good venues *so* far out."

"What about here at the Big House?" I ask, though I can't even imagine what that'll take to pull off. I'm not a wedding planner by any stretch of the imagination.

Emma shakes her head. "No, Tahlia. It's too close to finals for you. I can't ask you to do that."

I'd nodded, mostly relieved, then feeling guilty about being relieved.

Now, standing in my foyer, I'm that same yo-yo of emotions I've been since Emma and Aaron got engaged in early November. Happy—desperate—glad for them—worried about my bank account—celebrating as they shop for a dress, taste cake, and book bands.

Then crying in the shower so no one can hear.

And now I stand ready to leave the Big House by myself. I'll meet up with the others at the Dorothy, where Emma will walk down the aisle first, with Lizzie behind her.

"So you'll get married with me." Lizzie had beamed with the words, and her selfless suggestion carries enough energy to propel me out of the house. On the way there, I repeat the same mantra I've said at least five hundred times in the past six months.

"It's going to be fine." Check my mirror. Flip on my blinker. "It's a few hours, and you'll know a lot of people there."

Additional words flow through my mind, but I don't acknowledge them. I don't have to dance, though the ballroom in the Dorothy is made for such things. I don't even need to stay much past the ceremony and the dinner.

At the same time, I don't want to miss a moment of this dual wedding.

So I won't be leaving early, and, "It's going to be fine. It's a few hours, and I *want* to be there. These are my friends, and they're not abandoning me."

They're moving on, and moving on is what humans are meant to do.

Not only that, but Donald has confirmed that he and his still-nameless client will be arriving next weekend.

I'm going to be able to keep up with the maintenance on the Big House, and I've lived with five other women before. I can handle two proper men who each have their own floor.

Before I know it, I'm parking at the Dorothy, and walking in with other fabulously dressed people. Claudia rises from a couch just inside the door and links her arm through mine with the words, "Wow-wee-wow, T. This dress is Bonanza Blue and looks amazing on you."

I relax at her side, because Claudia is glamorous and always knows exactly what to say to put me at ease. I grin at her, and she smiles and leads me through the foyer and down a hall, away from where the other guests are being directed.

"They're down here." Claudia brushes her own curled hair out of her face. "We've been waiting for you."

"I'm not late, am I?"

"No," Claudia says with a wave of her hand. "Not really. Becks and I were just early, because I was worried about traffic. Hill just got here, and we haven't seen Ry yet."

"I bet she's freaking out about her dress." I give Claudia a raised eyebrow, and she doesn't argue.

"She's seven months pregnant," Claudia says instead. "And no dress is going to conceal that."

"I don't know why she even wants to. They've been so ridiculously excited about the pregnancy."

"And it's been so easy," Claudia says. Her phone chimes, and I have no idea where she's stashed that thing. She wears a deeper, darker shade of blue for her bridesmaid's gown, and hers has sequins—of course—and looks like it's been sewn onto her skin.

She turns down another short hallway and then pushes through ultra-tall double-wide doors. "Here we are," she says, stepping back to let me enter first.

The bridal suite is blindingly white everywhere. The summer sunshine streams in through walls and walls of windows, and I pause on the threshold of the room to take it all in.

"I want to get married here," I say.

Lizzie turns to look at me, and her face lights up. "Tahlia's here."

Emma comes around a dressing screen, fiddling with the glittery belt around her waist. "Tahlia's—oh, Tahlia's here." She rushes toward me, and because she's not wearing her shoes yet, she can move quite fast.

"You look beautiful," I say as we embrace. She's opted for a ballgown with layers of uneven tulle that fall in carefully designed layers from her waist to the ground.

"This dress is the real showstopper," Em says as she steps back. "I mean, holy hydrangeas, Tahlia. You look *amazing*."

I smile at her and cock a hip in my own gown. It's not as fabulous as Emma's ballgown, nor Lizzie's mermaid gown, but it fits me well, and it's well-suited to my personality.

Hillary steps into my arms and says, "She's right. You look fabulous."

"No one is fixing me up with anyone," I say. "I don't need you to fill my dance card or anything."

Hillary pulls back, her auburn hair shining in all the

bright light. She too wears blue, and she's done her makeup to match, of course. Subtle hints of eyeshadow and liner, with a pale pink lip that only draws my eyes back to hers.

Her dress is lighter than mine, but not quite sky-blue, and it seems to be made of wispy, cottony clouds that have been dipped in the ocean, caught the deep blue sea, and been hung to dry.

It's a fit and flare—like mine—but mine is satin and lace while Hillary's is feathers and gauze.

I love that we have a range of blues, and that Lizzie and Emma both love the color enough to use it in their weddings.

"All right," Ryanne says in her grumpy-cat voice. "I'm here, and I didn't fall down. Go find Liam and Beckett."

I turn toward the still-open doors to see Elliott kissing his wife, and then Ryanne faces us in her version of the perfect blue bridesmaid dress while he waves to us all and then turns his guide dog around to go back the way he came.

"They're in the groom's room," Hillary calls after him. She moves to the doorway and adds, "To your left, El. The next hallway on your right. It's the only door there."

"Thank you," he calls, and then Hillary brings both doors closed. She leans against them and smiles around at all of us.

"I swear, he thinks I can't go anywhere by myself," Ryanne says.

"I think it's adorable," Hillary says. "He takes good care of you, Ry."

I nod even as I hug her. "He is amazing," I say. "And so are you. Your dress is stunning." Her baby bump keeps us apart, and as she steps back, I rest my palm against it. "How's the baby?"

"He's grumpy today."

"So like his momma, then," Claudia says as she eases into a Ry-hug too.

"I'm not grumpy," Ry says. "It's just so *hot* outside." She falls back and then sucks in the biggest breath ever. She makes a big fuss over Lizzie's dress, and then Emma's, though we've all seen them both. But if you want a big reaction, Ry's your girl, and I do love that about her.

Two of my best friends marrying their perfect matches in one gorgeous ceremony. It should be the stuff of fairy tales—and it is, for them. For me, it's a bittersweet reminder that after tonight, I'll officially be the only one left in the Big House.

Just for a week, I remind myself, the *It's fine*, immediately following.

With all of us there, we help Lizzie put on her veil, as it's a Whole Thing that pulls behind her for fifteen feet. She'll go second down the aisle to the altar, and when she's ready, she stays by the door, her bouquet clutched in her hands.

I turn my attention to Emma, who's had Hillary braid her hair into a crown. Now, we all place tiny, delicate flowers into the plaits until she's a queen and completely ready for her groom.

I meet her eyes, my smile big and bright as I nod. "You're ready."

"I'm ready?" Emma's voice cracks, and Claudia swoops in.

"No crying," she says. "Em, you promised me."

Emma shakes her head. "No crying."

The problem is, Em cries about everything. Happy things. Sad things. Frustrating things. Amazing things. All things.

"Come on, ladies," Hillary says. "It's our time to shine." She stands in front of Lizzie, who hasn't moved a muscle. Her father should be waiting in the hall, and since Emma doesn't have her dad in her life, she's opted for her grandmother to walk her down the aisle.

I love my friends and the way we've all managed to find each other, find the people who care about us, and not worry about what anyone else thinks.

"I want to be on the end," Ry says, and I step to her right side. Claudia joins me, with Hillary on the other end. The four of us will walk down the aisle first, the entire wedding party for the brides. Aaron said his brother doesn't care to walk down the aisle, and Matt's sister is already married and doesn't need to be in the spotlight all the time.

That leaves it for the four of us and the brides, and my heart bobs around in my chest as we walk down the hall. Thankfully, Claudia seems to have gotten all the memos, and she knows to take us to Door B—"B for bride," she says—where we wait for the wedding planner to open it.

It only takes a few minutes, and then the doors open, seemingly on their own. Golden light fills this room, with its marble floors and pillars with the inlaid metallics that surely influence the sunlight coming into the ballroom.

The space is one enormous round, with a huge domed top that steals my breath. I manage to take a step when my girlfriends do, and the crowd rises to their feet when we start down the aisle.

Aaron stands there, looking stunning and dapper in his jet-black tuxedo—with a black leather tool belt under his jacket and around his waist.

"What's he got in that thing?" Claudia murmurs, but I don't answer. I have no idea what Aaron has equipped his tool belt with, because it looks empty to me.

Matt steps forward, and I grin at him too. He's also wearing an all-black suit, with a shockingly white jacket with huge lapels and a very chemist-lab-coat pocket on the right side.

"Mm, I approve," Claudia says.

"They both look great," Ry says.

We reach the end of the aisle, where I hug Matt first, and then Aaron, and I follow my friends to the first row, where Chanel has saved a seat for me with her husband and daughter.

I give her a side-squeeze and a smile, glad I have a place here.

The string quartet transitions to Pachelbel's Canon, and everyone ooh's as Emma appears at the entrance, her grandmother beaming beside her. Grams wears a perfectly Southern hat in pale blue on her head, perched just like a bird's nest. It seems like Emma walks her down the aisle more than the other way around, but they both shine with pure radiance.

Emma reaches Aaron, who says right out loud, "You're gorgeous," and kisses her cheek. They link arms, and Claudia guides Grams over to her side of the first row.

The music shifts again, and Lizzie appears. Her blonde

hair cascades in soft waves over her shoulders, and her dress—a stunning off-the-shoulder mermaid that showcases her curves perfectly—makes several guests audibly gasp. Matt stands at the altar, looking at her like she's the only person in the room.

I blink back tears. These are happy tears, and I don't need a mantra to feel it and know it. My friends found their people. That's worth celebrating.

The ceremony blurs by in a haze of vows and rings and perfect kisses. I cheer with everyone as Aaron dips Emma low to seal their I-do with a kiss, and then wipe my eyes when Lizzie and Matt kiss in a more subtle way.

The crowd moves on to dinner, where I'm seated with Claudia and Beckett, Hillary and Liam, Ryanne and Elliott, and Grams. I chit and chat, keeping my smile fixed on my face, but there's an empty ache in my chest that won't go away. I love these women fiercely—my college roommates, my found family, my support system through every up and down of the past decade. And now they're all paired off, moving forward with their lives, while I'm still… me.

Tahlia Tomlinson, middle school art teacher, owner of a too-big house, perpetually covered in some form of glitter and paint, or flour and chocolate.

There's dancing. A cake cutting. Bouquet tossing—which I'm conveniently in the restroom for. Through it all, I maintain my smile, even as the evening wears on and my face begins to ache from the effort.

Finally, I hold a two-foot sparkler in each hand and stand with dozens and dozens of other guests as the newly-weds, now changed into less formal clothes, come out of the Dorothy. I yell and scream, congratulating my friends as they get into a limousine and drive away.

Others turn toward each other, hugging and smiling, the energy falling fast now that the subjects of our celebration are gone. I don't have anyone, and I stand there in the darkness, wondering if anyone would notice if I simply... melted into it.

———

THE DRIVE back to Cider Cove is quiet, just me and my thoughts and the occasional flash of headlights from passing cars. The June night is thick with humidity, pressing against my skin even through the car's air conditioning.

I turn down the familiar lane to the Big House, the road as familiar to me as breathing. The moon is high and full, casting silver light across the front lawn and making the white columns of the porch glow like ghostly sentinels.

Still in the road, I slow to a stop, squinting at the house, knowing immediately that something isn't right. There's a light on in one of the second-floor windows—a window that should be dark because Emma moved out last week.

My heart rate kicks up a notch. Did I leave a light on? No, I'm obsessive about turning everything off before I leave—and I haven't been up to the second floor since I went through it after the cleaning service came five days ago.

I blink, my eyes moving to the front of the house, where I was going to park. Nothing looks amiss there, so I park and sit for a moment, debating my options. Call the police? Go in and confront whoever it is? Drive back to the Dorothy and pay an astronomical amount for a room?

"Get it together, Tahlia," I whisper, reaching into my purse for the pepper spray I keep on my keychain. "This is your house."

I slip off my heels, grab my phone, and quietly make my way up the front porch steps. The key turns silently in the lock, and I step into the foyer, listening intently.

There's movement upstairs. Footsteps. And...is that humming?

What kind of burglar hums while robbing a place?

I tighten my grip on the pepper spray and creep toward the staircase, wincing as a floorboard in the living room creaks beneath my bare feet. The humming stops abruptly.

"Hello?" a male voice calls down. "Is someone there?"

The voice is smooth, cultured, with just a hint of an accent I can't quite place. European, maybe? Definitely not local.

Before I can respond, footsteps approach the top of the stairs, and a figure appears.

In the dim light of the bedroom light he's turned on upstairs, I make out broad shoulders, tousled dark hair, and a strong jaw. He's wearing what looks like expensive loungewear—dark pants and a fitted T-shirt that hints at a well-maintained physique.

For a split second, I'm too stunned by his appearance to remember I'm supposed to be terrified.

Then reality crashes back, and I raise my pepper spray, finger on the trigger.

"Don't move!" I shout, my voice embarrassingly shaky. "I've already called the police, and they're on their way."

The man freezes, save for his hands lifting in surrender. "Easy, there." He for-sure has an accent, but I still can't identify where it's from. He takes a step down the staircase. "I'm not—"

I mirror his forward movement by going backward, out of his sight. My hand shakes, and I've never sprayed pepper spray before. I don't even know if it'll work. He probably thought this house was abandoned, though that makes no sense.

He keeps coming, and I'm over by the arched entry when he reaches the bottom of the steps. "Don't come closer to me," I say.

A flicker of amusement crosses his face, quickly replaced by concern. "Tahlia? It's me, Callan Irwin."

I blink, pepper spray still aimed at his face, though he's too far away for me to incapacitate him now. *Callan Irwin.* That name strikes a gong in my memory, and it's beautiful music in the beginning, and then the sound goes dissonant.

"There was a change of plans," he explains slowly, keeping his hands visible as he does the unspeakable—he comes closer. "Donald sent an email this morning. When we didn't hear back, he called and left a message explaining we'd be arriving tonight instead."

I haven't checked my email or voicemail all day. "How did you get in?"

"The key was under the fake rock in the back parking area, exactly where you told Donald it would be." He actually hooks his thumb over his shoulder, which seems too casual of a movement for someone as sophisticated as him.

My emergency key. Of course. I'd told Donald about it in one of our exchanges, in case there were any issues with the move-in.

"What's your name again?" I ask. "And where's Donald?" Not that I can confirm anything by meeting him. We've never met in person, nor have we exchanged pictures. "You're not supposed to be here for another week."

As the initial surge of adrenaline fades, embarrassment floods in to take its place. I lower the pepper spray as Callan reaches to snap on a lamp.

Light floods the living room, and that alone would stun me for a second. Callan's good looks do it for a lot longer than that. He's clean-shaven and simply gorgeous with the light in his eyes now. His hair makes me want to become a stylist, just so I can drag my fingers through it.

The man works out, and all worries about my mystery tenant being a seventy-year-old hermit working on his boring European memoir vanishes.

I can't get a proper breath, especially when Callan smiles. "We did email and call," he says.

"I was at a double wedding all day," I say, surprised my voice works at all.

He runs his hand through that hair in a completely unfair move. If he knew what that did to females, he wouldn't do it.

There's something familiar about that smile, about the way his eyes crinkle at the corners, about his nervous hair-pushing gesture. Something that tugs at a distant memory I can't quite grasp.

"Have we...?" I start, then shake my head. "Never

mind. I should probably put this away before I accidentally blind you." I tuck the pepper spray back into my purse.

"Probably wise." Callan moves closer, showing off his striking blue-gray eyes. "It's nice to finally be here, Tahlia. I've been waiting a long time."

I frown. "Donald said—"

Callan reaches the end of the couch, and he's only two paces from me when I gasp. I know this man. I know those eyes. I know this name.

He emerges from the depths of my memory like a ghost rising from another world, another life.

"Cal?" I whisper, the nickname falling from my lips before I can stop it.

His smile falters for just a moment, then returns brighter than before. In the next moment, it also falls into something far more sad, more anxious.

Yeah, he should be worried.

He has some nerve showing up here. How did he even find me?

He ducks his head, and I tell myself it's *not* the most adorable thing in the world. Maybe twenty years ago, it was. *Maybe.*

Then he lifts his eyes to mine, where they hook and don't let go. In fact, Callan Irwin has never really let me go. Especially when he says, "Hello, Tally," in that super-smooth, ultra-sexy, perfectly recognizable voice. "It's been a long time."

CHAPTER TWO

CALLAN

I can't believe I'm standing here, in South Carolina, with the gorgeous Tahlia Tomlinson in front of me.

Finally, I think, so many stars filling my bloodstream. They fizz and sparkle and foam, making my whole body tingly.

Unfortunately, Tahlia wears a look of complete distaste, colored by pure shock. My carefully laid plans of the past nine months crumble before me. Faced with her, I have no idea what to say though I've practiced and practiced for this moment.

I've planned what I'd wear, and where I'd stand in her house—the Big House, she calls it. I've studied the land, the house, where the parking is. Google Maps is an amazing thing, after all.

I can't even tell you how many hours of sleep I've lost as I've stood at the table in my study, the blueprints of this house spread before me.

Now that I'm here, face-to-face with the stunning

woman my teenage best friend has become, my mind blanks.

Gone are the speeches—and I've delivered plenty of stupid speeches.

Gone are the witty barbs I'd rehearsed with Donald.

Gone are all my defenses.

"What are you doing here?" she gasps out, one hand pressed to the middle of her chest. She wears the sexiest dress I've ever seen, and I've been to parties and dinners with princesses and duchesses. They're nothing compared to Tally in that blue gown. I close my eyes to imprint the memory there, almost overjoyed to have this new image of her.

"Things didn't end the way I wanted them to the last time we were together," I say simply.

Tally falls back another step, fire entering her expression. She cocks one curvy hip, which nearly sends me toppling to the ground as she weakens me. I reach out and grip the back of the couch.

"You left in the middle of the night," she says. "The last time we were together." She scoffs, holds my gaze with her fierce glare as she turns on her heel, and marches across the tiled foyer. "It's late, and I'm tired. You're a week early."

"Tally." I take a few steps to fill the doorway as she opens the door to her master suite.

"We'll talk in the morning." She turns back to me in her open doorway, and we face off there, the innocent foyer between us. "Or maybe we won't. Then *you'll* see what it's like to wake up and have the person you're waiting to talk to gone."

She snaps her fingers, and I flinch. "Poof. Disappeared. Vanished."

"Tal—"

She backs up and slams the door, effectively silencing me. I sigh and hang my head again. "Well, that didn't go so well," I mutter to myself.

Honestly, what did I expect? Tahlia Tomlinson to open her arms and welcome me back into her life without a single explanation?

I have explanations, but some of them I can't say. Some of them I don't want to. Nothing was ever good enough for Tahlia, because I know I've hurt her.

I've never forgotten her, and I've always felt terrible about the way our friendship ended. I scoff at myself and head back to the second floor. "Friendship, right," I say as I climb the steps in this gorgeous Southern plantation house.

Both Tally and I know we were *way* more than friends when I "poof. Disappeared. Vanished," on her. That's what happens when you tell someone you love them.

I groan as I roll my neck, going past the first two bedrooms to the last one at the end of the hall. It's bigger by twenty square feet, and it has the most comfortable bed.

I flop down on that bed and stare up to the ceiling. When I first returned to Notavella to take my role as the Special Envoy of the Crown, I never spoke of Tahlia. Not a single person besides the two of us knows what we were to each other—and that poses a huge problem for me.

See, Don goes everywhere with me, and he's not a stupid man. In fact, Donald Hastings is the one and only person my mother trusts to do this "ridiculous experiment" with me, and I'm quite fond of him too. I certainly don't want to lie to him.

He's known since the get-go that I have ulterior motives for this...sabbatical to the United States. He's never asked what they are, but the moment Tally and I get in the same room, Donald will see and feel the fireworks.

Because, oh, the sparks between us...hot. Instant. Powerful.

"She slammed the door in your face," I whisper to myself. After all, I don't know how sound-proof this old house is, and this bedroom sits directly above Tally's master suite. "Perhaps she doesn't feel those sparks the same way you do."

Perhaps, I grant to myself, and the thought makes my eyes sigh closed in a combination of disappointment and annoyance. I know how to hide these emotions from my parents and my older brother. I have no idea how I'm going to keep them from Don.

There will be so many questions, and now that we're not under the protection of the Vellation palace...he's going to want answers.

Tally wants them too.

I sigh, wondering how in the world I can answer her question. *What are you doing here?*

I can't speak the truth—I've never forgotten her, and we have unfinished business.

But if I don't, I don't think she'll let me stay in her house for longer than this one night.

Perhaps I don't want morning to come after all.

Perhaps, I agree with myself.

MORNING ARRIVES, as it always does, and I go through my normal AM routines. Shower, shave, scrub my teeth, dress in slacks and a white shirt. I have no meetings this morning, so I leave the tie hanging in the closet, and then I face the closed door of the bedroom.

"Can't stay here," I tell myself, and it's not the first time I've given myself this pep talk.

I leave the bedroom and take the stairs down to the first floor slowly, one hand skimming the pristine dark wood banister. The Big House is quiet. Not silent, like the palace at night with its marble corridors and servants who speak in "Yes, sir," and "Right this way, sir."

Oh, how I hate the word "sir."

Worse is "your majesty."

And don't get me started on "his highness."

If I hear that one more time... Thankfully, here in Cider Cove, I won't.

The kitchen is quiet, which I should be used to, but this is a different kind of quiet. The kind that hums with memory and stillness and something else I can't quite name.

Maybe it's hope. Maybe it's dread.

My stomach tightens at the emptiness of the room. I'm not sure what I expected—Tahlia in another ballgown the exact crimson of my country's flag, her hair swept up in a messy bun, flour on her cheek as if she's stepped out of one of my daydreams?

Instead, the kitchen is empty.

Except for the tortoise.

He's a foot across if he's an inch, and I can't move. The tortoise with a faint trail of strawberry across its beak sits in the middle of the kitchen floor like a forgotten sculpture from a modern art exhibit. It doesn't move. Just stares at me with centuries-old judgment and the energy of someone who's witnessed empires fall.

"Good morning," I say, because I was raised properly, and because this reptile might very well be Tally's first line of defense.

It does not respond.

It does not blink.

I think it might be breathing, but how can one truly know through the shell?

I take a slow step around it. The creature's eyes track me like a security camera in a museum. I nod respectfully and skirt the perimeter of the room. If this is some kind of ancient guardian or enchanted roommate, I'd rather not trigger a curse.

I open the fridge, find the orange juice Don put there last night, and pour a glass. The tortoise shifts—barely— and now it's facing me, its beady gaze unrelenting.

"I'll leave the lettuce untouched, Your Majesty."

It exhales through its nostrils like a tired librarian.

Tally appears in the doorway then, and suddenly the air leaves the room. She's wearing leggings and an over- sized T-shirt that says *Support A Local Artist* in glittery letters. Her hair is twisted up with a pencil—an actual pencil—and she's barefoot, her toenails painted a soft peach.

She looks exactly like herself, and nothing like the girl I

left behind. A woman now. One who could break me with a look—and did last night.

"Morning," I say, too casual, too light.

Her eyes narrow slightly. "You're still here."

"I live here now." I lift my juice in salute. "Or so I was told by your lease agreement, which I read quite thoroughly."

Her lips twitch, but she doesn't smile. She doesn't move either.

The tortoise takes a single step forward. I swear I hear the echo of doom.

Tally follows my gaze. "I see you've met Shellvador Dalí."

"That's...yes. We met."

"He's got a surrealist soul." She crosses to the stove. "Don't get on his bad side. He's chewed through better men."

"I believe you," I say, watching as she opens the oven and the scent of cinnamon and sugar wraps around me like a memory. Sweet, warm, unforgettable.

Like her.

Tally pulls out a tray of golden spirals, her movements efficient, practiced. She sets them on the stovetop and turns toward me, arms crossed now.

"So, Callan," she says, her voice as cool and sharp as the edge of a paper cut. "Are you going to explain why you're really here?"

I lift my juice to my lips, having dodged far harder and harsher questions than this. I've never wanted to tell the truth more earnestly than I do right now. But honestly, my reappearance in America—in Tally's life—has already shocked us both.

"I needed a change of scenery," I say with perfect neutrality. Mother would be so proud. "Somewhere quiet. Peaceful. Where one can walk into a kitchen and find a giant tortoise."

She doesn't laugh, but snorts. "He's not a giant tortoise. He's a regular pet-shop-tortoise."

"Yes, I see that."

She eyes me. "You could've gone anywhere."

"I wanted to come here."

"Why?"

I hesitate, because the truth is far too messy to deliver over cinnamon rolls and citrus.

Because I've never stopped thinking about you.

Because I watched your life unfold from a distance and realized I wanted to be in it again.

Because you're the only person who ever saw me without the title, without the pressure, without the expectations.

But I can't say any of that.

So I go with, "Because I remembered the fountain."

Her brow furrows. "What fountain?"

"In your back garden. You used to pretend it was a wishing well. You said if you made a wish and threw in a gumball, it'd come true."

Her arms drop slightly, and the air whooshes right out of her lungs. She looks at me with pure vulnerability, then seems to realize it and stitches it all back together. "I don't know what you mean."

I keep my distance, but I want to run to her and

remind her of everything we shared. "Yes," I insist. "You told me you used to come here in the summers and throw gumballs in your aunt's fountain."

"My aunt's?" She echoes my accent, and a very strong urge to leave the room races through me. So I say *ah-nts* instead of those pesky little creatures who invade picnics.

It's not a crime. It does, however, clue her in to where I've been living.

Perhaps.

"You don't remember?" I ask.

She brushes frosting over her baked goods. "I haven't thought about that fountain in years. Aunt Fern had it removed years ago."

"That's too bad," I say softly. "I wish I could've seen it first. I've been thinking about it a lot."

It. I nearly scoff but manage to keep it in.

I've been thinking about *her*.

The silence that follows is thick, stretched tight between us like an old swing set chain. And then she blinks, shaking herself free.

"Well," she says briskly. "Wishes don't always work out the way we want."

"Perhaps not," I say and finish my juice. My stomach just feels like acid now, and I'm sure it won't be the only thing I regret today. "But sometimes they still bring you where you're meant to be."

She exhales, and for a moment, I think she might soften. But then she motions toward the cinnamon rolls. "Take one and go. I have to deliver the rest."

"To whom?"

She hesitates, eyeing me like I'm still the burglar in her

house she wants to get rid of. "There's an old man who lives behind us. Me." She takes a quick breath. "He's eighty-seven and thinks I'm his granddaughter."

I grin. "I can't help but feel like I'm being set up." Is this a test to see if I'll eat an elderly man's breakfast?

"Only if you're allergic to raisins."

I take a cinnamon roll anyway and bite into it. It's warm and gooey and perfect.

"Still the best baker I know," I say, reaching for a paper towel and dabbing at my mouth.

Tally watches me intently, her eyes actually narrowing. I quickly throw the paper towel down.

"Flattery's not going to work," she says. "I never baked for you when we—before." Her face turns a delicious shade of pink I'd like to see over and over again.

"I wasn't trying to flatter you," I say. "I speak the truth."

She opens a Tupperware container and starts transferring the rolls from the pan to it. "You're going to need to tell me the truth eventually."

"I will."

"When?"

I pause. "When I know you won't slam the door in my face."

Her hands still, the cinnamon roll halfway to the container. "Then you might be waiting a while."

I nod, though my heart twinges in my chest. "I've developed quite the sense of patience."

She looks up, and our eyes lock again. That same magnetic pull I felt last night tugs at my spine. She breaks the moment with a sigh and turns away. "Come on," she says, grabbing the container. "If you're going to live here, you might as well meet Mr. Beasley. He hates everyone under forty and thinks Elvis faked his death."

"Perfect," I say and follow her to the back door. "We'll get along splendidly."

She snorts, and it's the closest I've heard her come to laughing. As she opens the door, sunlight spills in—bright, golden, and relentless. I blink against it, stepping out onto the deck beside her.

"Are you going to church?" she asks.

I frown. "No. Why?"

"You're wearing church clothes." She shoots me a look out of the corner of her eye, then moves down the steps. "In the summer heat. You're going to melt."

I've lived the past twenty years being uncomfortable. A little heat isn't going to touch that. "I'm—"

"Good morning, sir," Don says as he rises from the sleek black rental we'll have during our time here in the South.

"Sir?" Tally echoes.

I glare at Don, but it doesn't stop him from straightening his tie and fancy sweater vest—talk about being overdressed for a quiet Sunday in our new home—and opening the back door of the town car.

A man rises from the back seat—one on each side. Honestly, I'm surprised the second man had the wherewithal to open his own door. But he did, and the pair of personal security men step out, button their jackets, and face me as a single unit.

For the love of the crown.

Tally turns to me, confusion dawning in her eyes. "Don? Is that Donald?"

"Yes," I say tersely as my personal assistant starts toward us, his meticulously shiny shoes crunching over the gravel. The security detail comes with him, and all the oxygen in the air gets sucked right out of the sky.

"Why does your assistant have a security team?" Tally asks.

I open my mouth, but I have no idea what to say. What I know: There's no way I'm keeping my royal status a secret for very long. Heck, she could type in my name to her Google search and know ninety percent of my public life in less than point-two seconds.

And just like that, the very private door I've been hoping, praying, and planning to reopen between us slams shut all over again.

Acting quickly, with three men advancing toward me, I take a step and move in front of Tally, turning my back on them. Our eyes meet, and I ask, "Could you make me a simple promise?"

She stiffens, her eyes flicking past me—toward the suits —and back again. They're hard, guarded, and I hate the way she looks at me. "What is going on? Are they all going to live here?"

Unfortunately, I think.

"I'll tell you everything," I say. "I swear. But not here, not right this second."

She glares, and I'm certain she'd pop that curvy hip and fold those arms if she wasn't carrying the cinnamon rolls.

The crunching of their footsteps come closer and

closer. "Don't take everything you hear at face value," I say quickly, dropping my voice to something just shy of a whisper.

She says nothing, but her eyes don't leave mine.

"And I'd love it if you could promise me—don't look anything up online until I can tell you everything from my own mouth."

She doesn't respond. Her eyes flick to Don, to the guards, then back to me. There's fire behind them. Uncertainty. Hurt.

I take a breath. Step closer. Flutter my fingers against hers. She sucks in a breath, and I lean closer. Don's going to say something at any moment.

Your Highness. Majesty. Sir.

They all echo through my head as I whisper, "Tally, please."

CHAPTER THREE

TAHLIA

I can't believe this man in front of me. He's demanding promises? How does he know I haven't *already* looked him up online?

I have. Rather, I did years ago after he ghosted me literally overnight. Maybe a time or two—fine, maybe fifteen or sixteen times—since too. In college. Every time I feel so lonely, I'm sure the ground will open up and swallow me whole, or the wind will blow fiercely enough to push me across the ocean.

"Sirrrr—*Mister* Kingsley, I need a few moments of your time." The very proper, very foreign, gentleman settles only a few feet from Callan.

Whose last name is not Kingsley.

Cal sighs like a horse who's displeased that his stablemate got a treat and he didn't, his lips flapping and everything. He turns to his assistant, a man I've only corresponded with via email and text. "Yes, in a little bit," he says. "Have you met Tahlia Tomlinson? It's her house we're invading."

"Renting," I say. "You are paying rent." And trust me, that's the only reason I stitch a smile on my face and step to Cal's side to shake Donald's hand. "We haven't met in person, but I feel like I know a lot about you."

"Likewise," Donald said, his smile polite and reserved, just as I imagined it would be. "It's wonderful to meet you in person Tahlia."

A slick sheen of sweat decorates his forehead, because it's June in South Carolina, and he's wearing a sweater vest over a long-sleeved white shirt. The vest is gray, and cabled, and it matches the color of his tie, which also has green and blue thread stitched throughout it, and I swear it sparkles in the Southern sun.

He wears a pair of pressed brown slacks and the shiniest pair of wingtips I've ever seen, and I'm starting to feel like I've stumbled onto some strange science fiction movie set.

One can dream, as my aunt used to say, because that might be better than the reality I'm currently living.

"Have you guys settled in?" I ask, refusing to look at Cal. "I know Callan—I mean, *Mister Kingsley*—was here last night."

At my side, Cal doesn't move a muscle. He's always had great self-control, a fact I've spent too much time crying over, actually. After all, who can be best friends with someone, then vanish into thin air without a call, a text, a social media message, nothing?

Someone with great self-control. That, I'd reasoned, or someone who'd gone on the run. Or entered Witness Protection.

Funny, Cal doesn't seem to have done any of those things.

"This is Ajax," Donald says, indicating the first enormous man on my right. "And Titan."

"Wow," I say. "Are those real names?" I grin at both of them and nod, because it doesn't look like the security detail are hand-shakers. And huggers? *Forgeddaboudit.*

I laugh internally at my own mafia joke, but then a thread of panic starts to push through me. Are these guys mob bosses? In my quiet little suburb in Charleston?

My eyes flit back to Donald, and then over to Cal. "We, uh, were—"

"We're taking breakfast to a neighbor," Cal says, gently putting his hand on the back of my elbow. "I'll stop by after we're back."

"Yes, si—sss, that would be great," Donald says.

I narrow my eyes at him but let Cal prod me past the three of them. I can only imagine what they're thinking of me. You see, I'm wearing light blue leggings and an oversized T-shirt that probably has paint splatter on it.

Hey, it could be blood, I think as the summer sun continues to beat relentlessly down on me.

I cross the immaculately graveled parking area in the back and duck down a path that leads through the trees. I put a bench out here a couple of summers ago, and I love to bring my iced tea outside, sit in the shade, and read.

I glance to the side, almost checking to see if Cal is behind me. Of course he is, because while he's played the perfect part of a ghost before, right now, his footsteps land perfectly sound behind me.

"How big is this place?" he asks.

"Five acres," I say. "It meets up with the orchard next door, and then we get to the sidewalk that leads right along Mister Beasley's fence." It's a quaint neighborhood, and I've lived here for ten years. Everyone's been here that long, and we watch out for each other.

When the AC in the Big House went out, I had at least eight fans on my back porch within thirty minutes. When we had that high-wind advisory a couple of years ago, I showed up with my hands gloved up and ready to work. I'd never dragged as many tree limbs as I had then, but it was good, honest work and had forged a bond between neighbors.

Cal comes to my side when we emerge from the trees and move onto the sidewalk. I glance over to him, wondering how many questions he'll answer right now. After all, there are no doors between us to slam.

"Talk to me about the names," I say.

"Oh, those guys." Cal waves his hand in a purely dismissive way. "It's this...codename type thing. Everyone in the industry has one."

"I meant *your* name," I say. "I'm not deaf, Cal, and Donald called you Mister Kingsley." I look over to him, eyes wide so as to not miss anything.

Sweet potato pie. There's something going on with his name.

Cal's pressed his eyes closed, and he exudes grace and power while continuing to walk. He breathes in through his nose and then blows it out as he opens his eyes. "Yes, he did."

I take another two or three steps before I huff out the

air in my lungs too. "And?" I prompt. "That's not your last name."

"I mean…"

"Cal," I bark. "If you can't even tell me your name, you'll need to have one of your dog-named security men pack your bags." I throw him a dirty look and turn the corner. He hastens to follow me, and I march up the sidewalk to Mr. Beasley's door while glaring at him.

He thinks he's so great for walking with his eyes closed? Like it's hard.

I ring the doorbell, knock, and open the door in quick succession, all while Cal says, "Technically, you know more of my names than most people."

"You know what?" I round on him from the doorway of Mr. Beasley's living room. "I'm too old for games. I needed to rent the rooms in the Big House in order to keep it, but had I known it would be you and your…your…crime family, I wouldn't have done it."

I grip the plastic container of cinnamon rolls while Mr. Beasley yells from the back of the house, where the kitchen is. He doesn't like it when his front door is open for longer than three-point-two seconds, and it's been twice that.

"Go pack your bags," I say. "You probably don't need to, though. I mean, your servants just got here this morning, didn't they? If you call them right now, they can probably stop unpacking for you."

I start to swing the door closed in Cal's face, noting the pure shock in his soft brown eyes before the satisfying slam comes between us.

As I stand there, chest heaving, I can't help but wonder

how many more innocent doors will have to slam before Cal will tell me the truth.

"Martha?"

I round on Mr. Beasley and hold up the cinnamon rolls. "Hello, Mister Beasley. It's Tahlia from next door, and I brought breakfast."

"I thought you'd be here a half-hour ago," he says grumpily, then gestures me into the kitchen. "Well, come on. I have coffee ready."

And I go, because spending time with my elderly neighbor who doesn't even know my name is preferential to going back to my own house and seeing my tenants there.

———

AN HOUR LATER, I've overstayed my welcome at Mr. Beasley's, and I have no reason to stay for another moment. I finally finish cleaning up and hang the tea towel on Mr. Beasley's stove handle. "Okay, I have to go."

"Tell your sister to give me call," Mr. Beasley says from his back sunporch.

"All right." I let myself out the front door to another brutal wave of heat. The Big House has always been my sanctuary, and I find myself standing at a dead-end side-walk with nowhere to go.

I pull out my phone and tap a couple of times. To my great relief, Hillary picks up after only two rings with a, "Hey, Tahlia. What's up?"

"What are you and Liam doing today?"

"We're on the way to Columbia," she says.

"Oh, right. Sorry."

Hillary's parents live in Columbia, and she and Liam usually take their bikes and ride the trails up there when they go visit. She says they have to do something fun to offset the time at her parents' stuffy Southern mansion.

"We won't be back until Tuesday."

An idea pops into my head. "Hey, uh, could I—do you think I could stay at your place?"

"Yeah, but...why?"

I can just see the gears in Hillary's head turning, and I won't be able to keep anything a secret for very long. My silence stretches for too long, and the next thing I know, there's a rushing sound coming through the line.

"I put you on speaker," she says.

"That doesn't help."

"You'll just have to text everyone anyway," Hillary says. "I can back you up."

I roll my head to stretch my neck and move into the shade of the trees. It honestly doesn't help, but maybe telling Hillary and Liam about Cal will.

"Remember that boyfriend I told everyone about? The guy I went out with my senior year?"

Hillary lets a beat of silence go by, and then she asks, "Calvin? Kevin? I know it started with the K-sound."

"Callan," I say miserably just as I make it to my bench and collapse onto it. "Cal Irwin. I think. I don't know."

I launch into the story of how he had his manservant rent the place, how there are two probably-mafia-bosses living with me now, and how I just need somewhere to stay for even one night while "I figure out what to do."

"What are you gonna do?" Liam asks.

"I don't know," I say. "He makes me so mad, and he speaks with this infuriatingly sexy accent, but he doesn't have any answers. And my questions are really simple, you know? Like, how hard is it to tell someone your last name?"

"Not that hard," Hillary says.

"Exactly."

"I'm going to have to ask them to leave." I get back to my feet and start pacing in front of the bench. "There's just no way I can forgive him, especially if he won't tell me the truth."

"Why do you think he won't?" Hillary asks.

"I don't know, but he hasn't, and I've given him a couple of chances."

"Why do you think he's there?" Liam asks. "It surely can't be a coincidence."

I frown. "What do you mean?"

"I mean, the guy has a personal assistant," Liam says. "Two security guards? It sounds like he has plenty of time and money, and I don't think—I mean..."

A pause, with that car-whooshing sound coming through the line.

"What Liam's saying, Tahlia, is that Cal knew whose house he was renting before he showed up."

"He sought you out," Liam says. "Dude, you're coming into my lane." A honk fills the line, but his words are echoing through my head.

He sought you out.

Could that be true?

"She's gone silent," Hillary says. "This isn't good. Tahlia? Tahlia, are you there?"

"I'm here," I say, sinking back onto the bench. "I just

don't know what to do. Why would he seek me out after all this time?"

"Stay at our place," Hillary says. "Think about it for a couple of nights."

"Go into text mode," Liam says, a grin in his voice. "I mean, that worked for me and Hill."

"I don't have his number."

"Then get it," Hillary says. "Sometimes it's easier to type something out and send it than it is to say it out loud."

"Yeah." I sigh and hang my head. "I can really stay at your place?"

"We'll be back on Tuesday afternoon," Hillary says.

That gives me two nights, and I wonder what Cal will do when I don't come back to the Big House tonight. An insane hope fills my chest that he'll run himself ragged to find me, and then I remember that he walked out on me in the middle of the night.

He's not going to care at all that I'm not in the house slamming doors and demanding answers, and that thought is more depressing than I want to admit.

CHAPTER FOUR

CAL

I don't know when I turned into such a mother hen, but darkness has fallen, and the Big House is silent. Tahlia is not here. I haven't seen her since this morning, when she closed the door in my face.

For the second time in as many days, I run my hands through my hair and eye my phone, which has three missed calls from *The Queen*, in one moment, and then Tahlia's giant turtle in the next. Oops, tortoise.

"She's a hard nut to crack, isn't she?" I ask Shellvador Dalí, chuckling internally at my own lame reptilian joke.

I knew Tahlia would be hard to get through to, but naively, I'd planned to be on our first date tonight in a nice restaurant, where I could explain everything to her.

"Well, not quite everything," I mutter as my phone blares to life with another song. At least this one isn't *Bohemian Rhapsody*—the sound for my mother. But *We Will Rock You* isn't much better. It means my father, the sitting king, is on the other end of the line, and I quickly calculate what time it is in Notavella. Too early to be calling, which means he hasn't slept well.

I sigh like talking to my parents is the greatest challenge of my life, because sometimes it is. I swipe on the call. It takes a moment to connect, during which I also tap on the speaker, as I don't have enough energy to pick up the phone and hold it right now.

"Hey, Dad," I say, fixing my eyes on the back door. Where could Tahlia be? Why didn't she text anyone and let someone know she wasn't coming home? Does she seriously think I won't notice—or worry?

"...see if you're settling in?"

I blink and look at my device, having missed the first half of my father's question.

"Yeah, I'm fine," I say, my irritation already up at a level ten. "My location is on. Can you guys not see me?"

Dad doesn't say anything, and that clues me in that this is a group call. *Ravens and crows and all things sparrows.*

"Yes, of course I can see you," my mother says in her crisp, accented English. "I've called three times today, and you promised you would answer."

I sigh and cradle my face in my hand. "I know, Mother."

I did promise.

"I'm sorry, it's been..." I trail off, because I'm not quite sure what to put in that spot.

"I told you he probably has jet lag," Dad says.

I seize onto that. "I *am* tired. It's not an easy travel day here. And then Donald and the twins showed up, and they immediately pulled me into briefing meetings *all day.*"

I know that directive came from the Queen, though I don't say it out loud.

"Well, it's important that *everyone's* on the same page," Mom simply says.

"Did you really have to send *two* bodyguards?" I ask. "I was under the impression that it would just be me and Don here."

"I don't know why you thought that," Mother says.

"Because you told me that."

"Let's not—" Dad starts.

"Mom," I cut him off. "You know exactly what this is for me, and I don't want them here."

"Callan, you are a prince. You can*not* just go gallivanting around the world because you're trying to win back the woman you *think* you love."

"I'm not having this argument, Mother. If you want me to keep answering your phone calls, perhaps you should have something important to say when I pick up—*and* you should have kept your end of the agreement in the first place."

They say nothing, and honestly, I know they're worried about me abdicating completely and never coming home. Honestly, right now, I wish I was the raven on our stupid family crest, and I could grow wings and fly somewhere far from Notavella for good.

"And Dad? If you're going to call and ambush me with a group call with Mom, I'm not going to pick up your calls either."

"I'm sorry," Dad says, as he's always quick to apologize. My mother, on the other hand, has never had to apologize for anything, as every single person in her life bends their will to hers in order to make her happy. Including me, until very recently.

"You're still planning that trip to Washington, D.C., correct?" Mother asks.

"I'm not even going to answer that. You have my calendar and my schedule. You have access to Don, who knows everything the moment I do. And you can see my location. For crying out loud, I'm thirty-five years old, and I know you don't understand how I could be unhappy in Notavella, because of all you've given me. And I'm not *completely* unhappy. I do love the job. But Mother, there has to be more for my life than this."

I've begged and pleaded for her to understand this in the past, and she simply doesn't. Because she was born to be queen, and she's fulfilled that role flawlessly. My older brother is cut from the same cloth as her, and he steps into every expected role with infuriating precision.

I have attempted to do the same, but the fact is, a second son in a royal family is not important. I will never sit on the throne unless my brother's entire family gets wiped out in one fell swoop on their way to their summer home, or something of the like. In fact, John travels with two of his children, while his wife Helena travels with their daughter in separate convoys, simply to ensure their safety and the security of the throne in Notavella.

I try not to let it bother me, and in truth, ninety-nine percent of the time it does not. But in that one percent, the whisperings of my heart and soul become so loud that I cannot quiet them—and I don't want to quiet them.

"Let's let him go, dear," Dad says, and then he adds,

"We trust you, Cal. Of course, both of us wish you the very best of luck in winning back Tahlia's heart."

A slip of humiliation pulls through me, but I nod and say, "Thank you, Dad," and then reach out and tap the red button to end the call.

I tried to earn my way back to South Carolina and the United States without bringing Tahlia into the equation. But my mother is exceptionally smart and astronomically gifted in rooting out the true cause of something. It had only been the second conversation before I'd confessed to her how lonely I was, how every woman I'd been out with in the past five years had bored me or scared me, and that I couldn't stop thinking about Tahlia Tomlinson.

The high school girl? Mother had asked, her voice pitching up in a way I'd never heard before and have not since.

"She doesn't understand how regular people live," I remind myself and Shellvador.

I'd shown her the layout of the Big House and where I would be sleeping, and the security measures between me and every door and window. Tally has a security system with doorbell cams on the front and back doors, as both of them face a parking area, and I can't even open my window without a voice on the central hub going "Second floor window," in a cool, robotic voice.

I'd managed to convince Mother that I didn't need security detail in a small suburb of Charleston, and she'd agreed not to send anyone. So seeing Titan and Ajax this morning had been as much of a shock to me as Tahlia.

Fine, maybe not. Perhaps that's going a step too far.

Shellvador takes a step toward me, and I quickly reach

out for another piece of lettuce, lest he get too close and I find out if he's a snapping turtle or not. I throw it near him, and he juts out his neck to pick it up.

He's creepy in all ways possible, and I wonder what Tahlia was planning to do with him when she decided not to come home.

Her security cameras pop into my head at the same time a loud, booming wave of thunder fills the air. I pull in a breath and look up to the ceiling.

Of course it storms in Notavella too, but I have never heard thunder roll through the sky the way it does now. Almost as if it's clinging to the clouds and can't quite let go until it's had its final say. It sends a thrill through me, because I do have an adventurous heart and a gypsy soul, and I remind myself that my mother *did* authorize my travel and my stay here simply because of those two things.

Yes, she arranged meetings at the U.S. Embassy and with the President of the United States—because *we have to have something to tell the people.* Her words, not mine. No one in Notavella cares what I do, unless it could potentially become a scandal.

I've had more written about my love life and my public appearances than any non-important person should, and I desperately hope that Tahlia is at least somewhat the girl she used to be. Because that person kept her promises.

Tahlia is also extraordinarily organized, and she provided Don with a binder that has everything we need to know about the house—from the codes to get in the front and back doors, the Wi-Fi password, and how you have to hold the trim down on the dishwasher's left side when you close the door before you start it.

I have not looked at the binder, because Don makes sure that I'm connected to everything I need to be, that I know my schedule, and that I'm able to have access to what I need to get my job done. He's already hooked my phone, computer, and tablet to the Wi-Fi, and he made me a digital cheat sheet of the codes for the doors.

I can't swipe my phone up fast enough now. "I wonder if he got me on the security system too."

I type in my passcode and navigate to the apps that have been installed on my device. Another clap of thunder fills the room and rumbles through the air, and in the next moment, rain hits the roof.

It sounds like missiles dropping, and once again, I look up just to make sure that the whole house isn't going to cave in on me. This place is old, but I know exactly why Tahlia likes it. The Big House has character and charm, and while I've noticed a few things that could use some fixing up, she stands strong and proud and welcomes anyone who approaches.

Because my mother sent extra detail, my living conditions have been rearranged. I'm no longer on the second floor right above Tahlia, but the third.

When I can't find the app, I get up from the barstool and walk to the back door. Upon opening it, the sound of the rain hitting the porch roof, which is so much closer to my head, sounds like literal gunfire.

"Sparrows and larks," I mutter as I step out and peer at the camera there, finding the name of it before quickly ducking back inside.

The motion sensor light came on when I poked my head outside, and I stand just inside, in the warmth of the

Big House, with that golden glow cast over my phone as I find the app and tap on it.

It requires authentication, and I quickly navigate to my digital cheat sheet and find the information I need about halfway down.

Perhaps Tahlia is home and she simply ignored my knocking and pleading twenty minutes ago. If so, that will be the third cruel thing she's done, and I'm not sure I should even be here. I thought I had a chance, but everything in my body feels heavy, indicating that I don't.

I make it into the app and tap on the events for the back door. There's a flurry around ten-thirty when the twins moved in. Nothing after that. We'd gone next door closer to eight, and I back up all the way to that and see us leave. The camera reaches out far enough to record the arrival of the twins and me begging Tahlia not to look me up online.

Twenty minutes later, I return. Boy, I look angry.

And another hour after that, at 9:26, Tahlia bustles into the frame, up the steps, and through the back door. She doesn't come out again.

So I navigate away from the back door camera and move to the front. The master suite sits right off the front foyer of the house, and she could easily slip out her door and take the six steps to the front door and be gone. Her car still sits in the back lot, beside the shiny black town car that I'll be driven around in.

My heart continues to wail as I back up the time. It doesn't take long to find the 10:34 time stamp, where Tahlia steals out the front door with a bright pink overnight bag in one hand and a black backpack slung over her shoulders.

"That little minx," I mutter to myself, my heart now pounding behind my breastbone. She used the noise of the twins moving in and me moving to the third floor to sneak out.

She has not texted or called since she left, and the front door camera shows her making a right turn and cutting across the lawn the moment she gets down the few steps from the porch. I quickly leave one app and tap into another. This one—the Maps app—shows me what's around here.

I've studied the neighborhood so much I think I already know that there's only one house down this lane, and then the road dead ends into orchards. The only logical explanation is that Tahlia went next door to spend the night.

I can't fathom such a thing, but I also don't live in a small suburb where I know all of my neighbors intimately enough to take them cinnamon rolls on Sunday mornings and ask them to come stay over if necessary.

I look up, and for a moment my surroundings completely disorient me. I *have* only been here for a day and a half, and the mudroom is meant to be passed through, not lived in.

I leave it, and pause once again at the counter, where Shellvador has moved over to the plate of lettuce I got out to feed him. I don't even know if you're supposed to feed tortoises lettuce, but he seems happy enough.

I, on the other hand, am not.

And while part of me says that I absolutely should let

Tahlia have her space, the other part can't stand that she dislikes me so much that she can't even sleep under the same roof as me.

The rain eases up, and that solidifies my decision. I hurry up the two flights of stairs to the third floor and all the way down the hall to the last room on the right. Don and the twins now each have their own bedroom on the third floor, and they went to bed a half-hour ago, as they made the treacherous journey across the sea and back in time nine hours today.

I have no idea what I'm doing, but I throw a pair of pajamas in a bag, an extra pair of socks and underwear, and hurry into the adjoining bathroom to grab some deodorant and my toothbrush and paste. I tell myself I need clothes for tomorrow, and I jet back into the bedroom to grab a new set of slacks and another polo. I turn in a complete circle, then rush back into the bathroom to grab my comb.

I stand there and look at myself in the mirror, trying to think rationally, with my heart beating so loud it booms in my ears. "By the royal crest and ravens," I say, a measure of disgust in my voice. It's my way of saying, *This better not be the biggest mistake of my life.*

Then I zip close the bag, pick it up, and leave the Big House, making that same right cut across the lawn that Tahlia did twelve hours earlier.

CHAPTER FIVE

TAHLIA

The thunder drives me out of bed and into the kitchen. I've never been good with storms, as they remind me a little bit too much of a childhood I'd rather forget.

Liam has a state-of-the-art sound system threaded throughout his entire house, and I know how to run it because I've been the DJ at past Halloween parties hosted here. I queue up my favorite classic rock and crank the volume before moving into the kitchen. Maybe the drumbeat will drown out the sound of thunder and the storm will pass quickly, so that by the time I go back to bed, all will be silent.

I open the freezer and stare into the depths of it. Hillary loves ice cream bars, and a few different choices come into view.

"Coffee toffee crunch," I say, pulling out one of the boxes. "Vanilla, caramel, double chocolate chip. Ooh, a drumstick."

I reach for the variety box of those, which has vanilla, chocolate, and caramel in it, and I pray that Hill hasn't eaten all the caramel ones. They're the best, with vanilla ice cream inside, gooey caramel around it, all covered in chocolate and dipped in nuts.

You don't have school tomorrow, I tell myself. And while I don't exactly tolerate dairy super well, I also have nothing going on tomorrow. So if I want to lay in the shade of the orchards, that'll be close enough to a bathroom, should I need it.

I slide all the other ice cream bars back into the freezer just as one of my favorite Queen songs comes blaring through the house. I unwrap my drumstick and use it as a microphone, as it sort of mimics the homemade one we've used at the Big House when we had roommate meetings. Really, that was a paper towel tube that I'd fashioned into a point at one end, attached a tennis ball to the top, and then spray-painted the whole thing pink.

A sense of missing lashes through me at the thought of those meetings and how we'll never have another one. I find I can't sing, so I might as well eat the ice cream before it starts to melt.

My spirits get buoyed by the delicious chocolate, caramel, and vanilla that explodes across my tongue. I'm glad for the cold in my mouth too, as everything else in my face feels so hot. I'm so sick of crying, and I've already deemed this summer a tear-free time.

After a few bites, and as the song reaches the chorus, I lift my drumstick microphone back to my mouth and really belt out the words.

I'm only a couple of bars in when the music suddenly goes silent and a male voice says, "I hate this song."

I scream, whip toward the sound of the voice, and

throw my drumstick in that direction all at the same time. As it arcs through the air, I take in the tall form of Cal Irwin, and I manage to blink once before my vanilla caramel drumstick splats against his pristine shirt.

He barely flinches, but he does look down at his chest and then lifts his eyes back to mine. "Did you just throw ice cream at me?"

The cone sticks for a moment, then slides down a couple of inches before releasing and plopping to the ground with a sickening crunch of cone on hardwood.

"What are you doing here?" I ask.

"You didn't come home," he says. "I was worried."

"I don't owe you any explanations."

"No," he says. "You don't. But it's the *courteous* thing to do, to let someone know if you're coming home or not. I was *worried*."

He's said that twice now, and it honestly makes no sense. He stoops, picks up the ice cream, moves over to the garbage can, and drops it inside. "I can go get you more of these."

A new round of thunder fills the air, and I lift my hand to press it against my floundering heart. "It's fine. There's more in the freezer."

He rips off a paper towel from the roll next to the sink, gets it wet, and cleans up the floor before dabbing at his shirt. He's brought with him the scent of cedar and fresh air, and a sense of comfort that I won't have to spend my night in the storm alone.

All of it is ridiculous, because I don't want to be around him either. Just as I'm about to ask again what he's doing here, I realize his hair is dripping wet and his shirt along his shoulders is soaked.

"You came through the rain?" I ask.

He looks at me again, a measure of distaste in his expression. "Yes."

"But you hate the feel of rain on your skin."

His eyebrows go up in a silent challenge. "I'm surprised you remember that."

Oh, I remember it all right. I'd laughed and teased Cal relentlessly about his "indoor cat" nature. He doesn't like being too hot or too cold. He doesn't like being uncomfortable. And when he told me he couldn't stand the feel of rain on his skin, I'd curled into his chest and giggled. After that, every time it dared to rain, I'd pretend like I was going to drag him outside.

During one particularly enjoyable spring sprinkle, I'd gone out and spread my arms wide and tilted my head back and let the rain wash over me. I'd never felt so clean. So free. Because we only had a couple of months left of high school, and then I was going to be gone from my parents' house and from the life I'd been trying to escape for years.

"You came outside with me that one time," I say, moving to the counter opposite where he still stands at the sink. "Remember?"

"Yes," he says.

I smile at a memory I've kept locked away for a long time. He'd spread his arms too, let the rain soak through his clothes and run rivers through his hair. He'd smiled and laughed, caught my hand, and pulled me into his chest. He'd danced with me, and as the sudden microburst softened, he'd kissed me.

I try to shove the memories away, but they won't go.

"What are you doing here, Cal?" My voice is soft, full of pleading, and I mean so much more than just here in Liam's house.

He makes one final swipe at his shirt before sighing. "I'm sure Don can get this out in the laundry."

He moves to the end of the counter and drops the paper towel in the trash before facing me. He seems to war with himself for several long moments, and then another shuddering sigh comes out of his mouth.

"I'm really sorry for leaving the way I did. It wasn't what I wanted. I did attempt to get in touch with you after I left. It wasn't until later, when you hadn't responded for months, that I realized none of my letters or emails or texts had reached you."

I fold my arms and cock my hip. "How is that even possible? Texts go through, Cal."

"Not when your mother blocks them," he says. "Not when she's changed your email address and I didn't notice. Not when you find a stack of letters you've written bound up and sitting next to the fireplace, and you realize she's been using them to start fires instead of mailing them as promised."

I blink at him, sure none of that is true. I don't quite know what to say, and I come up with, "You always spoke so highly of your parents."

"Yes," he says. "And I still would. But that doesn't mean they haven't done things that upset me. That hurt me." He takes a step toward me. "Surely you understand that, Tally."

I take a step back. "Of course I do. I just..."

The piece of my heart that always hopes for the best pinches at me. "Once you knew she was doing that, why didn't you try again?"

"It had been eight months," he says. "And I didn't want to hurt you any more than I already had." He drops his chin, his expression so sad and filled with regret. "I was thrown into my new role, and I became very busy for the next several years. First with military service and then acclimating back to regular life." He scoffs. "I mean, as regular as my life gets."

Another clap of thunder fills the air, and I jump along with it. Cal sees me, though I wish he wouldn't, and sudden understanding dawns on his face.

"I forgot—you're afraid of storms."

"I'm not afraid," I say. "They just make me nervous."

He nods and turns back to the fridge. He opens the freezer, pulls out the box of drumsticks, rifles through the plastic packages, and then turns with the caramel one in his hand.

"It's the last one," he says. "Do the people who own this house know you're here?"

A tiny smile accompanies the challenge this time, and I practically growl as I walk over to him. I snatch the ice cream out of his hand.

"Yes, of course they do. Believe it or not, Mister Irwin, I don't need a babysitter."

"What if I *want* to be your babysitter?" he asks.

My heart comes to a full stop right there in my chest. He's *flirting* with me, and while there are plenty of doors I could slam between us, I find I don't want to.

I unwrap my new drumstick and throw away the

wrapper before looking at him. "Why do you hate *Bohemian Rhapsody?* Everybody loves Queen."

"It's my mother's ringtone," he says. "And I'm not very happy with her right now." He shivers, reminding me that he's soaking wet in a house I've spent all afternoon cooling down to sixty-eight degrees.

I nod to his bag. "Do you have a change of clothes in that?"

"Yes."

"So you thought you'd spend the night here?"

"I wasn't sure what was going to happen," he says. "I just knew you'd come this way, and I wanted to make sure you were okay."

"Did you think I was camping in the orchard?" I grin at him, recognizing my own flirtatious tone.

"Knowing you," he throws back. "It's possible."

And he came to check anyway. The thought warms me, because Cal doesn't like being outside at night or in the rain.

"I decided to try this house first when I heard the music pumping inside. I *was* surprised to find you didn't lock every door."

"I thought they were locked," I say.

"Not the back one." He lifts his bag. "If I go get changed into something dry, will you promise not to disappear?"

"No. I'm sick of making promises to you."

Pure fear marches across his face. "So you looked me up online?"

"No. I hadn't gotten to it yet."

Everything that had turned tense inside him relaxes.

"Good." He sweeps his gaze across the dining room and then through the arched, double-wide doorway into the living room. "Maybe we can meet in there in about fifteen minutes, and I'll answer as much as I'm able to."

I take a big bite of my drumstick and nod, because I don't trust myself to speak. I used to have a list of questions to ask Cal, but I don't anymore.

Maybe if I say, *Tell me what I need to know*, he'll do it.

He nods too and turns to leave the kitchen. I don't tell him where a bathroom or a spare bedroom is, but he navigates through the house as if he owns the place. The soft click of the bathroom door reaches my ears only a few seconds later.

"He's not going to tell you what you need to know," I mutter to myself. So I better come up with a list of questions—specific questions—in the next fifteen minutes.

CHAPTER SIX

CAL

I can't get the sight of Tally in an oversized T-shirt and nothing else out of my mind. I wonder if she even realizes what she was wearing as she danced around the kitchen and sang into that ice-cream-cone-slash-microphone. She's literally the sexiest woman I've ever met, and everything about her lights up everything inside me.

I look down into the bag I brought, really only needing to change my shirt.

I open the cupboard under the sink and find a towel, then scrub it through my hair to get as much water out as I can. For some stupid reason, I brush my teeth, and then I choose my royal blue silk pajama shirt and pull it over my head.

Just as I'm about to leave the bathroom, I realize the cuffs of my pants are soaking wet as well. I kick them off and pull on my pajama pants. I could go out there with tousled, damp hair, but I brought a comb, so I use it to quickly put every strand back in place.

I leave everything in the bathroom because I'm not sure if I'm going to be staying here for the night or not. With the way the rain continues to pummel the house, I certainly hope so, as this place seems big enough for multiple bedrooms.

"Sweet banana pudding," I hear Tally curse as I approach the doorway of the living room.

It only makes me smile because I'd forgotten that she swears in Southern foods. I prefer birds, as our family crest bears a raven, and they don't get me in trouble with the King and Queen—or the press.

I move into the living room and find Tally perched on one end of the couch with a blanket tucked all around her legs and waist and all the way up to her armpits. So she realized she was wearing a T-shirt and nothing else, and my stupid imagination can't help wondering if she went and put on a pair of shorts or not.

She looks up at me and drops her phone to her lap as she blinks. "Wow," she says. "You brought pajamas and everything."

"I was taught it's always best to be prepared," I say as I sink onto the other end of the couch. It's soft and squishy, and I sigh in happiness as I lean back against it. "I'm so tired."

"Yeah?" she asks. "Today was just a really rough one for you?"

I note the sarcasm and ignore it as I let my eyes drift closed. She has no idea who she's dealing with, because I have ignored a lot of barbs, horrible articles, and other awful things said about me—some right to my face.

"Yes," I say. "It was just supposed to be me and Don in the house, but with the arrival of the twins, I had to move upstairs."

"*You* did the moving?" she asks.

This time, I open my eyes and send her a glare. "Yes. They were busy bringing in their own things. I'm not sure if you saw them clearly or not, but they don't have patience for very much—including me."

"So you're on the third floor now?" she asks.

"Yes."

"Are they really twins?" she asks next.

I smile this time and shake my head. "No. That's just what we call them."

"Who's 'we'?" she asks, and I have a feeling this night is going to be a lot longer than I imagined.

"My family and I," I say. "They work for us."

"I figured that part out," she says. "So what are you guys? Like...organized crime?"

A laugh bursts out of my mouth. "Organized crime?" I laugh again. "You really think I'm a mob boss? From where?"

"I don't know," she says, her voice tight and defensive. "Italy. There are a lot of Italian crime families."

"Crime—families." I gasp and wheeze and laugh some more. When I finally manage to calm down, I shake my head. "No, we're not a crime family."

"Then what are you?" she asks.

"We're rich," I say, sobering. "And powerful. Some of us hold government positions. We have press assigned to us constantly, day in and day out, and no move is made and no car leaves the property without someone knowing and someone speculating about where we're going and when we'll be back."

Fine, maybe there's some bitterness in my voice.

"But you do live in Europe." She doesn't phrase it as a question.

"Yes," I say. "Though not quite as near to Italy as I would like."

"Oh, I bet it's *terrible*," she says.

"Yeah. The Amalfi Coast is gorgeous, but it's so far away."

"Biscuits and gravy," she mutters.

"You knew I was an exchange student," I say. "You knew I'd be leaving after graduation."

"No, I *didn't* know that," Tally says. "We'd started making plans, Cal, to go to the same college. That's not leaving."

I nod, my jaw tight, because she's not wrong. "I underestimated my mother," I say. "And I'm not using her for an excuse. I swear I'm not. And I can give you a play-by-play of that night if you'd like, but I truly left against my will."

"I believe you," she says quietly.

Those are the best three words in the world. "Thank you," I say just as quietly.

A flash of lightning fills the front window, and Tally gasps. In the brief moment between it and the gong of thunder that follows, she pulls her blanket tighter, and I take the opportunity to move down the couch and slide into her side. I put my arm around her and pull her into my chest, and it takes almost no effort at all.

She leans into me and puts one arm around me, and I

feel like I could do anything, be anyone, rip the sky away from the earth for her if I had to.

"I'm so sorry," I whisper again. "I hope you can forgive me one day."

She nods, and in the next moment, the power goes out. She cries out, and I grip her tighter and shush her. "It's fine. It's all right."

She holds me tighter, like I matter, like she needs me, and my heart fills my entire chest as it floods with hope.

"I'm right here," I tell her. "And this time, I'm not going anywhere."

She nods against my chest, and I press a kiss to the top of her head and subtly take a breath of the scent of her hair. I get caramel and peaches and sunshine, and I'm once again reminded of how much Tally meant to me back then. It testifies of how much she could mean again.

And though I haven't quite worked out every detail of how to get her back and keep her in my life, I know I want to try.

I know I have to do more than tell her my family is rich and important.

But how does one say that their family runs an entire country, and that when they walk in a room, everyone bows to them? It sounds ridiculous in our modern day, and yet it has been my life for the past seventeen years.

I know I can't outrun it forever, and that my time in the U.S. is limited and will be brief.

As my eyes adjust to the darkness, I tell myself that Tally deserves to know. And that she won't be able to glare at me in the dark. I press my eyes closed, and the blackness that had already started to surround us gets deeper.

Tally is still kind and still perceptive. She's still quiet and only says what needs to be said. She's still afraid of storms, and she still loves chocolate and caramel together.

And if there's any chance at all that she still harbors some feelings for me, I have to tell her—and tell her now.

I take a deep breath, hold it for a count of four, and as I exhale, I say, "Tally, my family is more than rich and powerful. They're royal."

She lifts her head, but I don't open my eyes, and I don't look at her.

"Hawks and sparrows," I murmur.

"Keep going."

"My mother is queen of a country called Notavella, and she has been for thirty years. I'm the second son and will never be king, which affords me more freedom. It's what allowed me to come to the U.S. to study as a teenager, and why I'm able to be here with you now."

I pause. "I'm the Special Envoy to the Crown, and I do have some work to do here in the United States, but the real reason I came back—" My voice falters, and I grind it through my throat, unsure if Tally needs me to be quite *this* honest.

She reaches up and touches my face, and my eyes fly open. Somehow, in the darkness between us, they meet hers.

"I came back for you," I say, every barrier against her undone with her touch. "I have missed you every hour and every day since I left. Every other woman I've been out with gets compared to you and is found wanting. Somehow, I convinced my mother to give me six months to see if we could somehow start over and be together again."

I swallow, and my brain goes blissfully blank. "That's it," I whisper, and I let my eyes fall closed again. "That's what I'm doing here, and who I am."

Now all I can do is hope and pray that Tally doesn't growl, shove away from me, and march into the nearest room to slam the door behind her.

CHAPTER SEVEN

TAHLIA

Before I can even formulate a response that it isn't *Kentucky Fried Chicken*, Cal goes on.

"Irwin is my middle name. Well, one of them. Callan Irwin Rockwood Kingsley." He shakes his head and lets out a frustrated sigh. "It's ridiculous, really, but at least I don't have a number after my name like my brother."

I'm still touching his face, and he seems to be turtling his head forward the way Shellvador does, as if he wants to maintain the contact.

He's a prince, and while that had definitely been tossed around on the friends' text, it was something I had dismissed immediately. I'd thought his bodyguards and personal assistant had more to do with his work than his personal life. Turns out, it's both.

"Do I have to call you Prince Cal?" I ask.

He chuckles and shakes his head, which causes me to drop my hand. "No, and in fact, if you do, I will not answer."

He leans back against the couch as if he's truly tired. "I

don't want to be a prince while I'm here. When I go to Washington, DC, I'll step back into that role. But at the Big House, with you, I just want to be Cal."

There's more to that, but I don't press him on it.

It feels late, and the storm continues to rage beyond the windows, so I tuck myself in Cal's arms, close my eyes the way he has, and let the silence drown out the terror of the storm. With Cal at my side, it's able to do that in a way nothing and no one else ever has.

———

I STIR, almost reaching the surface of consciousness, as a wisp of air glides across my cheek. Then Cal says, "Go back to sleep, Tally," and I snuggle down into the pillow he's just placed beneath my head. The surface beneath me is soft and the blanket over me fuzzy, and I don't hear any rain or thunder.

The past couple of days have drained me. I feel tired and gross the way I do after eating a family feast meal of fried chicken, so I do what he says.

The next time I wake, I become aware of the brightness of day falling across my face. My eyes pop open, and I say, "Strawberry shortcake," right out loud.

I don't usually sleep very late, and I didn't even hear my alarm. I look around, realizing I'm not in my bedroom and I have no idea where my phone is. Any of those would make my heartbeat erratic, and combined, it's thrashing against my ribs.

"I'm so late for school—"

Then my mind catches up to reality. I don't have

school today. It's summertime. I'm at Liam and Hillary's, where I slept last night.

A groan trickles out of my mouth.

Cal.

Cal was here. I definitely remember Cal.

I whip around, looking behind me, down to the other end of the couch, and toward every doorway that leads in and out of the living room. I don't see him. Thankfully, I have more than one sense, and my ears pick up some humming coming from behind me in the kitchen.

A moment later, the scent of coffee hits my nose.

I quickly reach up and run my fingers through my hair in an attempt to make it look less like a three-year-old toddler's.

I'd claimed the bedroom behind the kitchen in the corner of the house, tucked away from everything, and my toothbrush is back there. Hilary had told me that she and Liam had toiletries in every bathroom, and I was welcome to shower in any of them, so I'd only brought my hairbrush, toothbrush, and toothpaste for my mini-vacation from the Big House.

Really, from Cal.

"Good morning, Tally," he says, as if he finds me waking up on this couch every morning. He's smiling, and he holds a pale blue ceramic mug in his hand that looks like one of my seventh graders made it for their mom.

He extends it toward me. "Two cream and one sugar, if my memory is right." Something flashes across his face. "But if you take your coffee differently now—" He pulls the cup back just as I start to reach for it.

"No, that's great," I say, though part of me definitely

wants to hiss and rattle and push him further from me. He said such nice things last night, and they accompanied me into my dreams, which always fade before I can truly grasp them. I remember being happy, though, and I wasn't alone.

I take a sip of the coffee, and it's hot and creamy and delicious. I smile, but Cal has already turned around to go back into the kitchen.

I push the blanket from my legs, suddenly too hot, and then remember why I'd pulled it onto my lap to begin with.

I'm wearing an oversized T-shirt I got from my grandfather two decades ago, and a teeny tiny pair of booty shorts that no one can see when I'm standing up. I'm sure Cal got an eyeful in the kitchen last night, what with the way I was dancing and singing into that ice cream mic.

Even now, my face heats with embarrassment.

After another fix of my hair, I quickly tuck the front of the shirt into my shorts, so he'll know I'm wearing pants. Then I promptly untuck it. I'm not the skinniest person on the planet, and I certainly don't know how to rock my curves the way Claudia does.

I end up tying a knot in the shirt to sit over my hip, so that a swash of fabric still falls across my stomach and my shorts are visible. Then I take another sip of liquid courage-caffeine and head into the kitchen.

Cal stands at the stove built into the island, wearing a polo the color of ripe red cherries and a denim apron that says *The Alamo* on the front.

"Where did you get that?" I ask.

He looks at me, and I drop my eyes to his chest.

"I found it in a drawer." He lifts his spatula. "I'm making eggs and bacon for breakfast."

"This isn't my house, you know."

"No, I know," he says, and then he clears his throat. And while Cal is definitely twice as old as he was last time I knew him, a lot of his mannerisms are the same. I can't even imagine the things that he's seen and done in almost two decades as the "Special Envoy to the Crown" and a prince of Notavella. But he still clears his throat when he has something to say he doesn't want to.

I move over to the island, pull out the barstool, and sit down. I cradle my chin in one hand and say, "Go on," clearly teasing and flirting with him.

"It's just... you left your phone in here, and it kept buzzing and buzzing and *buzzing*, and it was the same person over and over again. Hillary?" His voice goes up at the same time his eyebrows do. "Anyway, I finally answered, and I'll have you know that I didn't even say hello. I just said, 'This is not Tahlia, but I can tell her you called. She's alive. She's just asleep.' Literally, verbatim, that's what I said."

I grin at him. "Oh, so you answer other people's calls?"

"Your phone would—not—stop. It was driving me nuts."

"How long ago was this?" I ask.

"About a half-hour," he says. "Hillary sat there for a minute, and then she said, 'Who is this?' And I said, 'It's Cal. I'm Tahlia's roommate. So don't worry, she's not going to think anything happened.'"

Oh, Hill's gonna think something happened, all right. But I don't tell Cal that, because I don't want to disclose that I've already discussed him with my former housemates on a group text.

"What else did she say?" I ask.

"She just wanted to make sure that everything was okay in the house. And I said it was."

"Oh, so she knows you stayed here with me."

"I didn't say that." Cal shoots me a look, and then uses a pair of tongs to flip over a slice of bacon. "For all she knows, I came over this morning. Anyway, that's when she told me that we could eat anything we wanted out of the fridge. And, well..." He gestures to the stove. "Bacon and eggs sounded very American. And I seem to recall that you like all things bacon—including lip gloss, soda, and air fresheners. Which—gross, by the way."

He grins at me and then goes back to frying bacon.

"You're wrong," I say. "The bacon soda is totally disgusting."

He laughs and shakes his head, and I have forgotten how good it feels to make a man laugh and have one look at me the way Cal does.

He pulls the bacon out of the pan and lays it on a paper towel, then cracks three eggs into the still-sizzling grease. "Over easy or fried flat?"

"It's not fried flat," I tell him.

"Oh, right." He snaps his fingers. "What did you call it? A rubber shoe?"

"A rubber *sole*, and yes, that's what I want."

"So you still don't like runny yolks?" He looks at me for half a heartbeat and then uses the end of one of the broken shells to break the yolk on all three eggs.

"No," I tell him. "And I don't need three eggs."

"Great," he says without missing a beat. "Because some of these are for me."

I barely know what to do with this man, with this situation. I had been planning to make a bagel run this morning, because I didn't want Hillary and Liam to know I'd been in their house at all.

"So," Cal says. "What are you going to do today?"

I blink at him, wondering if he can read minds the way he can say such perfect things. "I don't know. I'm still coming down off the end of school and the weddings, and that takes me a few days to recoup and feel human again."

"Mm. Yes, the time difference is catching up to me, I think." He yawns and turns to get plates out of the cupboard. How he even knows where they are, I can't fathom. "So, do you want one or two?"

"Two," I say, which leaves only one rubber sole for him.

He plates two on one and pushes the bacon closer as he sets the eggs in front of me. He keeps the last egg near him, and then cracks two more into the pan, which he leaves with intact yolks. He sprinkles salt and pepper over them while I marvel at every move he makes.

"You can cook," I say.

"The number of lessons I've taken in my life would terrify you," he says in a dry voice. "From languages to diplomatic introductions to—yes—cooking. It's what I did instead of college."

"So you never went to college at all?" I ask.

"No." His voice is flat and tells me in only two letters to drop the subject. But I don't want to. I watch him while he finishes his eggs and then joins me on my side of the island.

"You really wanted to go to college," I say, finally picking up my fork.

"Yes, well, men in my position don't always get to do what they want." He looks at me with a somber expression painted across his face. "I've had my fair share of education, though none of it ended in a degree."

I cover his hand with mine, an electric thrill moving through me. "I'm really sorry, Cal. Maybe you could do a few classes while you're here."

He shakes his head as he cuts his runny yolk and it seeps out across his plate. "No. That's not part of the deal. And if I expect my mother to hold up her end of the bargain, I have to play by the letter of the law."

"You always did do that." I smile at him and pick up a slice of bacon. It's not too done, but not flabby either, just the way I like it.

He watches me take a bite, and then says, "I can only be in the States for six months, Tally."

Surprise sears through me, but I manage not to choke or cough on my bite of bacon—that would have ruined it. I manage to get it down and then say, "Oh. Six months?"

He nods. "Legally. It's part of the visa I got to be here, and it's all my mother agreed to."

He turns back to his breakfast, but I don't know if I'll be able to take another bite. Yes, Donald only signed a six-month rental agreement, but I had assumed that if things went well, he and his tenant would stay longer. Now that I know his tenant is Cal—and what Cal is and does—of course they won't be able to stay longer.

I reach for the saltshaker and add a few extra shakes to my eggs.

"You haven't even tasted them yet," Cal chastises. "You're always doing that."

"Some things about a person don't change all that much," I say. "But some things do. So don't pretend like you know me, just because you know how I take my coffee and that I add extra salt to eggs before I taste them."

I take a bite, and they are perfectly delicious and salty. "Eggs always need more salt."

He nods, a brilliant smile showing all of his straight white teeth fixed on his face. "Well, if you don't have a lot going on today, I'd love to take you to lunch. Or dinner. Or we can just go for a walk."

I shake my head. "If we're doing anything, it's inside air-conditioning, Cal. It's June in the South. Are you gonna try to kill me while you're here?" I shoot him a mock glare and pick up another piece of bacon.

He chuckles—a gloriously rich sound that makes me remember why I liked him so much. A new thread of hope winds through me. Maybe I can find a way to forgive him. Maybe we *can* have our second chance.

So I look at him and say, "I'll give you one hour to prepare your lunch date options and your dinner date options, and then I'll decide if I'm willing to do any of them."

I grin at him, and he grins right back, then throws his arm around my waist and pulls me closer to him, barstool and all.

"You might be different in some ways, Tally-Lou," he says. "But there's a lot about you that's the same."

I can't deny it, because how much does a person change, really? Their habits, their taste buds, the things they like—those tend to stay the same without some sort of major intervention.

While I have gone through a pretty significant transformation, it didn't influence the way I drink coffee, or eat eggs, or want my boyfriends to plan dates.

He is not your boyfriend, I tell myself sternly.

But when I glance at him out of the corner of my eye, I think, *But he could be.*

CHAPTER EIGHT

CALLAN

IF I WAS AT HOME IN NOTAVELLA, I'M CERTAIN MY presentation for lunch options and dinner dates would wow Tally to the stars. As it is, she started the clock while we were still eating breakfast, and after she disappeared into the bedroom behind the kitchen to shower and get dressed, I've only had my phone and a semi-stable data connection to try to come up with something that will get her to say yes.

Unfortunately, Charleston seems to have only outdoor attractions, from a food truck rally that evening, to Folly Beach, to backyard barbecues.

I know Tally loves museums, especially art, which would provide the required air-conditioning. But there's also the classic steakhouse, a lantern dinner festival, historic downtown walking tours, a huge farmers market, the botanical garden, and a riverboat lunch cruise. Unfortunately, ninety percent of those are outside, and as I look at my top three picks for lunch and then dinner, I'm pretty sure I'm going to be shot down on all six.

Tally returns to the kitchen wearing a pair of skin-tight shorts in a deep purple and a tank top the color of the pale peach Italian soda I like, tie-dyed with pink. It is once again oversized and tied in a knot on her hip, accentuating every female curve and making me forget my own name.

"So," she says as she opens the fridge. "What did you come up with?" She pulls out a pitcher of sweet tea and turns toward me, her eyebrows raised. Her blonde hair falls in loose curls past her face and over her shoulders, and that smattering of freckles across her nose only makes me want to kiss each one—the way I have before. Her blue eyes sparkle as if she knows she's thrown me a hard challenge, and I give her the best glare I can.

"All right," I say, taking a deep breath. "I'm going off old information here, but I think I've narrowed it down to a few things you'll like."

I glance at the list on my phone, and suddenly, none of them are good. "The Charleston Museum," I say anyway. "It's inside, and I'm pretty sure they'll have some art exhibits that you'll like. They have a Lowcountry History Hall, and they're the oldest museum in the entire country, and that sounds kind of cool to me."

"You're so nerdy," Tally says with a grin. She turns back to the cupboards and gets down a couple of glasses.

"There's a riverboat lunch cruise," I forge on, knowing this suggestion will be met with boos. I continue before Tally can say or do anything. "There's a café at Magnolia Plantation, the botanical gardens, or we could wander the farmers market and pick out ingredients and take them back to the Big House, and I'll cook them for you."

I really hope she doesn't pick that one, because she'll

choose things like shishito mushrooms and make me pair them with grape soda. Tally says nothing as she pours the amber liquid into cups and pushes one toward me.

"For dinner, I read about the rooftop dining scene in Charleston, and I think that would be pretty fun. There's also a great jazz scene here, and we could enjoy some music and dinner at a club. Of course, I would love to see the beach, and we can take a blanket, wine, cheese, dinner, and head out to Folly Beach."

I pause to take a breath while Tally swirls her sweet tea in a way only maniacal villains do.

"I have a couple of bonus dinner ideas, including a progressive dinner, where we visit different restaurants in the city, and you can give me a little historic down-town walking tour as we make our way from place to place. Or we could do a Southern food tour." I glance up at her. "Because I know you like to curse in fried green tomatoes and shrimp and grits, so I figured I should sample them again after being gone for so long."

Tally takes a sip of her tea, holds up one finger, and says, "One, the riverboat lunch cruise is going to be completely bugified. We'll be lucky if we don't eat more bugs than food, so that's out." Another finger comes up. "Two, the botanical garden café is completely overrated."

I look down at my list as she shoots down my carefully done research so quickly.

"Third, the farmers market is outside, and while I would like to see you cook something, I'm not sure I trust you in the kitchen at the Big House quite yet. Fourth, I do like jazz, but it is terribly loud and we won't have much opportunity to talk. And the beach? Really? Did you not get the memo about the heat and humidity?"

"I got the memo," I mutter.

"Or the bugs," she adds on for good measure, and I give her another mock glare.

She appraises me, scanning the parts of me she can see sitting at the island. "The progressive dinner sounds fine," she says. "It feels very European. The rooftop idea might work, though I'm pretty sure you need reservations for that pretty far in advance, and again, we'll be outside."

She grins at me and takes another sip of her sweet tea. "And holy fried pickles, I do love Southern food. I suppose that would combine your insane desire to take a walk *and* give us an opportunity to chat."

"We would only be outside sometimes," I say, returning her smile. "Is the Southern food tour your final vote?"

"Yeah, that is my final vote," Tally says. "Though some of the other ones aren't bad." She walks to the end of the island and glares at me out of the corner of her eye. "But the Charleston Museum? No. Never suggest that again."

I chuckle and turn off my phone as I flip it over and lay it face down on the counter. "No, ma'am," I say in the best Southern accent I can muster. "I will never suggest another museum again."

She gives me a brief smile and then nods to the back door. "There's a price of admission for this date," she says. "Especially since some of it is outside."

"A price of admission?" I get to my feet and follow her as she heads toward the back door. "Are you staying over here again tonight?"

She exits the house the way I came in—through the back door—and crosses the back porch to the steps, where she pauses and looks out across this beautiful backyard. A huge garage sits off to the right side and orchards meet the grass and fill the space beyond.

"I don't know," Tally says. "I probably don't need to. We can come back later today and clean it up before we get ready to go out."

I nod as I settle at her side. "What's my price of admission for the date?"

Tally takes a big breath and exhales. "Not sure if you noticed the detached garage at the Big House."

I have seen it in floor plans and blueprints, but I don't tell Tally that tiny online-stalker detail.

"No," I say. "Wait, is it that shed in the corner of the yard that we passed today?"

She nods. "It's a double-car garage on the road, and..." She trails off, and I know I'm not going to like this price of admission. I start praying it'll be something I can pay at all.

"Well, what?" I prompt, because I have no idea what she's going to say next. Her aunt could have buried all of her cats in there for all I know.

"My roommates say I have a little bit of a hoarding problem," Tally says. "I like to call it being sentimental."

I look over to her, but she refuses to meet my eye. "I have to clean out the garage before our date?"

She releases a laugh that is not quite happy, and in fact, carries some hint of bitterness. "Oh, honey, you can't clean it out in one day." She turns toward me and puts one hand against my chest. "If you want me to go out with you and do some outdoorsy things—because Folly Beach *is* fun and

I'd go there with you—you have to help me clean out that garage." She grins at me. "We can do it a little bit, every day, this summer."

"Can I see what's in it first?" I ask.

She grins at me, pure teasing in her dancing expression. "I want to know if you've ever cleaned out a garage."

A sting moves through my chest, and I'm not really quite sure why. "What if I haven't?" I ask. "Is that a strike against me?"

"Not necessarily," Tally says, and she turns and goes down the steps. "Let's go look at it right now, because it'll be shaded in the morning."

I hurry to follow her and match my stride to hers fairly easily.

"I just think it will give me a lot of fun things to tease you about."

"Great," I say dryly.

We leave Liam's land and step back onto the property of the Big House. The structure stands tall and brightly lit in the morning sunshine, and because I texted Don last night, he didn't send out a search party to find me. He did say he would feed Shellvador, and I find it surprising that Tally hasn't asked about her turtle, not even once.

She takes me around to the front of the garage, where sure enough, two single doors stand solidly closed. The scent of dust and cobwebs fills the air, and I wonder when Tally last opened this garage.

She flips open the cover on a keypad, taps in a few numbers, and then jams her thumb against the big *ENTER* button at the bottom. The first door starts to rumble upward ominously. She steps back and gestures to the space, though the door is only halfway up and groaning like it is about to fall off the tracks and obliterate us both.

"Go on," she says. "You can tease me about what's in here, just like I'll tease you about never having to do anything for yourself."

"Hey," I say. "I do *plenty* for myself."

"Yes, I see. You got dressed and brushed your teeth this morning."

"*And* I made breakfast." As the door finally stops growling and comes to a screechy halt, I turn back to the garage. The only way to describe the scene is...*horror.*

Pure horror.

A dank smell comes out of the garage that could be from water—*Or blood,* I think—and I see an assortment of sagging cardboard boxes, black garbage bags filled with who knows what, lawn tools, a pile of bricks, a couple of broken-down bicycles, and there—just peeking out of the shadow of the second garage space—the edge of the fountain I had already asked Tally about.

I cannot seem to get a proper breath, and not just from the smell.

"Eagles and owls," I swear.

"Indeed," Tally says gleefully. "What do you think? You'll help me clean this out as the price of admission for our Southern food tour date tonight?"

CHAPTER NINE

TAHLIA

"Okay, what about this dress?" I ask, stepping out of my closet and in front of my phone, where my friends have been kind enough to stay on video with me for the past forty-five minutes.

"That's a ten," Claudia says before anyone else can chime in. "Tally, that's *it*."

I smooth my hands over the scuba fabric of the royal-blue dress, keeping to myself for now that it's the same color as Cal's silk pajamas.

"I love those sleeves," Hillary says. "Where did you get that?"

"It was one of the rejects for Emma's wedding," I say.

"It's *amazing*," Emma says just as I reach up to touch one of the puffy sleeves. It has an elastic band that cinches around the middle of my upper arm, and then the scuba fabric has enough form to stand up tall over my shoulders. It has a sweetheart neckline that doesn't give away too much and leaves plenty of room for my favorite necklace—

one from my aunt that she gave me on my birthday the year before she died.

The fabric hugs my body to my waist, where another ruffle hides the extra weight I carry there, then swells over my hips and tapers to my knee.

"Is that the Charles Anson?" Lizzie asks. "*Sacramento* —it is." She breathes out her awe. "Tahlia. Why didn't you wear this to the wedding?"

"It's gorgeous," Ry says.

"What shoes are you going to wear with it?" Lizzie asks. "Because you're walking a little bit tonight, right?"

"Yeah," I say, suddenly self-conscious in my own skin. I've left my hair down all day, and I've added a little bit of curl to it tonight to go with my mascara, lip gloss, and smoky eye makeup.

"Before we move on to shoes, I just want to point out," Claudia says. "That Tahlia has her blue butterfly eye shadow on."

"How can you tell that?" Ryanne asks. "She's not even close enough—"

"Oh, loaded baked potatoes, she does!" Hillary shrieks. "Tahlia, come closer."

I grin while also internally sighing, and I move over to the dresser to pick up my phone. Yes, I've put the blue sparkly powder in the corner of my eyes.

"Mm, you *like* him," Emma says.

"What part of the last forty-five minutes has not given that away?" I ask. "Or any of the texts I've sent today?"

"I want a selfie by midnight," Claudia says. "Or I'm looking this guy up."

I've told them he's a prince and what country he's

from, and that he made me promise not to look him up online—and that I wanted them to do the same. They'd all promised, and as I look at Claudia's determined expression, I know I'm going to have to send her a picture or deal with her Googling Cal.

"I'll get a selfie, I promise," I tell her. "And yes, Lizzie, we're doing a Southern food tour. We're probably going to have to walk, or maybe ride one of those rail cars."

I sigh and set the phone back down. "I should maybe change the plan. Maybe a progressive dinner instead. This dress is too nice for a *food tour*. There's going to be tourists on that, and they'll be wearing their gross Hawaiian shirts and mismatched plaid shorts."

Lizzie shudders. "You're probably right."

"You cannot *not* wear that dress," Hillary says. "I mean it, Tahlia. You're wearing that. And you're going next door to my house, and you're making him come to the door and pick you up, all proper and prince-like."

I grin at her, because she knows how romantic I am about some things—including how I want my dates to go, and the men I go out with to treat me like a princess. And who better to do that than a prince?

"I think if you're going to change the plan to the progressive dinner," Ry says. "Any shoes are fine, but maybe those really cute black sandal wedges. You know the ones?"

"Yeah," I say. "I know what you're talking about."

"If you're going to be doing a lot of walking," Lizzie says. "You could try that pair of low silver heels I left at the Big House. They have a big, chunky, square heel, and I think they're only one inch."

"I've never worn those." I hold up my finger. "Give me a second." I jet back into the closet and find the black wedges easily, and they'll add at least three inches to my height. I teach in ballet flats or Crocs or sneakers, and I can't imagine having to walk very far in wedges.

I have to dig for a minute to find the silver heels Lizzie left behind, because her fashion sense and mine hardly align. I take both pairs of shoes back out to the bedroom and hold them up.

"Put one on each foot," Hillary says.

I sit down on the edge of my bed to do that, as the silver sandals require me to buckle something around my ankle. When I stand up, I put one hand on my hip, cock the other, and move the black sandal forward. "This one?" I pull it back and put the silver shoe forward. "Or this one?"

I look up at my friends on my phone to make sure they can see me. "I'll give you ten seconds to confer." I continue the movement a couple more times, showcasing each shoe.

"Do both silver ones and both black ones," Claudia says.

I demonstrate that, and then say, "Lizzie, you're on the top left of my screen. What do you think?"

"Silver," she says.

"Hill?"

"Silver."

"Ryanne?"

"I'm going to go with the black wedges."

"Emma?"

"Black wedges," she says.

"Claudia, you're the tie-breaking vote."

Really, I get to make my own decisions, and I know

which pair of shoes I like more. Claudia takes an extra moment, and then she says, "Becks and I both vote silver."

"Becks doesn't count," Lizzie says. "*Boooo.*"

But Claudia only laughs.

"What are you even doing here?" Ry asks. "Aren't you on your honeymoon?"

"It's not quite dinner time yet where we are," Lizzie says. "And Matt's in the shower."

"I think I'm going to go with the silver ones." I retrieve my phone and take it back to my bed to remove my shoes. "What if this is just all stupid?"

"Hey, don't say that," Hillary says. "The man came back from his own country, after begging his mother, mind you, so he can try to win you back."

She watches me with her dark eyes, so solemn and seeing so much. "Let him try."

I nod, though a thread of unease moves through my stomach.

"Just try to have an open mind," Claudia says. "Isn't that what you always told me about Becks?"

"Yeah, but that's because you hated him."

"Yeah? And you hate Cal," Claudia shoots back. "Stormclouds and Steel. It's like you've forgotten how much you trash-talked him, how much he hurt you."

"I haven't forgotten," I say, every cell in my body turning tight.

"Just the fact that we all know about him," Emma says. "Speaks about how much you liked him."

"Yeah, in *high school*," I say.

"And he was in high school too," Lizzie says. "And yet,

here he is. I don't know...there's something written in the stars about you two."

"Don't say that," I say, frowning at my friends. "There's nothing written in the stars. There's just the choices we make about the situations we find ourselves in."

No one says anything after that, because it's a lecture I've given them before.

"Tahlia," Hillary says, and I look at her tiny square on my screen. "You're right. So you're in a situation where you have a very royal roommate—whom I'm assuming is also very handsome—and he came to Cider Cove *for you*. He wants to get to know you now, as you are. So my question is, what are you going to *choose* to do in this situation?"

"Don't sabotage yourself," Ry says.

"Yeah, because we only need one friend to tease about that," Emma says, grinning, and I smile at her too. She and Aaron did sort of self-sabotage their relationship until they got out of the way.

"Just make the best choices you can," Claudia says.

"And don't do it with a mind in the past," Hillary adds. "Just focus on the here-and-now. The Cal Irwin in front of you—not the boy he used to be."

"It can be hard," Lizzie says. "I know what it's like to take someone you know really well and then turn them into a boyfriend. Especially if you've sort of held them on a pedestal and had feelings for them in the past."

I nod, because Lizzie and Matt did take their amazing friendship and turn it into something romantic. And no, it wasn't an easy road for her.

"Okay," I say. "I'm going to take off my dress and get over to Hillary's."

"Selfies!" Claudia calls, as if I've forgotten.

"You're gonna have so much fun tonight," Hill says.

"Yeah, just have fun," Lizzie adds.

I don't want to tell them that I don't know how to have fun, that the junior-high teacher in me tends to squash fun so we can get projects done before the bell rings, and the responsible homeowner in me is the one who has to worry about the mortgage, and the yard getting taken care of, and the bills being paid.

"It's going to be an amazing night," Emma says. "I mean, he's a *prince*, Tahlia. Can you imagine? I can't wait to see what he wears."

"Ooh, yes. Try to get a full-body shot," Ry says.

"Holy tater tot casserole, you guys," Hillary says, her voice made mostly of air. "We have a ring cam on the house."

"I'm hanging up now," I say. "Hillary, don't you dare share out that footage."

"Oh, I'm sharing out the footage," she calls. "You guys, watch your texts!"

I groan, but I can't help smiling as everyone waves and blows kisses and the video call ends. I'm left in the silence of my bedroom, and while I usually crave silence above the constant chatter of eighth graders, right now it only allows my mind to conjure up horrible situations—where I trip and fall because I haven't worn sandals like this in forever —and allows it to whisper that I'm not pretty enough for a prince. That nothing I own is nice enough to go out with Cal. That what about me could possibly intrigue him and hold his attention long enough to eat dinner and walk around downtown?

I shimmy out of my dress and grab my earbuds from my nightstand. Once they're in, I turn on the playlist I was listening to last night, gather up everything I need, and head next door.

I change right back into the dress and secure the sandals to my feet, leaving myself only ten minutes before Cal should arrive to pick me up for our dinner date. I wonder if he'll drive himself or if Don will chaperone us. Then I worry about if I'll have to sit in the front seat with Don while Cal rides in the back between Ajax and Titan. Will it be five of us on a date, because Cal can't be left to his own devices in a foreign city?

I shake my hands, because I just don't know, and I'm not great going into situations where I don't know what's going to happen.

Precisely at six o'clock, the doorbell rings, and since I'm standing in the kitchen, I hear the patriotic tune Liam has programmed on his doorbell cam. The screen brightens, and sure enough, Cal stands there.

He's wearing a full suit.

"Holy mother of catfish," I whisper, because the light gray looks amazing with his sandy hair and his oceanic eyes. He wears a pale purple shirt underneath his jacket and black shiny shoes on his feet. He must be sweltering hot, and yet not a bead of sweat shows on his face.

He looks right at the cam and waves. "It's just me, Tally," he says in that ultra-smooth European accent that makes my knees weak and my stomach vibrate with nerves.

As I spin away from the security camera and start toward the front door, my phone starts buzzing like mad, and I know that means my roommates have seen him.

They've heard him. They know about the sexy accent now and the way his hair swoops just-so, and they're going to be listening when I open the door.

They're listening. They're watching. They're listening. They're watching, I tell myself with every step. Then I open the door and see him standing there in the flesh.

He's a god in human form, and his smile radiates absolute sunshine and positivity.

"Good evening," he says, oh-so-formally. He holds up a bouquet of flowers that he had to have bought from Emma's shop. "I had Don get these while he was in town today. I told him something bright and pretty—like you."

I can practically hear my friends *aww*-ing, and I step forward and take the flowers from him with a soft, muted, "Thank you. They're beautiful."

I glance at the camera. "Do you want to come in for a minute while I put them in water? Because, full disclosure, all of my previous housemates are currently watching and listening to this conversation."

Cal looks at the ring camera too, a look of pure horror crossing his face. "Really?"

As if we'd choreographed it, the doorbell cam beeps, and Hillary says, "Yes, really. You look very handsome tonight, Cal."

"Oh, it's Hillary," he says. "I recognize your voice."

"Liam wants to know if your suit is a Calabachi or an Intamin," she says.

"Lizzie says it's an Intamin," Liam yells. "But I don't believe her."

"We think—" Hillary starts, but I step in front of Cal

and peer into the camera. "Are you serious right now? You're asking him what designer-brand his suit is?"

Cal chuckles from behind me, and I cover the camera with my hand. "Let's go inside. They've had enough of a show."

I march in first, and Cal follows, closing the door behind him.

"Are there cameras in here too?" he asks.

I continue on toward the kitchen, where I'm sure I'll be able to find a vase. "I don't think so," I say. "Sorry about them."

I pull down an extra-tall cup from Hillary's cabinet and fill it with water before I plunk the flowers into it. They are happy and bright—pink and yellow and orange— and they make me smile. I touch the petal of a daisy and then look at him. "Thank you. These are beautiful." I scan him right down to his shiny shoes. "And you do look good enough to eat."

He chuckles and comes closer to me. And then closer. And then closer.

"This dress is the most fabulous thing I've ever seen." He slides his hand along the top of the ruffle at my waist and pulls me right against him. "And you can let your roommates know that my suit is actually a Matinetini, which *is* Italian."

"I'm sure it is," I say dryly.

"Did you decide on the walking tour or the progressive dinner?"

I look up at him, suddenly nervous again. "I don't know. What do you think?"

"I'm thinking we switch to the progressive dinner," he

says. "Then we can have longer conversations, and I can hold your hand when we walk down the sidewalk to the next place. Then, it won't be you playing tour guide or us in a crowd of tourists."

I nod and note the way his eyes drop to my lips. He reaches up and tucks my hair behind my ear as he leans close. He touches his temple to mine and whispers, "You are the most gorgeous woman in the world, and I'm the luckiest man to go out with you tonight."

With that, he steps back and offers me his arm. "I think our ride is about here. Let's go out front."

I link my arm through his, the thrill of having his body so close to mine echoing through me. "Is Don driving us?"

"No," Cal says. "And let me tell you, it was quite the fight."

"Will they be shadowing us?"

Cal clears his throat, and I know the answer before he says, "Yes. But they promised we wouldn't see them."

"I won't even look," I tell him. "So how are we going to get downtown?"

He opens the front door and leads me out onto the porch, where a perfectly normal, white SUV waits in the driveway.

"I called a RideShare," he says. "Apparently it's how you get around here if you don't have a car."

I grin at the driver and then at Cal. "It's perfect," I tell him, a brand new giddiness galloping through me that maybe Cal and I will be able to have the perfect first date after all.

CHAPTER TEN

CALLAN

I PRETEND NOT TO SEE THE BLACK TOWN CAR halfway down the block that leads to the parking area behind the Big House. I purposely sat on the left side of the car behind the driver so I could block Tally's view of this very road. Donald, Titan, and Ajax have been sitting there for at least twenty minutes, though I've given them our full itinerary.

I pull in a breath, and Tally turns toward me.

"What?" she asks.

"I just realized." I turn toward her, my eyes wide and pure wonder wandering through me. "I gave Don the itinerary for the Southern food tour."

Tally's eyes zip between mine. "And we're not doing the Southern food tour."

"No," I say. "We're not." I look forward and catch the driver's eye. "Can you just pull off right here?"

"Right here?" he asks.

"Right now," I say, in probably one of the most commanding voices I've ever used.

He slams on the brake, wrenches the wheel to the right, and pulls down the street we were almost past.

"Pull into the driveway up here," Tally says. "See that one with the big truck in it? Can you park behind it?"

I love that she's picked up on this so quickly.

The guy goes, "I guess," as he pulls into a stranger's driveway and puts his SUV in park. "You guys aren't going to kill me, are you?"

Tally laughs and says, "I'm a junior high art teacher. Of course we're not going to kill you."

"You never know," the guy says. "There's all kinds of whack teachers in the news these days."

"We're not going to harm you," I tell him. "We're just trying to throw off my bodyguards."

That raises his eyebrows. "Yeah? Where are you from, man?"

Tally slips her hand into mine, and my mind goes blissfully blank.

"He's from overseas," Tally says when I don't tell this RideShare driver every intimate detail of my life.

"Why you got bodyguards?"

"I just do," I say. "And if you can give me ten minutes right here, I'll double your fee."

"Yeah, no problem, man." He removes his phone from the holder on his dashboard and starts to scroll.

I look over to Tally. "I gave them the starting point for the food tour and the different restaurants we were going to, and then said that we would be walking around downtown, maybe on the boardwalk, and then calling a RideShare from that beachfront park."

Her grip in mine tightens, and I squeeze back. I'm

going to have to face some seriously loud music eventually, but right now, being with Tally alone is worth it.

"This is so exciting," she says. "I was a little nervous about how we'd get around tonight. I thought Don and the German Shepherds might be chaperoning us."

I chuckle, adding the sound to her giggles. "The German Shepherds?"

She grins at me. "Titan and Ajax. I mean, come *on*, Cal. Those are *total* German Shepherd names." She laughs fully now, and it's gorgeous and free.

I suppose Titan and Ajax are a bit like German Shepherds.

"But it was a fight for you?" she asks after she sobers, clearly prompting me to tell her more.

"Oh, it was a fight," I say. "No one seems to understand that I'm thirty-five years old and know how to get around on my own."

"Do you though?" she teases. "Can you even drive in America?"

"I mean, I haven't for a while," I say. "But how hard can it be?"

"It's hard if you're not used to driving on the right side of the road."

"I think I could pick it up again pretty quick," I say. "But part of the deal was that I would call a ride and they would follow."

"I can't believe you're breaking the deal at all," she says. "You should have texted Don before we even left Liam's house."

A thrill runs through me that I've never experienced before. "I can't believe it either," I say.

"You always play by the rules."

"Well, not tonight, Tally-Mae." I too pull out my phone and look at the list of restaurants I'd put together for the progressive dinner. I'd also told the RideShare driver that we were going to be going on the Southern food tour. I lean forward. "We want to go somewhere else. Can you change our destination?"

"Yeah, but it might cost more," he says.

"That's fine," I tell him, because my mother has given me a generous budget for my escapades here in the United States.

"Where are we going now?" he asks. "And you understand that if someone calls in to RideShare and wants to know where you went, that we legally have to tell them, right?"

I meet his eye in the rearview mirror again, my heart pumping out an extra beat. "Is there a way to delay that?"

"I don't know, man," he says. "Sounds like you two have some problems you need to work out."

"Yes, thank you," Tally says briskly with a hint of sarcasm in her voice. "Where are we going for our appetizers, sweetheart?"

Sweetheart.

I gape at her, and she looks at me meaningfully. I startle and look at my phone again. I had picked a restaurant & bar on the outskirts of the city, not quite in the suburbs, called Whiskey Way, and I turn my phone toward her and show it to her.

"Yeah, that should be fine," she says.

"Have you been there?" I ask.

She shakes her head and lifts her own phone. "I can look up the menu."

She does that while I give the address to the RideShare driver.

"This looks really nice," Tally says. "We can have drinks and apps here."

I nod and settle back into my seat, take Tally's hand in mine again, and say, "We can probably go now."

The RideShare driver backs out of the driveway and gets us on our way, and we arrive at the restaurant only twenty minutes later.

I put my hand on the small of Tally's back as we move into the building, which is dark inside, though it's still plenty light outside, and filled with the vibe of young people, though it's too early for any of them to be here yet.

"Two?" a woman asks, already picking up menus.

"Yes," I say. "And can we have somewhere in the quietest corner here?"

"You got it, hon." She leads us through the restaurant and up to the second floor. It's far quieter up there, away from the bar and the makeshift stage, even though there was no one on it.

"How's this?" She indicates a cozy booth for two in front of a window that overlooks the street.

"It's great," Tally says. "Look at this view, Cal."

She slides into the booth on one side, and I nod to the hostess and take the other side. She sets down the menus and says, "We have a couple of specials on drinks and dinner tonight, so be sure to ask your waiter about that."

"Sure," I tell her, and she walks away.

Tally's nose is pressed against the window, and when

she turns back to me, she radiates the energy of a golden retriever. "I do love the city," she says.

"Do you?" I ask. "I thought you craved the quiet."

"I do," she says. "It's really both. There's something about coming and feeding off the energy here and then being able to retreat to my quiet house on Cherry Lane."

"Hmm." I hum at her and realize I sound very much like my father.

The waiter arrives and tells us about their drink and dinner specials.

"We're doing a progressive dinner and just want drinks and appetizers," I tell him. "Is that okay?"

"Yeah, that's fine," he says, though I'm pretty sure he'll probably barely check on us, assuming his tip won't be very big. My parents taught me to tip well, and I hope to prove him wrong tonight.

"I want that Main Beach Squeeze," Tally says. "That specialty drink with the pineapple sherbet."

"You got it." The waiter looks to me, the same way Tally has.

"And I want the virgin Paloma."

"Do you guys know what you want for apps yet?"

I shake my head and pick up the menu. "No, we need a minute on that."

"You got it. I'll be right back with those drinks." He walks away, and I peer at the appetizer menu while Tally watches me.

"What?" I finally ask. "Do you want the artichoke dip? The pimento cheese?"

"You don't drink?" she asks.

I shake my head. "We *hold* drinks at social functions,

but we don't actually drink them. My mother has drilled into me that alcohol consumption only happens at home, behind closed doors, when you have many days to sleep off whatever might happen."

"Wow," she says.

"I don't care if you drink."

"Oh, I'm a lightweight," she says. "I'll only have one."

I tip my menu toward hers. "The pimento cheese?"

"Yeah, we've *gotta* have the pimento cheese," she says. "It's a classic Southern appetizer, and I want you to try it. Oh, they have the street corn dip. We should get that too."

The waiter returns with our drinks a few minutes later, and we put in no less than four appetizers: the pimento cheese, the street corn dip, the hot artichoke dip *with* chicken, and a nice, tall, greasy stack of onion rings.

I make a face at the last one, and Tally laughs as she hands her menu to the waiter. "You're going to love them, I promise."

"I doubt that highly," I say.

"Try to have an open mind." She unwraps her straw and pokes it down into her tropical drink, which starts out yellow like the sand, moves up into green and then blue, and is topped with a white foam of whipped cream.

"That looks amazing," I tell her.

She takes a sip and goes, "Ooh, that is boozy." She blinks rapidly and pushes it further from her. "Yeah, that's got a *lot* of rum in it."

I smile and take a drink of my Paloma, which doesn't have any alcohol. The smoky flavor almost chokes the back of my throat, but I manage to get it down without making a fool of myself.

Our eyes meet, and I notice the sparkles in the corners of her eyes from her makeup. She makes everything tense inside of me release, and I smile at her.

"I thought we could start with maybe something new about us that the other doesn't know."

She nods. "You go first."

"I have to go first? I've already told you that I'm a prince from a foreign country. I don't have much else."

She cocks her head, considering me with those bright blue eyes. "Well, I'm a junior high art teacher, and I still like my coffee with two creams and one sugar, and I think everything needs extra salt."

"And you like Queen," I say. "I don't think I knew that."

"I like all the classic rock," she says. "It has such a good vibe, you know?"

I nod. "I suppose I could say I served in the Notavella military for five years. I don't think I told you about that."

"You did mention military service," she says. "So it's just for your country?"

"Yes," I say. "The Royal Navy, in fact."

"Ooh, it sounds fancy." She smiles at me. "I used to love to chew bubble gum, but now I can't." She reaches up and touches her jaw. "Well, I can for a few minutes, but it hurts my jaw after that."

"I'd forgotten about the bubble gum," I say, so many memories coming forward. "You used to be able to blow bubbles as big as your whole head."

Tally laughs, the sound infusing me with happiness. "I did. Sadly, not anymore." She quiets and watches me for a moment. "Let's see...you know how to cook now."

"Yes," I say. "As do you."

"I *bake*—but you don't know how to drive."

"Hey, I know how to drive."

She grins. "Do you know how to run a dishwasher?"

"Yes. You left detailed instructions in your 'Welcome to the Big House' binder." I point at her. "So you're still organized and like to make lists."

"Guilty," she says.

"And you look amazing in blue."

She looks down at her dress. "Did you notice this matches your royal pajamas?"

Oh, I'd noticed. But I simply nod. "The royal colors are blue and red and black."

"Oh, the *royal colors*," she says, and laughs again. "Are you allowed to wear other colors?" She nods to my shirt. "You're wearing purple tonight."

"Oh, Tally." I lean closer. "Haven't you figured out yet that I'm the black sheep of the family?"

She giggles and shakes her head, but I'm speaking the truth. "If I were to wear this in Notavella, there would be no less than three articles about it the next day. Probably some by that evening."

She sobers. "You're kidding."

"I can assure you, I'm not."

"So let me ask you this," she says. The moment between us shifts from playful and teasing to something more serious. "And you don't have to answer right now or anything." She glances out into the restaurant as the hostess brings another couple upstairs. "In fact, I'd like it if you *didn't* answer right now."

"Okay," I say, my guard all the way up.

"So you're only going to be here for six months," she says. "And then what, Cal? What's the plan? Let's say me and you decide we want to be together. Am I moving to Notavella and having my every clothing choice scrutinized? Or will you be able to come to Cider Cove and live here with me?"

I should have known Tally would pull out the big guns on the first date, because she's never been one to hold back or pull punches. She's asked me to think about this and answer later, and oh, how I want to give her what she wants.

I think of my mother and how most of my decisions are not wholly mine. It takes a special person to be with a prince and be his princess. And while I want Tally to be that, it's a *huge* expectation she'll need time to come to terms with. So I simply nod and say, "Those are great questions."

She nods as well and looks up as the waiter arrives with our tower of onion rings.

"Just think about it," she says, and then squeals, her demeanor changing on a dime. "Look at these, Cal."

All four plates get delivered, and Tally pulls off the smallest onion ring from the top of the tower and hands it to me. "You get the first bite."

I shake my head, but I take the piping hot onion ring from her and pinch it between two fingers. "I don't know about this."

"You can have it with the chipotle ranch," she says, moving the tower platter closer, which also has three dips in little cups along the bottom. "I think that one's blue cheese, and this one is fry sauce. It's ketchup and mayo."

"Ketchup and mayo." I eye the peachy-orange sauce like a tidal wave of it will lash up and drown me. "I'm not touching that."

None of the sauces sound good, and they certainly don't seem like they'll amplify the taste of this fried onion ring. So I put it in my mouth plain, and it's hot, and salty, and crispy...and yet soft. It feels like joy dancing across my tongue. My eyes widen, and I nod at her as I chew and then swallow. "Yeah, that's not bad.

"Not bad." She scoffs and takes the next onion ring and dunks it in the chipotle ranch. "It's the food of the gods." She takes a big bite, and I can only laugh at her exuberance for onion rings.

By the time we leave Whiskey Way, I'm pretty sure I'm sliding down into falling all the way in love with Tally again, and it's only the first date.

Still, her question weighs on me even as we walk down the block to an Italian place I'd mapped out as the second stop on our progressive dinner.

In a perfect world, Tally would come to Notavella and live with me in my castle as my princess. My mother would give us official titles, and we'd live happily ever after in a tiny European country too far from the beach for my liking.

But as I settle across another table, in another booth, in another restaurant, from Tally, I wonder if she'll ever be able to leave everything she's ever loved and known here in the U.S. and follow me across the sea.

CHAPTER ELEVEN

TAHLIA

"All right." I reach back and pull my ponytail tight, ready for battle mode. As the garage door lifts on my side, Cal finishes punching in the code on the left, and his door starts to screech and howl as it rumbles up as well.

I've decided I want to start parking in here, and I've had the Big House now for ten years since my aunt died. It's time for me to clean out some old things and move on. I've been putting this off for way too long, and now that there's no one here to share the rent with me, I've decided I have to be the adult that paperwork everywhere says I am.

Still, the thought of working through the physical items in this garage makes my stomach twist. Not only that, but I'll have to face emotional demons and sift through the ghosts of my past at the same time.

I glance over to Cal, realizing that I've made a grave mistake by asking him to help me. I won't be able to break down into sobs at the sight of a picture or a coffee cup. I tell myself that I'm stronger than that now. Besides, if Cal can't handle me crying a little bit, that sounds like a him-problem that he'll have to figure out.

"Wow. Look at this," he says, his voice filled with far more excitement than it should be for anything this garage may contain.

I can admit I don't know everything in here, as my aunt cleaned out the Big House before she died, and I've never gone through the boxes. Yes, I have a little bit of a hoarder tendency, because I grew up so poor with so little, and I can't stand seeing things go to waste or discarded and left behind.

I myself was discarded and left behind, and I can't stand doing that to anything, even something as insignificant as a lawn mower that doesn't run anymore and that no one has used in fifteen years.

It's not the lawn mower that Cal pulls out of the garage now, but a dull orange canoe. He looks at me, his blue-eyed gaze filled with wonder and light. "Look at this, Tally," he says. "We can go *canoeing*."

"You're out of your mind," I shoot back at him. "I'm not going canoeing."

He releases the watercraft, and the heavy wooden boat thunks to the ground. He bends over and lifts out an oar that has a cracked yellow paddle and is missing the top half of the stick.

"I can fix this up."

"You can fix that up?" I snort and then start to laugh. "Cal, I had to help you call the RideShare so we could get home the other night."

"That was because I had no service on my phone," he

says. "Not because I couldn't navigate to the app." He shoots me a glare and then dives back into the canoe, pulling out a helmet.

"I'm good on the water," he says. "You have everything you need. Why are we not out on the lake right now?"

"What lake?" I challenge. "You had to give the guy the address to the Big House four times before we got back here the other night."

"Oh, come on," he says, his grin refusing to be dulled by anything I'm saying—though everything is true.

He steps forward with that once-red helmet in his hand. "You liked the other night, didn't you?" His grin grows. "It's kind of fun having an adventure and figuring things out as we go. Nobody wants someone who's perfect, do they?"

"I do," I say, raising my chin in defiance. "I expect and want pure perfection."

He looks at me and searches my face, finally rolling his eyes and turning away from me when he realizes I'm teasing. He stands in front of the canoe, his back to me, inspecting something inside. "Are you going to get rid of this?" he asks over his shoulder.

I move over to stand next to him, looking at the canoe I've ridden in many times. "It's my uncle's. He used to take us fishing on it in the summer."

"So you *do* participate in outdoor activities in the summer," he says.

Peaceful memories of still water like glass, trees in the distance, and the hot, baking sun overhead flow through my mind. "It wasn't so bad back then," I say. "Because it was an escape from my real life, and heat, humidity, and bugs were minor inconveniences compared to that."

He puts his arm around me and pulls me into his side. "Hmm. So you just don't do much canoeing these days."

"No," I say. "That thing probably has a ton of leaks in it."

"If I fixed it up, maybe we could go—maybe when it's cooler, you know, in the fall."

I look up at him and see the hope shining in every pore of his face. "If you fix it up with your two hands—no help from Thor and Atlas, no calling in a handyman—then I'll go canoeing with you."

He tips his head back and laughs. "Their names are Ajax and Titan, not Thor and Atlas."

"It's about the same," I say. "They're all names for a German Shepherd."

That sets him off on another round of glorious laughter while I face the left side of the garage where he pulled out the canoe. It's barely made a hole in the items that have been left here, and I take a deep breath and dive into the mess.

"I've got a dumpster coming on Monday," I say. "And they'll come pick it up anytime I call and say it's full."

"Well, I don't want this to go in the dumpster," he says. "I'm going to give it a real American try to fix it up, because I think it would be super-fun to go canoeing."

He starts to drag the canoe across the small cement pad to the side of the garage while I wonder if he knows how adorable he is when he says things like *super-fun*.

I move over to the wire shelves attached to the side of the garage and look up at the dingy coolers I've never once had an occasion to use. I have cute sweet tea containers and pitchers in the house, and it's not like I go camping, hiking, or canoeing, where I need to take an ice chest with food into the wilderness.

"I think we should make a pile for garbage," I say. "And then one for me to go through, and one for things to keep."

"All right," he says. "I know I'm just here for the muscle, so tell me what you want me to do."

"I think we should put the garbage pile around the other side of the garage from where you just put that canoe. We can put the keep pile over there, and the pile for me to go through can stay here in the garage."

"All right," he says. "So what's going in the keep pile and what's going in the trash pile, right off the top of your head?"

I gaze at the shelves again and see a bag that probably contains an old air mattress, a filing crate that I have no idea what's inside, and two bags that hold shades—the kind my aunt used to put up in the backyard and put tables under to serve lunch for her friends out of the direct sunlight.

"I think everything on these shelves can go in the garbage pile," I tell him. "Except that black crate. I don't know what's in it."

"All right," he says, and Cal, while wearing a polo and a pair of dark brown slacks, starts pulling off dusty, disgusting coolers and walking them around to the *Trash* side of the garage.

I push out the lawn mower and add it to the pile, then tell him, "Both bikes too," with a mighty frown on my face.

He's just passing me, and he stops and puts his hand on my arm. "Hey, are you all right?"

I hate that the question undoes me so completely. My eyes burn with unshed tears as I shake my head. "The big red bike was my aunt's," I say. "And she got me the blue one the summer before you moved here. We rode those bikes all over that summer, and she got in a real big fight with my dad when she sent it home with me."

He watches me carefully, a contemplative look in his eye. He doesn't rush in to apologize or hold me, but says, "I remember that blue bike. You rode it everywhere."

I sniffle, wipe my eyes, and nod. "It was the only way I had to get around. That bike represented freedom for me."

"Well, maybe we should fix it up," he says. "Maybe you could ride it around the neighborhood; put those cinnamon rolls for Mister Beasley in a basket." He tries a smile, but it fades quickly.

"I don't really ride a bike anymore," I say, though I think of Liam and the big shed he has in front of his orchard where he works on old bikes, cars, and trucks. He could definitely fix it up for me, even if no one ever rides it again. "I don't really have the money to fix it."

"All right," he says, and he continues past me, while I move to the back corner of the garage and take a moment to breathe in. The garage is shaded in the morning by the big trees that grow wild along the property line between my house, Liam's, and Mr. Beasley's.

Cal brings out one bike, and I turn to go give him more directions. I round the front corner of the garage just as I see him push the blue bike around to the *Keep* side of the garage.

My heart does a cartwheel in my chest, and I'm not sure if I want to yell out to him that he's putting it in the wrong place, or run over to him, hug him, and cry into his chest that he took this horrible decision from me and is keeping the bike.

He comes back and freezes when he sees me standing there. We're several yards apart, but I feel closer to him than ever, and he gives me a small, very European nod before going back into the garage.

He comes out with a wheelbarrow that's seen better days. "This looks like something your aunt used."

"Yes," I say, surprised at how strong my voice is. "I want to keep that, because I think I can fix it up, paint it her favorite color, and maybe put topsoil in it and grow her favorite flower in the front yard."

He pushes it toward me, the wheel bumping along awkwardly because it's been misshapen from years of sitting.

"What color will you paint it?" he asks.

"Red, of course," I say. "Like the bike."

"Like the bike," he echoes. "And what's her favorite flower?"

"Petunias," I say. "Purple and pink and white."

He nods, and as he pushes the wheelbarrow past me—surely getting splinters in his hands from those awful posts—he says, "I'd like to see that, Tally. I think it'd be real pretty out in front of the house."

Then he wheels around me and takes the wheelbarrow back to the Keep side of the garage. I go inside and look at the stack of boxes closest to me.

When he joins me, I take his hand in mine to anchor

myself. "These are my aunt's clothes. My roommates and I went through them all already, but I couldn't get rid of them." I look up at him. "I think I'm ready now. We can move all of these to the trash pile."

He doesn't ask me if I'm sure. He simply watches me, giving me space to feel and breathe and be who I am. I appreciate that more than anything, and I move my hand up and link it through his as I lay my head against his bicep.

"I told myself that this was going to be a tear-free summer," I whisper.

"Did you?" he asks.

"Yes," I say. "I don't want to cry myself to sleep at night anymore, and I don't want to be sad over the things of the past that were actually the only happy things in my life."

"You cry yourself to sleep?" he whispers, his arm tightening against mine.

I don't know how to explain to him the vastness of how empty I've felt for the past several months as Emma and Lizzie planned their weddings. There are no words to explain the hollowness and the fear of being alone forever. So I simply say, "It was very hard for me to watch all of my roommates fall in love, get married, and move out."

My voice moves up into my nose, and I take a moment to spell out *sassafras*—that always centers my emotions, as it gives me something else to focus on instead of the internal hurt and the endless pain. It's actually a trick I learned as a second grader, who thought that if they got perfect scores on their math tests and spelling word lists every week, that her mom and dad would pay attention to her, that there would be food in the house, and that they might start to care more about her than they did about their next fix.

I take a step forward, releasing Cal as I go, and pick up the top box. I move it to the *Trash* side with Cal behind me, and we work in silence for a few minutes.

"I'm really sorry about your roommates," he says.

"It's okay," I tell him. "They're really happy, and of course, I want them to be happy."

"You just want to be happy too," he says.

I nod, and I look at the little bit of space we've cleared in the garage. "The Big House makes me happy," I say. "And I love teaching. It's just—"

Cal moves to the back of the garage where my uncle had built in a workbench. "I felt the same in Notavella, you know," he says. "What do I possibly have to be unhappy about? My own castle, a great job, people at my side getting me anything and everything I've ever wanted. And yet..."

He moves down the workbench just a little bit, picks something up and then replaces it. He won't turn and look at me, and I've learned in only the six days that Cal has been in town that it's easier for him to say things when he's not looking someone in the face.

I pick up an old cat tower, thinking of my aunt's felines, and move it to the trash pile. I've never been overly fond of cats, and if I were to have a real pet, it wouldn't be a tortoise, but a little lap dog who would curl into my hip at night and jump up on my knees when I get home from school, because she's so excited to see me.

Cal meets me in the doorway of the garage when I return. "The main argument I used so that I could come here and live in the Big House with you was my unhappiness. Really, it stemmed from how lonely I was." He gestures behind him in the direction of the Big House. "And it doesn't matter if you have an amazing castle to live in, or an amazing house that feels like a sanctuary."

Tears come to my eyes, because the Big House has always represented safety for me. I'm *safe* within its walls, and I'm at peace, and the appliances work, and there is air conditioning in the summer and heat in the winter, and food year-round. There is love and acceptance and belonging, and I cannot imagine what my life would be without the Big House.

He brushes his fingers against mine. "But if you don't have someone to share it with, none of it really seems to matter, at least to me."

I nod and wipe at my eyes again, glad I've managed to contain the tears there instead of letting them stream down my face. "Did you date at all in Notavella?" I ask.

He scoffs and looks away. "Yes, but everything I do is under a microscope, and as I said, no one held my interest."

I look over to the wall where he's focused. "All of that is my uncle's fishing equipment. Maybe you'll want to go through it and see what's salvageable."

He lights up again and nods. "Sure," he says. "But what else do we need to take out first?"

I get him going on the old barrels in the back where my aunt kept dry beans and rice. "They're at least fifty years old," I tell him. "And no good. We just need to get rid of them."

He ends up turning them on their sides and rolling them out of the garage while I move out more boxes of my aunt's old gardening clothes, gloves, and aprons. Again,

I've already kept everything I want, and I'm ready to get rid of these things now.

"Why do I hold your interest?" I ask him when we've been working for about an hour.

Cal stills in loading a box we've emptied with old tools. "What do you mean?"

"You said no one in Notavella held your interest," I say. "How in the world do I do that?" He blinks at me, clearly surprised by the question. "Out of everyone I know, I'm the most boring," I say. "I'm vanilla when others are chocolate and rocky road and key lime pie."

He abandons the tool bench and walks over to me, but I don't dare look at him. "I teach junior high art, Cal. There's nothing interesting about that. I don't like doing outdoor things, and I can barely keep up with my responsibilities here at the Big House." I finally look at him, the challenge rising through me. "So how is it that someone with such a boring job and such a boring life can capture your attention?"

After all, I've never had much luck with men at all, but I keep that to myself.

"You don't see yourself clearly," he says. "You have an adventurous spirit. Need I remind you that I came after you on Sunday night, thinking you'd gone into the *orchards* to *sleep*?"

I smile, but it comes and goes as quickly as a breath. "I *used* to be adventurous, Cal. Now I'm practical, responsible, reliable."

"Those are all excellent qualities," he says. "And you're funny and beautiful and smart." He takes one of my hands in his and moves the other to cradle my face. "You make me laugh, and you make me think, and no one has done either since the day I left South Carolina eighteen years ago."

"That can't be true," I whisper.

Cal leans closer, his eyes falling closed, and he says, "It's true," right before he touches his lips to mine.

I've kissed this person before, but as a much younger version of himself. Heck, a much younger version of myself.

A flame ignites inside me, and I kiss him back with probably a little bit too much behind it. He keeps pace with me and then takes control again and deepens the kiss, holding me close against his chest and making me feel treasured and smart and beautiful and all the other wonderful things he says I am.

He pulls away and tucks his head into the hollow of my neck, his breath washing against my skin softly. He says nothing, and I find I don't have anything to articulate either. When he finally raises his head and looks into my eyes, I swear I see my whole future with him.

But I can't tell where we are, and I can't tell who else is with us. Everything in the background is blurry and dark, and a thread of fear moves through me at what I might have to give up to be with Cal.

"I'm going to Washington next week," he says.

"Yes." I back up and tuck my hands in my back pockets, feeling the summer heat now that we've been working for a while. "Let's be done for today, okay?"

He nods, and together we close the garage doors. Then he takes my hand and leads me back to the Big House, where Shellvador Dalí greets us in the kitchen with a look of total tortoise judgment about where we've been all morning and what we've been doing.

"Ah, there you are, Your Majesty," Donald says in his crisp accent, and while Cal shoots him a dirty look from where he's standing in front of the fridge, I'm bluntly reminded that Cal is a prince, and I'm nowhere near good enough to be his princess.

CHAPTER TWELVE

CAL

"Okay, I have to go." Tally picks up her oversized tote bag with a variety of paintings all over it. She's signed up for a summer gardening class, and it happens to be starting the same day I'm headed to the airport to go to Washington D.C.

Donald gets to his feet and goes to open the back door for her. Titan and Ajax track his movement, but their eyes switch to me as I stand too. She flicks a look to Don first, then to me as I approach.

Yes, I kissed her a week ago, but I haven't done so again. I don't know why. Maybe because the first time happened while she was semi-crying, and I want the next time to be more about passion than *com*passion.

"Have fun," I say, easing her into my arms. "I'll text you when we're settled at the hotel." I step back and smile at her, then sweep a kiss across her cheek. She presses into the touch but falls back quickly.

Her smile is a little tighter than usual, and I know it has everything to do with the other three men in the room.

"Your Majesty," Titan practically growls. "We need to head out too."

"Yes," I say, shooting him a death glare for using the YM-words. "My briefcase bag is still upstairs." I hold my ground while Tally leaves through the back door, but when Don meets my eyes, I can't linger any longer.

I sigh and turn away from his raised eyebrows. He must be bored out of his mind, babysitting me while I feed Shellvador lettuce for breakfast, lunch, and dinner, or following Tally and I around as we get to know each other again.

I have plenty to say, but I don't want to press my luck. Ditching my detail for my first date with Tally earned me an hours-long meeting where-in plenty of threats were made, all including looping in the Queen and-or buying a one-way return plane ticket to Notavella.

So I leave the kitchen, though my irritation boils in my blood. The silence of the Big House feels like a heavy shroud, far more oppressive than the usual quiet of the palace back home. There, silence means efficiency, the smooth operation of a well-oiled machine, and no scandals to deal with.

Here, it just means no one's home. I'm not thrilled about leaving her here, even for a few days. The thought of her navigating the empty rooms alone, or worse, cleaning out that infernal garage by herself, twists my gut.

At least we got the massive fountain out. She considered putting it back in, then decided she didn't want to deal with a water feature. It took me, Don, and the Shepherds to get it in the Dumpster.

My phone whizzes and chimes with Tally's assigned

sound as I reach the third-floor hallway. I tug it out of my slacks pocket and smile at the message sitting on the screen. The top of the screen sucks it away, and I quickly tap in my passcode to read the whole thing.

Don't be too princely in Washington D.C., she says. *Just be yourself.*

I scoff, because that's so easy for her to say. I duck into the last room on the right and pick up my black briefcase bag. I pause for a moment, though I should return to the kitchen immediately. I can text from the car.

But I stay in the doorway of my room and tap out a quick response to Tally. *I miss you already. Promise me we'll find a way to be together without my irritating security guards when I get back.*

I tuck my phone back into my pocket and return to the kitchen. Titan indicates the back door, where Ajax meets me on the porch. Donald is already waiting by the shiny black Town Car, holding open the back passenger door. Titan comes to my side as I start down the steps, and Ajax joins him, giving me more room on the right than the other guard.

Even in the humid morning air of Cider Cove, they manage to exude a sense of serious, unyielding duty. I see Tally's old blue bike sitting by the side of the garage, where I'd moved it to the Keep pile last week. I made a promise to her, an unspoken one, to fix it up. It represents her freedom, she'd said, and I understand that deeply. It's a stark contrast to the life I'm about to step back into.

"Your agenda, Your Highness," Donald says, his voice crisp and professional, entirely devoid of the mild exasperation I've grown accustomed to since his arrival in South Carolina.

Great. He's back to protocol, and we haven't even left town yet.

A heavy, internal sigh builds beneath my breastbone that I try to keep from escaping. "Thank you," I say, a brief smile touching my lips as I slide into the backseat of the car.

Donald gets behind the wheel while Ajax closes the door and claps a couple of times on the roof. He and Titan then pile into a second car, where they'll lead the way to the airport, clear everything there ahead of my arrival, and ensure I get to my private jet without incident. I do appreciate the smoothness this trip will have, and the frustration I have about having my detail around fades.

My phone whizz-chimes again, and I tug my phone out of my pocket again. *That seems like something you need to promise me,* Tally's said. *You're the one with the detail, not me, Cal.*

Cal.

Here, in Tally's world, I just want to be Cal, and seeing that title on my phone makes my chest warm, a small rebellion against the inevitable.

"We'll have dinner at the embassy tonight, sir," Donald says, a clear prompting for me to stop flirting through my phone and get to the agenda. We always talk everything through during the travel to the airport, and I flip open the portfolio.

"I'm looking at it now, Donald," I say, a warning in my tone. He gives me an imperceptible nod, understanding that I don't want to take this trip. I don't want to be in rooms with important men, pretending like I'm the same as them.

I'm not, and everyone—except my mother—knows it.

The air in the car feels thicker, constrained, compared to the open freedom of Tally's house. Flight to Washington, D.C. Dinner at the US embassy, with my usual contacts—a man named Steven Hopper and a woman named Rhonda Caster. I actually like them both, and they'll have my favorite foods on display for tonight's meal, and then I'll meet with the US Ambassador in the morning.

"What's on the menu?" I ask anyway, because it's always been part of the transcript.

"It's beginning with oysters Rockefeller," Don says. "And beef carpaccio."

I flip the page and find the menu. "Oh, I see," I say. "Then there's the choice of Beef Wellington or rack of lamb."

"Which would you prefer?" Donald asks. "I've been asked to let them know before we take off."

I scan the sides—haricots verts almondine, potatoes dauphinoise, or honey-glazed baby carrots. Of course, there will be an assortment of breads and compound butters, and when my eyes land on the European cheese course, I begin to relax.

"I'll take the lamb, please," I tell him, flipping the page again. Donald has prepared the topics I need to discuss with Steven and Rhonda, which includes a discussion on the current stock market, the exchange rate of the US dollar, and our exportation of olives and olive oil to the States.

I sigh and flip the page, where a briefing of each topic waits. I don't look at it right now, because I still have a flight ahead of me, and I'll want to be buried in something so I don't have to glare at Titan or Ajax and wonder what they're thinking.

The drive to the Charleston airport is blessedly short, a blur of green landscapes and familiar suburban houses I only glimpse as I go over tomorrow's agenda to travel to the White House, where we'll have a welcome reception at four p.m.

To get through, I try to hold onto the image of the Big House, the way it welcomes everyone. It's a place of comfort, of real life, and I already miss it.

At the private terminal, the usual fanfare of security is amplified by our presence. Donald handles everything with effortless grace, his impeccable attire and calm demeanor smoothing over any potential hitches. Ajax and Titan form an impenetrable wall around me, their stoic faces and broad shoulders deterring any curious glances any of the airport employees might dare to throw my way.

Not that it would matter. None of them knows who I am; they know they need to make sure I have secure passage to the jetway and that's it.

I keep my gaze straight ahead, because there's only white-gray walls to see. One moment, I'm a simple renter, helping Tally clean out a dusty garage, and the next, I'm royalty, shielded from the world by a phalanx of security.

Once I'm on the jet, the transition is complete. The cabin is opulent, silent save for the hum of the engines. Donald immediately opens his laptop, a stack of briefing papers already laid out on the table in front of him.

"We have an early start tomorrow, Your Highness," he says. "Do you want to go over your notes for the International Trade Summit?"

I nod, flipping open my booklet again, moving quickly to the right page. "Are these updated with my thoughts?" I ask, referring to the speech notes I've already been over once.

"Yes," Donald says. "The Queen specifically requested some revisions after your last debrief. She's particularly keen on the details concerning the cultural exchange program."

The Queen is relentless, brilliant, and utterly devoted to Notavella. And while I respect her immensely, her constant presence in my life, even from across the Atlantic, is stifling.

I scan the bullet points for my speech, but my mind keeps returning to Tally's questions from our date. *So you're only going to be here for six months, and then what, Cal? What's the plan? Let's say me and you decide we want to be together. Am I moving to Notavella and having my every clothing choice scrutinized? Or will you be able to come to Cider Cove and live here with me?*

The questions hang in the air, follow me around like demons. They're valid, important questions, and I don't have answers. Not yet. I've been so focused on simply getting back to her, on convincing my mother to allow this sabbatical, that I haven't fully considered the endgame.

Living in Notavella means a life under constant scrutiny. Every move, every choice, every outfit scrutinized by the press and the public. That's always been my life, but it's not Tally's. She loves her quiet house on Cherry Lane, her teaching job, her mundane, glitter-filled life.

I sigh and look over to Donald. "The notes look fine. Do I have the personal gifts from my mother and father for the POTUS?"

"Yes, of course," Donald says just as a flight attendant approaches us.

"Sorry to interrupt," he says, his accent from some-where outside the US as well. "Do we want drinks? Some-thing to eat while the pilots go through their final checklist?"

"I'd love a club soda," I tell him. "With all the citrus you have."

"Yes, sir." He looks over to Donald, who orders a Coke Zero with a smile.

I find myself grinning at him too, because he's filled a mini-fridge in his suite with the cola he can't get back home. He chuckles and shakes his head before saying, "Your Highness, Ambassador Rogers is particularly inter-ested in the renewable energy initiatives Notavella has implemented." He raises his eyebrows at me. "He's aware of your personal interest in sustainable development."

I force a smile, acknowledging his words. This is my duty, my job, the very reason my mother sanctioned this trip. My role as Special Envoy to the Crown is more than just a title; it involves real work, real diplomacy.

The flight to D.C. feels endless, filled with briefings and strategic discussions. Donald is an invaluable assistant, anticipating my needs before I even voice them. He waves the flight attendant over for snacks just before my stomach growls, reviews all necessary information, and listens when I give my speech for the Summit, just to practice.

Upon arrival at Joint Base Andrews, the reception is even more formal, every detail choreographed with military precision. The massive hangar lights bathe the tarmac in an almost theatrical glow, bouncing off the polished black sedans and SUVs of the waiting motorcade. The vehicles stand at attention just as firmly as the uniformed servicemen who flank them, their posture rigid, their salutes crisp.

The late afternoon air hums with restrained energy—an arrival like this is as much ceremony as it is logistics. An Air Force honor guard lines the path from the aircraft, their flags catching the light, their presence a reminder that this is no ordinary landing. Cameras flash in the distance, the press kept carefully behind barriers but close enough to capture the moment.

At the head of the delegation stands Steven Hopper, assistant to the U.S. Ambassador. He isn't the most senior official present, but his presence is deliberate—chosen as the ambassador's right hand, the man trusted to shepherd high-profile guests through the carefully curated welcome.

Steven's suit is immaculate, his tie knotted with the kind of precision that suggests rehearsal. His smile is diplomatic, warm without being overly familiar, the sort of expression honed by someone used to smoothing first impressions.

My stomach hisses with snakes as I wait for Titan and Ajax to allow me to leave the plane. Donald stands in front of me, both of us out of sight of the open door leading off the airplane.

Finally, just when I'm sure my patience is about to snap, Donald steps aside and gestures for me to go ahead and leave the jet.

I step forward and frame myself in the doorway, pausing to button my suit jacket and painting my royal smile on my face. After all, everyone in Notavella will be watching this, and that includes my mother. They're all counting on me to be a good representation of them, and I definitely want that too.

I lift my hand in a wave and start forward again, noting the press back behind the barrier that's been set up. Only Steven and a pair of military men stand on the other side of it, and I find Ajax and Titan flanking the bottom of the steps.

As I descend the stairs and step onto the red carpet they've laid out, Steven moves forward, extending his hand with practiced grace. "Your Highness, welcome to Washington on behalf of the Ambassador, and the United States." His voice is steady, carrying just enough gravitas to suggest authority, though I recognize the subtle humility of a man who speaks for another.

After all, my whole job is me speaking on behalf of my mother. Steven and I, we're not different at all.

"Thank you, Steven," I say. "I'm delighted to be here." We shake hands, the cameras snapping, my own face a mask of practiced diplomacy.

"How's Sam?" I ask, as Donald had all the details about Steven and his family in my portfolio. "Isn't your son going to college this fall?"

"Yes," Steven says, his smile getting wider. "Georgie's

going to Dartmouth, and Sam's hoping to make partner at her firm."

"That's wonderful." I fall to his side, and we walk down the carpet toward the legion of reporters. Ajax and Titan move into position behind me, and I return to my performance. The air smells faintly of jet fuel and polished leather. The salutes, the cameras, the gleaming motorcade—it is a tableau of power, stage-managed down to the smallest gesture. And I play my part by following Steven over to a small group of people who've been kept separate from the reporters.

"Your Majesty," Steven says. "These are fellow Notavellans."

"Oh, wonderful." I shake the hand of one man, then sign an autograph for his daughter. "What are you guys doing here in the States?"

"We're visiting my wife's family," the man says. "In Philadelphia."

"Mm, is it as muggy there as here?"

"Yes, unfortunately." The man laughs, and I move to the next person. There's only about twenty people here, and I make sure to greet them all, my cheeks aching by the time Steven gestures me toward the waiting, oversized SUV with the flag of Notavella on the antennae.

Donald is already sitting inside, and I glance over to him as he extends a bottle of water toward me. "Well done, sir," he says.

"Thank you." I twist off the top of the bottle and take a long drink.

"Texts from your mother are glowing," he says.

I only nod, because I don't keep my phone with me

when I'm in public. It's too distracting, and no one wants to see the shape of it in my pocket in photos.

"Tally also approves," he says coolly, and I whip my attention to him.

"She—what?"

Donald grins and hands me the phone, something he's never done before. "Did you think it wouldn't be streamed somewhere? You're a *prince*, Your Highness."

I one-hundred percent knew my arrival in Washington, D.C. would be filmed and streamed, talked about, written about, all of it. I don't come to the US very often, and my mother has only been once in her entire life—and that was to bring me here for high school.

I look at my phone, and I can't read fast enough.

Wow, Your Highness, you look amazing walking off that plane.

Is that your private jet? Why didn't I think you'd be on a private jet?

Holy cow, your smile...

I can't help smiling at that.

You are so handsome, and I can't wait until you get back to the Big House.

What's your agenda like tonight? Do you have time to call? Or is this classified information?

Anyway, I can see you landed safely—you just got in the SUV. Try to enjoy! I'm consoling Shellvador that he has to deal with me instead of you for the next few days.

A picture of her grumpy tortoise is the last text she's sent, and I look up, a measure of happiness settling inside me in a whole new way.

"Miss Tomlinson seems to really like you," Donald says.

I look over to him, pure shock flowing through me now. "You never comment on anything."

"Yes, well, you should see your face right now, sir."

I turn toward him fully and hand back my phone. "Have you ever been married, Don?"

"Yes, sir," he says. When he doesn't elaborate, I let him have his silence.

I look out the window as the SUV starts to move, and I sigh, my hot breath fogging the glass for a moment. "I don't know what I'm doing."

"Which part?" Donald demands. "I have everything you need right here, and—"

I hold up my hand to cut him off, and I swing my attention back toward him. "I meant with Tahlia. My mother asked me once what my end goal was, and I said I wanted to get back together with her."

Donald nods. "I think you've done that, sir."

"Yes, me too," I murmur. "So now what?" I meet his eyes, and we watch one another for a moment. He doesn't have an answer, and that only makes me slump in my seat and roll my head toward the window again.

"Black swans," I say. "What am I doing?"

CHAPTER THIRTEEN

HILLARY

THE SOFT CLINK OF SILVERWARE AGAINST CERAMIC and the low hum of conversation fill the air at The Anchor, making it feel like a cozy, secret haven. I trace the rim of my water glass, a nervous flutter in my stomach that has nothing to do with the exceptional shrimp and grits I've just devoured.

Next to me at the table, Liam, my incredible husband, beams at me, his eyes crinkling at the corners in that way that always melts my heart. Beside him, Claudia, draped in a deep, sequined blue tank-shirt that sparkles even in the restaurant's subdued lighting, is mid-anecdote about a recent City Council meeting, her dark curls swaying as she speaks. Beckett, her husband, listens intently, a faint smile playing on his lips, probably mentally crafting a witty, short, perfect response.

"And then Marshall, bless his heart, tried to suggest we use that *awful* yellow paint, you know—what they have in the gross library bathrooms?" Claudia rolls her eyes for dramatic effect. "I told him there is no way I'm putting *Nicotine Stain* paint anywhere in this city."

I burst out laughing, because I was just waiting for the name of the paint color to drop. Liam chuckles too, a warm, resonant sound that reminds me why I fell in love with him.

"Sounds like a typical Tuesday for you, Claude," I say.

"Indeed," she deadpans, lifting her glass of lemon water. "Some things never change."

But everything changes. That's what I'm here to tell her and Beckett, my best friends in the whole world.

My heart is doing a frenzied little jig against my ribs, a rhythm that reminds me of the chaotic beauty of Hollywood, where Liam and I called home for a little bit. It's good to be back in Cider Cove, with the familiar comfort of the Big House next door, and all my friends so close.

Liam senses my shift, his hand finding mine under the table, his fingers tracing soft circles on the back of my thumb. He's always been so attuned to me, capable of reading my moods even across a noisy room. I meet his eye, and he nods.

Claudia sees it all, because the woman doesn't miss anything. "I just—I have some news."

Claude's eyes narrow slightly, but she says nothing. Beckett glances at her, something nervous in his expression too. "Work news? The documentary has wrapped, hasn't it?"

"Yes," I say, because this isn't work news. Just thinking the words—*Liam and I are going to have a baby*—cause a genuine smile to spread across my face. I look at Liam, and he grins back, his eyes sparkling with shared excitement.

"I'm pregnant," I blurt out. "We're going to have a baby in January."

The words hang in the air, but at least my heart isn't jumping against my ribs anymore. For a beat, there's silence, broken only by the ambient restaurant noise. Then, Claudia's eyes, usually so sharp and knowing, widen, and tears well up instantly. Her lower lip trembles, and she drops her fork onto her plate with a clatter.

"Hillary," she gasps, her voice thick with emotion. She pushes back her chair, scrambling to her feet, tears now streaming freely down her cheeks. I expect a hug, a scream of joy, a dramatic "And I'm just finding out *now?*"

But when she says through her sobs, "So am I," my jaw drops.

"No." The word falls from my mouth, and I cover it with my hand.

Liam's eyes, which had been shining with happy tears, now snap to Claudia, mirroring my own shock. Beckett grins and grins like the golden retriever he is.

"It's true," he says, as if I was being serious when I said no. "I saw the test and everything."

Tears spill down my face too, and I quickly wipe them away. "Just—you're—this is *incredible.*"

Claudia nods and dabs at her own eyes. "We were going to tell you tonight. We wanted you to be the first to know."

"Besides my aunt and sister," Beckett says. "We've told them."

"We told my parents a couple of weeks ago," I say. "When we were in Columbia."

"And your mother let you come back here?" Claudia teases, and we laugh together.

Liam laughs and pulls me into his side. "It was a bit of a fight, trust me."

"I can't believe this." I shake my head. "When are you due?"

For some unknown reason, a wave of missing engulfs me. I should be telling my friends this after we've gathered in the living room at the Big House, while holding a pink sparkly fake-microphone.

I could've done that, but I've opted for telling people in smaller groups.

"January twenty-seventh," Claudia says.

"I haven't told anyone else yet," I say. "So you can't mention it to anyone."

"Same," Claudia says, and she takes another sip of her water, makes a face, and then puts down her glass. "I hate plain water."

"I should've known when you didn't order your usual mojito." I shake my head, a little surprised at myself for not seeing the clues. "I just thought it was this place."

She glances around, her black cat skin coming right back, and leans forward. "Well, this place doesn't have the greatest mojitos."

I grin at her and shake my head, then sober as I gear up to tell them my next piece of news—and Liam doesn't even know this one. "I, uh—" I clear my throat, and that brings everyone's eyes to me.

"I'm going to quit my job," I say. "At Christmas."

Liam pulls in a breath, and I know it's the quiet before the storm. The man doesn't know how to celebrate quietly, and I probably should've told him this news at home. Because he reaches up and grabs the golf hat he wears, tosses it up, and whoops.

I roll my eyes at him and look at Claudia. "Do you know if you're going to keep working?"

"I can't believe you're going to quit," Liam says. He leans over and kisses my cheek. "I'm so glad, and I promise I'll do whatever I have to in order to support us."

I lean into him, because I know he will. He works incredibly hard already, because he wants our life to be the best it can be.

"Well, I've already got a Christmas Festival theme picked out," Beckett says, his grin as wide as the sky. "Win—ter—Won—der—land—Babies!"

Claudia rolls her eyes, but she's still smiling. "He's been obsessed with Christmas planning for weeks, and it's not even July yet."

"So you're still going to do the Christmas Festival?"

Claudia's dark eyes fix on mine. "I haven't decided what I'll do after the baby comes." I see the flash of fear as it moves through her eyes, and then she blinks and looks over to Beckett. "Tell them your news."

"You have news too?" Liam asks. "Well, shoot. I'm going to have to come up with something."

"You're going to have an amazing crop of peaches this year," I tell him, almost tacking a question mark on the end of the sentence.

"That's what I get?" His disbelief rolls off of him in waves. "Peaches? You get a baby, and you get a baby, and Beckett gets..." He flaps his arm toward Beckett, who still hasn't told us his news yet. "Something awesome, and I get peaches?"

"You've been very excited about them," I say, grinning and grinning.

He smiles back. "They are going to be amazing this year. I've thinned them perfectly, and—" He cuts himself off, which is a miracle in and of itself. "No one cares about my peaches."

"I do, baby." I lean into him and look at Beckett. "But I want to know your news, Becks."

He practically bounces in his seat. "It's kind of a baby, but not the human variety."

Claudia grins at him, though she has that hint of wariness that tells me she's not as excited about Beckett's news as he is. "He's getting a new puppy."

"Wow," Liam says with a chuckle. "A puppy before a baby? That's brave."

"I'm going to work with Elliott and his dog trainer, and we're going to train him to be a guide dog."

"Oh, that's great," I say, and a yawn completely takes over my mouth. "I swear I'm so tired lately." I look at Claude. "Do you feel like that too?"

She nods, a small smile on her face. "Yeah, I take a nap every day after work now."

"Let's get going," Liam says, and he reaches into his back pocket for his wallet.

"I wanted to ask you if Tahlia has said anything more about Cal." I watch Claudia as she bends to gather her purse.

She meets my eye, something serious in hers. "Nothing

specifically about Cal, but she's working with him on the garage."

"Yeah, and that's got to be hard." I make a mental note to get next door to the Big House and see if she needs any help with anything. Everything in that house has meant so much to her for so long, and honestly, the fact that she's even opened the garage is a huge step for her.

"I know they're going out," Claudia says. "I've seen them on the doorbell cam at the Big House." She smiles as she gets to her feet and Beckett starts to talk to Liam about splitting the bill.

"She did tell me that he picks her up at the door of the master suite." I smile and link my arm through Claude's to walk out. "Isn't that so cute? They live in the same house, but he still comes to her door to pick her up."

"I really hope he's the one for her," Claudia says, the familiar worry in her voice. "She's got to be so lonely in that enormous house."

A twinge of guilt for blowing up the situation in the Big House tugs through me. It's irrational, I know, but I did fall in love with Liam—and leave—first. It's been a domino effect since then, and with the double wedding only a few weeks ago...

"I hope he's the one for her too," I say as we leave the restaurant. "Can you imagine having a prince come back to the States just to reconcile with you?" I shake my head. "That in and of itself is *so* romantic."

"Right?" Claudia sighs, and I glance over my shoulder to make sure Liam and Becks are still behind us. They are, so I face forward again.

"So, tell me for real," I say. "A puppy? *You're* excited about a *puppy*?"

Claudia tips her head back and laughs. "It won't be too bad, because I'll just get to cuddle him, and Becks'll do all the hard work."

"Talking about me again?" Beckett asks as he comes to Claudia's other side.

"All good things, baby," she says, dropping my arm and linking her other one through his. "Always good things."

"Mm."

Liam takes my hand, and we pause, since our car is to the left. I suddenly feel like crying again, which makes absolutely no sense. Stupid hormones.

"Hug me," I say to Claudia, and I practically throw myself at her. "Mm, I love you. Let's get together again really soon."

"Tahlia's having that Fourth of July party."

"Yeah, but maybe before then." I step back, smile at her, hug Becks, and then let Liam take me home and put me to bed.

He lays down beside me, and I snuggle into his side. "I love you," I whisper. "I can't believe we're going to have a baby."

He presses a kiss to my forehead and tightens his arm around me. "I love you too, Hill."

I close my eyes and let his words and the pure feeling of love wash over me, and I want this so badly for Tahlia that I say a little prayer for her and Cal right there on the spot.

CHAPTER FOURTEEN

RYANNE

The summer air hangs heavy and humid, pressing down on the house like a thick, damp blanket. It's almost July, and the sun, having put in a full day's work, is finally dipping below the horizon, painting the sky in fiery oranges and soft purples.

I stand at the kitchen island, trying to distract myself with a fresh batch of lemon bars I've attempted to make from Tahlia's recipe. They're usually a comfort, their tangy sweetness a balm, but tonight, even they can't cut through the strange, restless energy thrumming beneath my skin.

I've only got six more weeks until my due date, and every movement feels like an Olympic feat. My back aches, I can't even see my feet, and the baby, bless his little heart, seems determined to use my ribs as his personal trampoline. He's been particularly active tonight, a constant press, stretch, and kick that's now intensified into something more deliberate.

"Just Braxton Hicks," I mutter, popping a piece of

lemon bar into my mouth. I've read enough pregnancy books to self-diagnose every ache and twitch.

But suddenly, a sharp, clenching sensation wraps around my middle and squeezes. I drop the lemon bar, a moan coming involuntarily out of my mouth.

Another wave hits, stronger this time, at the same time panic grips my heart.

I'm home alone tonight, as Elliott's mother went to pick him up from work.

The pressure and pain rippling through my back and around my midsection steals my breath, making me lean heavily against the counter.

My thoughts scatter like starlight.

It's too early.

I can't drive myself to the hospital.

Anyone I could call is at least fifteen minutes away.

Do I call 9-1-1?

My mother isn't here to help me yet.

What time is it? Maybe Elliott and his mother are almost home.

The pressure and deep ache subside, and I manage to stand up straight again. I grab my phone, my fingers fumbling. My first instinct, the one that's become second nature since Christmas a couple of years ago, is to call Elliott.

"Ry?" His voice, warm and low, is laced with a hint of something familiar—that slight grumpiness I adore, probably because his mother is lecturing him on the drive home.

"Ell," I gasp, the word a tight knot in my throat. Another contraction rolls through me, forcing me to double over, and all I can do is groan. "Something's happening."

Silence stretches for a beat, and then he says, "Mom, go faster. Something's wrong with Ry." His voice sounds sharp with concern, all traces of grumpiness gone.

I gasp for air. "It's...it's like a giant fist is squeezing me," I manage to get out, trying to straighten.

"We're almost there," he says. "Just hang on, okay? Where are you?"

"Kitchen," I say, and I turn around as the grip lessens again. "I'm going to make my way out front."

"Five minutes," Joan says, and I swear Elliott's big beast of a car roars as she steps on the gas.

"Peanut butter and jelly," I squeeze out as another round of tightness pulls through me. Fear passes through me with it, because I've never gone into labor before, and I have no idea if what I'm experiencing is normal or not.

Elliott and his mother keep talking to me, but I put the phone down and focus on breathing. The pain passes quicker this time, and in the interim, I move as quickly as I can toward the front door.

I've just opened it when Elliott reaches the porch. His dark hair flies a little wild, his eyes wide and searching. Luna, his beautiful golden retriever guide dog, trots in beside him, her tail wagging gently, seemingly oblivious to the chaos.

"I've got you," he says, immediately moving to my side. "Are we thinking you're in labor? We're going to the hospital?"

Joan comes huffing up the steps behind him. "Has your water broken?"

"I don't think so," I say. "I just have a lot of tightness."

"Let's just go," Elliott says. "The worst they can do is send us home again."

I nod, because I don't really know what else to do. Part of me wants to just stay home, so I won't be humiliated when they send me home, but another part wants to move into a hospital room, so I'll be there when the baby comes.

"Luna, back to the car."

Luna immediately turns and heads back down the steps. She waits at the bottom for Elliott, and then moves right at his side though his step is agonizingly slow to match mine.

Joan gets behind the wheel again, and I want to argue. She's been a huge help, and it's not like I can kick her out of her own house. But sometimes, I just want Elliott to be the one behind the wheel, just the two of us.

And if I feel like that, I can only imagine how frustrated Ell feels. He reaches for the door handle, and while my internal grumpy-cat wants to bicker about who's driving, my body is failing me.

Luna hops into the car as the now-familiar tightening happens again. I grip Elliott's arm, and he says, "All right, my salty little peanut. One foot at a time."

He helps me carefully onto the seat, and I groan as he slams the door.

"Is it a contraction?" Joan asks.

"I don't know," I bite out.

Elliott gets in the passenger seat while Luna curls into my side, pressing gently against my baby belly. Ell glances at me, his face still etched with concern. "Ry, talk to me."

"It's coming and going," I say, focusing on my breathing. "It's just a *lot* of pressure."

He looks at his mother, but neither of them say anything before she starts backing out of the driveway.

The ride to the hospital only ratchets up my panic. "Are we going to have to get rid of my teal luggage?" I ask suddenly, a new wave of strange desperation hitting me. "If the baby comes early, I won't have time to pack anything for the hospital." Elliott had teased me about my bright teal bag with neon bubbles before. "And I won't need the luggage."

Elliott glances at me, his eyes twinkling in the dim dashboard light. "Ry, honey, even if you don't get a chance to pack, I'll bring you everything you need."

"Yeah-yep," I say, mimicking his go-to phrase. "What about names, Ell? We don't have a name for the baby."

"Ryanne, there's plenty of time for that."

"Not if the baby is coming right now."

Joan pulls into the emergency room bay, and Elliott is out of the car and at my side instantly. He helps me out, and Luna, ever the professional, guides him smoothly towards the entrance. The bright, sterile lights of the hospital are a stark contrast to the cozy cottage we've established as our home.

"Ryanne Huston," Elliott says to the triage nurse, his voice surprisingly steady. "She's almost eight months pregnant, and we think she's in labor."

That begins a whirlwind of questions, monitors, and a very kind nurse who keeps tabs on me as the minutes tick into hours. Joan gets a RideShare home, promising to come at any time to drive us back.

Elliott never leaves my side, holding my hand, smoothing my hair, and occasionally whispering silly Mars Rover facts to distract me. Luna lies quietly by his feet, a calm, fluffy presence.

I only have a few more bouts of tightening, and I know I'm not going to have the baby tonight. Despite my panic that he'd come too early, now only disappointment cuts through me. I finally look over to Elliott, who's got his eyes closed and his head cradled in his hand.

"Ell," I say.

He jerks awake. "Yeah. Yep?"

I smile at him, though tears crowd into my eyes. "Go find the nurse and ask her if we can go home."

He gets to his feet. "You want to go home?" He scans me in the hospital gown—and let me tell you, getting out of my clothes and into that was a feat that should've earned me an Olympic gold medal.

I let my tears fall. "I'm not in labor, and they're just going to send us home."

"I'll go—" He turns to go get the nurse just as the door opens. The nurse who's been helping us all night enters, with the doctor right behind her.

He holds a clipboard that probably has all my vitals and notes on it. "Well, Mrs. Huston," he says. "It looks like you're having some very strong Braxton Hicks contractions. Your cervix isn't dilating, and your water hasn't broken."

I nod. "Yes, I'm sorry. I just—it was pretty regular."

"All of your vitals are strong," he says, consulting the chart. "So are the baby's." He smiles kindly at me. "Just go home, rest, and let's see if we can't get him to stay inside a bit longer."

Elliott squeezes my hand. "Thank you, Doctor."

As we walk out of the hospital, the late-night air feels cooler, lighter. The panic has receded, leaving only exhaustion and a strange sense of emptiness.

"We were so close," I say with a sigh.

Elliott helps me into the car while Luna hops into the back seat. He gets behind the wheel while I stare through the windshield and into the night.

He starts the engine, but he doesn't pull out of the parking spot. "I can drive this car home." He turns to me, his hand resting on my knee. "We almost had a baby, Ry."

I nod, more tears coming. I swear, they're endless since I got pregnant. "And we don't even have a name."

His eyebrows, those perfectly expressive eyebrows, shoot up. "*That's* what you're worried about right now?"

"Yes," I say, my grumpy-cat voice making a strong comeback. "What if he was here right now, Ell? We'd be stuck calling him 'the baby'. Bring me the baby. Isn't the baby so cute? Text everyone that the baby is here."

I roll my neck, pure exhaustion weighing down my every muscle.

Elliott laughs, a real, full-bellied laugh that fills the car and somehow makes everything okay again. "You're right, you're right. Okay. We need a name." He exhales, as he's been up for most of the night too.

"It needs to be good," I say, wiping my eyes. "Something strong. Something...us."

"I know—Rover," he teases, and I elbow him as I glare.

"No, Ell, come on. Something that doesn't sound like he's a dog or a robot." I point at him. "Something *good*."

"How about a space name?" he suggests, his eyes bright. "Like...Orion? Or Cassian?"

"Cassian? That is not a name," I say, shaking my head. "What about something classic? Like James? Or, or, Neil?"

He bursts out laughing. "Neil? Absolutely not."

I lean my head back against the headrest, a comfortable silence settling between us for a moment. The immediate crisis is over, and the warmth of Elliott's hand on my leg, Luna's soft breathing in the back, it's all so comforting. I love him so much, his quirks and all.

"We don't need a name right now," I say. "Let's go home."

He leans over, his gaze soft and filled with so much love that it makes my heart ache in the best possible way. He cups my face in his hands, his thumbs brushing away the last of my tears. "We'll have a name for him before he's born, okay? I promise."

He kisses me then, a slow, tender kiss that speaks volumes. The kind filled with promise and a future that, despite his deteriorating vision and my grumpy tendencies, I know will be amazing. We'll figure out the rest, just like we always do. We'll be clumsy and bicker, and he'll tease me, and I'll love him no matter what.

Elliott pulls out of the parking lot, Luna stirring slightly in the back. As we drive home, the world feels a little less chaotic, and a lot more full.

I lay my hand on my belly, feeling a faint flutter, almost as if my little boy is already saying hello—and *oh, sorry for freaking you out tonight.*

TAHLIA

"You can put that pitcher right over there," I tell Donald when he comes out of the Big House.

Liam, Beckett, and Matt are still wrestling with the canopies that Claudia brought from the city of Cider Cove. She and Hillary have taken up residence in the rocking chairs on the back porch to keep Ryanne company after her false labor scare. She's made it another ten days, and while she looks the most miserable I've ever seen her, she and the baby are still doing well.

They're being very tight-lipped about what they're going to name him, despite our constant reminders that she's going to have to tell us sooner or later.

Claudia has Matt's Chem Cats in her lap—Purroxide and Purricell—both of them on leashes, though they certainly don't need them at the moment. They love her, and she scratches them lazily around the ears at the same time.

I go back into the house, where I find Cal standing with Elliott at the narrow counter next to the stove. "They go like this," Elliott says, doing something with his hands in front of him.

I move over to them and lean into Cal's side, sliding my hand along his waist. "They look great," I tell them. "They're just whoopie pies. You can't mess it up."

"I'm only supervising," Cal says. "Elliott told me he can't see very well, and he wanted to make sure these were straight."

"They're perfect, Ell," I tell him. "You can take them out on the table where Donald is putting the refreshments."

Ell picks up the platter of whoopie pies—neatly arranged in rows of chocolate, lemon, and peach—and heads out the door.

It's been propped open, letting in this July evening heat, but I don't care. I've closed off the rest of the house so the heat will be contained in the mudroom, back porch, and kitchen until all of the prep is done for the party.

"Excuse me, Your Highness," one of the German Shepherds says, and I turn toward Ajax at the same time Cal does. He's holding up a device, and Cal leaves my side instantly, saying, "Nightingales, what is it now?"

With the time difference between here and Notavella, he was certain that country business would not infringe on our Independence Day picnic—especially since we're not even beginning until eight p.m.

I do a quick calculation, and of course, that means it's almost five a.m. in his country, and he says his parents don't sleep much.

Ajax hands him the phone, and Cal moves into the

half-bath in the corner of the kitchen and closes the door behind him.

"You just took my hired help," I tell Ajax, but getting him to smile is like trying to push a two-ton boulder off a cliff. I simply haven't been able to do it yet.

"All right, get on over here," I say, employing my aunt's *Nothing gets me down* personality. Nothing was ever awkward for Aunt Fern, even when I was nasty to her or she knew my brother didn't want to come stay for the summer. She always had our favorite foods and our rooms made up and new toys to play with.

Ajax comes closer, and I wonder, not for the first time, how many black suits he owns. "Your jacket looks different today," I say.

He gives me a withering glare.

"What? It does." I grin at him. "I think it's slightly more charcoal than black, and you just won't admit it."

"The exact color is midnight," he says. "Just as all of my others."

I lean one hip into the stove. "And how many is that, Ajax? Come on, tell me how many suits you have upstairs in that closet."

"Enough," he says.

I've seen him carrying dry cleaning in and out, but there are four grown men who only seem to wear designer suits living in the Big House. I grin, remembering how their whole world changed when I told them they could schedule the dry cleaner to come pick up and drop off their clothes.

"What do you need help with?" he asks.

I point to the decorative container with pink lemonade.

"That has to go out on the table—the same table where Donald put my pitcher of sweet tea."

"Yes, ma'am," he says, and he turns dutifully and lifts it as if it doesn't hold ten gallons of liquid, but a few feathers.

I smile at his retreating back, my gaze switching to Titan, who's positioned himself at the corner of the dining room table, only three feet from the bathroom door, as if an assassin will swing through the window there, kick down the door, and attack Cal.

I meet his eyes, and he cocks one eyebrow. "You really shouldn't tease him about his clothes."

"No?" I ask. "Why not?"

"Probably because it's one hundred degrees here," he says. "And we're not actually allowed to wear anything else."

I sober, realizing that I may have hurt these burly security guards' feelings. "I'm sorry," I say quickly. "You realize you can wear whatever you want here, right? You're not in a castle or Notavella."

He gives me a smile, which is something I *have* earned from Titan only a couple of times previous to this. "You don't understand the way we live."

"No," I say, "I don't." That causes another round of frowning to cross my face. "Listen, Titan, do you think...?"

I trail off because I don't want to ask him his opinion on whether Cal will ever be able to leave Notavella or not. Just the fact that his mother or father called tonight and he ducked into the bathroom mere moments before our party is supposed to begin tells me what I need to know.

The part of my heart that knows he'll be returning to

his country, where he'll take his role as the second son, dies just a little bit.

I'm falling in love with him, and that means I'm going to have to let go of a lot more than my aunt's old clothes, and her bicycle, and my uncle's tools. I can't even imagine leaving the Big House.

And I can admit to myself that I've started making contingency plans. My mortgage isn't huge, because my aunt left me the house in her will, but it's a big house on a big piece of property. I got a home equity line of credit to pay for the repairs that it needed before my friends and I could move in. That's what I count as my mortgage, and the land and the house continue to need upkeep, repairs, and maintenance—all of which costs money.

I think of the five couples who have gathered here with us tonight, and if any of them would ever be willing to move into the Big House and take care of it for me, should I fall all the way in love with Cal and want to move overseas with him.

Liam and Hillary have their own beautiful estate right next door, so they're out. Claudia and Beckett moved half an hour away to be closer to Beckett's job, and I can't imagine he'd want to make an hour commute, even if he got to live in the Big House.

Ryan and Elliott live in a small house on the other side of town with his mother, and they're a definite possibility. Emma and Aaron live in a newly remodeled home that once belonged to Aaron's grandfather, so they're probably going to be out as well. But Matt and Lizzie live in Matt's townhome, and it's certainly not going to hold them forever, especially if they start having kids. So she's another possibility for the caretaker of the Big House.

"Tahlia," Lizzie herself says, and I turn toward her. "We have a little bit of an issue out here." She gestures for me to follow her, a hint of nervousness in her expression.

"An issue?" I go with her onto the back porch and down the steps, where Beckett and Matt have moved on from the canopies to the movie screen that we normally hang against the east side of the house.

"It's just right up there. See?" Beckett points, and I look up to where the chimney comes off the house. "When do you think that happened?"

"I have no idea," I say, and then I look around for Liam. "Where'd Liam go?"

"He went to get a ladder," Hillary says as she joins us. "He thinks he's going to fix it tonight." She folds her arms, cocks one hip, and looks up at the damage along the roof next to the chimney. "I told him to leave it for another day, but you know how he is."

"Yes, I know how he is," I murmur.

I glance back to his house to see him trucking across the lawn with his ladder over his shoulder. "We really don't have to do this tonight," I call to him. "I can have you come fix the roof another day."

"I just want to see if it's going to cause any leakage," he calls back, and before I know it, he's got the ladder propped up against the house, and he's climbing it while everyone on the ground tells him to be careful.

"I'm a *general contractor*," he finally bellows down to us. "I know what I'm doing."

I don't like ladders or heights at all, so I'm glad that

Beckett is holding the ladder steady at the bottom as Liam uses both hands to take pictures with his phone. He then climbs up another couple of rungs and yells, "I think it's just superficial, Tahlia. There's no water or anything getting inside."

"Okay," I say.

"Now, come down," Hillary says. "We want to get this movie started."

I've planned appetizers and desserts, a movie, and fireworks once darkness falls. I told everyone to bring their own chairs and blankets and any snacks they wanted to share. As Liam descends from the ladder, I move over to the two tables I've set up for food. The stuff I've made—pimento cheese, crab cakes, brookies, lemon-zucchini mini loaves, banana pudding, and hummingbird cakes—takes up one table, along with all of the drinks.

My friends have brought potato chips—those had to come from Hillary—and Ry brought an assortment of M&Ms, including a couple of flavors I've never seen before. Emma brought mini cornbread muffins with honey butter, and there's also a chocolate mousse cake that I can't wait to taste, and some of Lizzie's father's homemade beef jerky.

As I'm surveying the scene, Donald comes back outside with an unmistakable tin in his hand. I suck in a breath and say, "You didn't!" as I rush over to him.

He grins and holds up the festive holiday tin in red, green, and white. "It's the cheddar and caramel mix."

"I love you so much right now," I say.

He sets the popcorn down on the end of the table, and I grab onto him in a hug. I haven't had nearly the opportunity to get to know him or Titan or Ajax the way I have Cal, and I'm pretty sure Donald has no idea what to do with me. It takes him a couple of seconds to even soften his muscles, and then slowly, he puts his arms around me and pats my back awkwardly.

I pull away and grin at him. "Thank you *so much*. Did Cal tell you this was my favorite snack?"

"One thing you should know about those who serve," he says. "Is we're always listening, and we're some of the most observant people in the world."

"Is that right?" Part fear and part amusement dances through me. I turn and face my friends, who are now setting up camp chairs, blankets, and—in the case of Elliott —wrestling with a giant beanbag from the back of his even bigger car. "Tell me what you've noticed about my friends."

Donald chuckles and shakes his head. "I don't think you want to know."

"Oh, I want to know," I say.

"Well," he says. "I noticed that Hillary, Claudia, and Ryanne did not help set up any tables or any canopies."

I say nothing, just expecting him to go on. They usually help me in the kitchen, but they didn't do that today either.

I watch as Hillary cuddles into Liam's side in the zero-gravity camp chair built for two that he brought. He always has the best outdoor gadgets, and I'll probably be the most uncomfortable one at my own party.

"They sat on the back porch rocking and talking," Donald says. "And when no one thinks you're listening, they'll say almost anything."

"Did you get the name of Ryanne's baby?" I ask.

His grin brightens. "No, but I know they've decided on one. And I know you can't quite tell from looking, but the way they were talking and sitting, and see how Hillary has her hand on her stomach? I think she's pregnant."

The air leaves my lungs. "What?" I stare harder at Hillary. Shadows are starting to fall across the backyard, and she's sitting in the shade to boot.

Ajax joins us. "I suspect Claudia is too," he says. "Because they're sticking close together, and always talking about doing things 'after.'"

I stand there dumbfounded, sure they're wrong. "What about Emma and Lizzie, or Matt and Aaron?"

"Aaron carries a lot from work," Donald says.

"He's checked his phone a bunch of times," Ajax says. "He even left for a minute to take a call—a lot like Cal."

It's the first time I've ever heard any of Cal's detail call him by his first name, and suddenly Ajax becomes more human.

"He's definitely duty bound," Donald says. "But I haven't decided if it's to work or his parents or something else."

Even as we stand there observing my friends, Emma reaches over and holds her hand out flat. Aaron looks at it and then at her. And though I'm too far away to hear the sigh, I can see it as it raises his shoulders and leaves through his mouth. He pulls his phone out of his pocket and puts it in her palm. She takes it, tucks it into her bag on the other side of her chair, and then scoots closer to Aaron and takes his hand in hers.

He definitely has something going on, but I'm not sure if it's work or family-related either.

"Matt's a little bit more of an enigma," Donald says. "Lizzie I've got figured out. She knows what she wants. She speaks her mind. She has a lot of confidence."

"Yes," Ajax says. "She reminds me a lot of the Queen, actually."

"Matt might be a little bit like us," Donald says, glancing over to Ajax. "Doing whatever he has to in order to make Lizzie happy. He sure loves her, and she loves him, and they're very cute together."

"That they are," I say, because that is true.

"Beckett is a jokester," Donald says next. "Though he's very intelligent. And Liam wants to be helpful more than anything."

I catch the smile in his voice, and it sits handsomely on his face too.

"They're all wonderful," he says. "I can see why you're friends with them."

"Can you?" I ask. "What did you observe about me when you first met me?"

"Oh, he's not answering that."

I turn as Cal takes the last couple of steps and joins us. "What are you three doing here? Gossiping?"

"No," I say. "Donald told me that he was one of the most observant people on the planet, and I wanted to know what he had observed about my friends."

"And you told her?" Cal sounds quite surprised, but Donald simply shakes his head and clasps his hands behind his back.

"I believe it's time for the party to start," Ajax says, once again surprising me.

"You don't have to keep Tahlia on schedule," Cal says, and he takes my hand and tugs me away from his detail. "He's probably just starving," he says, leaning closer as we go past the food.

Matt is still fiddling with the projector when I arrive in front of everyone, but I grin around at everyone. "Welcome to the Big House. I'm really glad you're here. Even though Cal isn't American, I asked him to host this Independence Day party with me, and we have tons and tons of food over on the tables. And we're going to be starting *Legally Blonde* at any moment. After it's over, Aaron and Matt are going to light all the fireworks."

"I got the most amazing assortment from the hardware store," Aaron says. "You guys are gonna *love it.*"

"I'll lead us out in food," Hillary says, and she gets up and heads for the tables. Others go with her, but some stay back to chat with each other and with me and Cal.

I lament that we didn't get to get out our pink mic and go around and say something, but we've never done that with our significant others.

"What do you want to eat?" Cal asks, breaking into my memories. "I'll get it for you. You've been working so hard. Why don't you just sit down?"

"I haven't brought my chair out yet," I say.

Cal's grin widens, and then he nods subtly to the back left corner of the group. My gaze flies in that direction, where I find Titan fluffing a bright pink blanket I've never seen before, and Ajax straightening the cushion on a loveseat.

A legit loveseat. On my back lawn.

Donald places an ottoman in front of it and swipes one hand across it as if there's dust there that needs to be wiped away.

"What in the world?" I don't know what else to say, and I turn back to Cal with wide, surprised eyes.

"I figured we'd need somewhere to sit," he says. "And I don't actually own a camp chair."

"I'm—yeah. We need somewhere to sit." Where did he even get that loveseat? Did he buy it just for tonight's party? Where is he going to put it after this?

He chuckles and presses his cheek to mine. "So tell me what you want to eat, and I'll get it for you."

"I like everything on that table," I say. "But if you come back without any popcorn, it's over between us."

He laughs fully then, and leads me over to the couch and tucks me in with the pink blanket before going to get my food.

I look around, hoping to catch Titan, Ajax, and Don so I can thank them for setting up the loveseat, but I don't see them.

I have Donald's number, so I pull out my phone and thank him via text, asking him to tell Titan and Ajax the same. Then I ask, *Where did you guys go?*

And how do they get away so fast? So silently? Maybe they're the ninjas.

Any time, Princess. And I know you won't believe this, but we've gone up to bed.

I glance up to the second-floor windows, all of which belong to Cal's detail. A light flicks on in one of them, and I smile as I return my gaze to my phone.

I hope you got food.

Ajax brought up an entire tray, Donald says. *Don't you worry.*

Enjoy your evening off, I tell him, though I wonder if he actually will.

I watch Cal as he laughs with Claudia, Beckett, and Aaron, says something to the conversation, and then listens when Emma chimes in. He seems to integrate into any group he joins, and that only makes my heart fonder for him.

He hasn't kissed me again since that melancholy day in the garage, and as he picks up the second plate full of food and heads my way, I vow that that's going to change tonight—when red, white, and blue explodes over our heads.

CHAPTER SIXTEEN

CAL

I don't think I've ever sat on a couch and watched a movie from beginning to end. Maybe I did in high school, but certainly not since I returned to Notavella.

Not only that, but I've never watched a movie outside.

And I've never done any of the above while holding the most beautiful woman in the world in my arms.

Tally loves all things sparkly and pink, which means she loves *Legally Blonde*.

I love her food, and the Big House, and the way she makes me feel like a normal person. I love the sound of her giggles, and the weight of her hand in mine, and the scent of her shampoo in my nose. While I've only been in town for about a month, I know I've fallen in love with Tahlia Tomlinson all over again.

The movie ends and the yard goes dark. My eyes can't adjust to it so quickly, and one of the men moves to the back porch, which activates the motion sensor lights there. They brighten the backyard, and I find Aaron coming back down the steps.

"Give us just a minute with the fireworks," he says. "You might want to move your chairs to face this way."

Everyone was instructed to park out front so that we could do fireworks on the back gravel lot, and now they stand and start turning their chairs around. Tally stands, and I look at her before jumping to my feet too.

Together, we manage to swing the loveseat around to face the graveled lot, and I sit back down and pull her next to me.

"Do you do fireworks in Notavella?" she asks.

"Yes," I say. "On Founder's Day. It's in March."

"Wild," she says. "I can't imagine fireworks in March."

Matt grunts and groans as he brings over a bucket full of water and sets it on the edge where the grass meets gravel. I have no idea what that's for, and I tell myself that I'm learning so much about Americans—what they do, the types of language they use to describe things, and so much more.

Before I know it, Aaron lights the first firework, and bright gold sparks shoot into the sky.

"Oh, that's a pretty one," Claudia says.

The firework stays on the ground, the sparks just fountaining out of the top of it. Matt lights one that spins on the ground, and then he and Aaron go through an elaborate setup of several pointed straight up into the sky.

They light those in what feels like a very unsafe manner, moving from one to the next in rapid succession. The fuses burn down, and the fireworks blast off from right to left, filling the sky with an array of screams, pops, and bright blasts of blue light, then green, then red, then white.

"*Wooow*," Tally says, and several others make similar sounds of awe and wonder.

She gazes up at me just as another firework explodes in the sky. She doesn't look at it, but keeps her eyes on me, and I wonder what she sees. She reaches up with her free hand, sliding her delicate fingers along my jaw and up behind my ear into my hair. She then draws me down, guiding my mouth to hers.

I have zero complaints about this, and as the fireworks continue to blast off around us, I kiss Tally like the hopeless fool in love that I am. Strangely, she kisses me back exactly the same way, and this is the passionate kiss I've waited eighteen years for.

The sky goes dark, and the noise stops, and I pull away from Tally.

"Sorry to make you miss the show," she whispers.

"I've seen fireworks before."

She curls into my chest, making me feel like I'm strong enough and good enough and worthy enough to protect her, while Aaron and Matt set up another round.

I smile as the show continues, and I get up and help Tally and the others take in the leftover food when the fireworks end. Her friends are fabulous, just like she is, and I can see why having them all move out has caused her to cry herself to sleep at night.

I help Liam, Aaron, and Beckett take down tables and canopies, while Tally boxes up leftovers, gives them to her friends, and puts them in the fridge. When the backyard is cleaned up, we go with everyone to the front of the house, where we stand together, my arm around hers, as we say goodbye to her friends.

"It was so great to meet you formally," Hillary says, and she grabs on to me in a hug.

I hardly know what to do, because while I know my parents love me, they're not the most physically affectionate people on the planet. I've lived a lot of my life without physical touch, and if there's one thing I've learned about myself since coming to South Carolina, it's how much I crave it.

I thought it was just Tally's that I needed—and she definitely feels different than Hillary—but it sure is nice to feel like someone likes me for me and wants me to be around because of who I am, not what I can do for them.

"Of course, it was wonderful to meet you too," I say. "All of you."

Claudia gives me an appraising look and then steps into me and sweeps a kiss across my cheek. "Please be gentle with Tahlia," she says in a quiet voice that only she and I can hear.

I nod to her as Beckett reaches for her hand and takes her down the front porch steps.

"I just don't think you should drive," Ryanne says.

"I know. I've already asked someone to take us," Elliott says. "Aaron's going to do it."

"Okay."

I can't even imagine what it would be like to live with a degenerative eye disease that makes it so I see less and less each day. Ryanne links her arm through Elliott's and leans her head against his bicep. The gentle acceptance between the two of them is beautiful to watch.

Emma finishes hugging Lizzie and then Tally, and she looks at me.

I open my arms to her, because it seems like everyone in the South hugs—even the more standoffish Emma.

Sure enough, she moves right into my arms, as if we're best friends, and hugs me tight. She steps back and smiles at Tally and then me. "I saw you two kissing," she says.

Heat fills my face, but Tally only laughs. "Yeah, we're dating, Em. Of course I'm kissing him."

Aaron shakes my hand, and then Matt and Lizzie come over, both of them offering hugs, before Matt picks up the leash and says, "Come on, Purricell and Purroxide. We have to go."

They head out too, and I stay on the front porch with Tally as they all leave, my arm hooked around her and keeping her solidly at my side.

"I see what you mean," I say.

"About what?" she asks.

"They're great," I say. "I really like all of them, and I see why it was hard for you to let them go and watch them move out."

She looks at me, something like wonder in her expression. "Thank you for indulging me in this very American party," she says.

"There is absolutely nowhere I'd rather be than here with you."

Because she broke the physical kiss barrier tonight, and it was a much happier occasion, I lean down and touch my lips to hers, getting a second fireworks show, this one even hotter and more explosive than the actual rockets that were lit.

———

A FEW DAYS LATER, I slip out the back door, knowing full well that I can count on Ajax and Titan to delay Tally should she come downstairs and head straight outside. For all I know, she might, because Liam has come to the Big House today to fix the roof.

I learned on the Fourth of July that he's a regular handyman, in addition to a general contractor—and a hobbyist at fixing up vehicles, including bicycles.

I catch him laying out a tarp on the lawn and then setting his toolbox on it. "Good morning, Liam," I say, and he dang near jumps out of his skin.

"Oh boy." He hops a couple of steps away from me. "Wow, you are like a *silent* prince."

I grin at him and then burst out laughing. "I've been called a lot of things," I say. "But never that. I apologize; I didn't mean to sneak up on you."

Though I totally did.

"It's fine," he says, returning to the tarp and opening the toolbox. "What's going on?"

"I heard that you know how to fix up bicycles," I say.

He abandons his toolbox, where he's laid out a hammer and a handsaw. I'm proud of myself for even knowing what those tools are.

"Yeah," he says. "You got something that needs to be fixed up?"

"I sure do," I say. "Do you have a couple of minutes to look at it with me? It's just right over by the garage."

He looks in that direction and then nods. "Yeah, sure. Let's go."

I lead him over to the side of the garage, where Tally's faded blue bike sits. "This was Tally's," I tell him. "And it means a great deal to her. Her aunt bought it for her when she was a teenager and staying here in the summers. I want to fix it up for her, and I want it to be a surprise."

Liam lifts the bicycle away from the side of the garage and examines it in a way that I'll never understand. I have no idea what he's looking for, but after several long moments of examination, he says, "Yeah, I can get this back to peak condition. This is a great brand." He smiles up at me. "It's a Boomer from the nineties."

"Okay," I say, having no idea what he just said. "How much do you think it'll cost?"

Liam looks at me, surprise crossing through his expression. "Oh, I can just do it."

"No," I say. "I want to pay for it. I know your time isn't free, and surely you'll need parts and supplies."

I look back at the bike. "New tires, yeah?

"Yeah, this thing needs a lot of new stuff."

"Precisely," I say. "I'll pay whatever it costs. I want the very best."

Liam grins at me. "I'm sure you do."

I don't know if that's a jab at me being a prince or not, but I like Liam, and I choose not to make it personal. "You'll let me know what you need? Money, phone calls to places to get supplies, whatever."

I'm not used to being told no, and in Notavella, whatever I want is found and given to me. I remind myself that I'm *Cal* here, not *Prince Kingsley*, and that I don't need to throw my weight around to get what I want. My money will do.

"Yeah, sure," Liam says good-naturedly. "I'll let you know."

"Okay," I say. "Thank you so much. And remember, it's a secret."

"Yep, it's a secret," he says. "I got it." He grins at me, and we start back toward the ladder. "So you and Tahlia seem to be getting along really well."

"Yes," I say. "It's going great."

"I'm glad," Liam says. "I've known Tahlia for years. She deserves someone good like you."

I nod as he continues toward the side of the house, but I want to go back inside. "Thank you, Liam. That means a lot coming from you."

"Does it?" he asks, pausing and turning back to me. "Why?"

I watch him for a moment, startled by the question. "Well, I mean, you don't know me," I say. "And...I suppose I'm used to being judged before people know much about me. They think I'm spoiled or rich or entitled."

He shrugs. "Well, aren't you?" He chuckles. "Who cares what other people think? You're nice to other people, and that's what I care about." He grins, then hooks his thumb over his shoulder. "I gotta get this done, though. I've got another job I've got to get to by ten."

"Yeah, go," I say. "Sorry to keep you."

"You didn't, man. You don't need to apologize." He sets the ladder against the house and scurries up it, and I hurry back inside, only to hear Ajax's voice echoing from the living room.

"It's got to be around here somewhere," he practically bellows.

Donald nods to my place at the kitchen table, and I rush to it, my eyes meeting Titan's, who's blocked the doorway—*physically blocked the doorway*—from the living room into the kitchen.

"Oh, look. Here it is," he says in the fakest voice I've ever heard in my life.

Herons in high water, I think as Titan turns in the doorway and takes a few steps into the kitchen, quickly followed by Ajax and then Tally.

"Oh, where was it?" she asks, and I realize he's holding her gardening apron.

"It was just underneath my suit coat," Titan says. "I'm really sorry, ma'am."

He hands her the freshly laundered apron, the one she's been using for the past couple of weeks to get her aunt's wheelbarrow painted and filled with topsoil. She had to drill holes into the bottom of it for water drainage, and she had me set it in the front yard last night, ready to be planted with petunias this morning.

She takes the apron, smiling, and then says, "Oh, it's fine, Titan. I'm sure you didn't do it on purpose."

I'm absolutely sure he did, but Titan simply wears a frown as he returns to his place at the table.

She looks at me with my still-full plate of breakfast in front of me. "I thought you'd be done by now. Are you still coming to the nursery with me?"

"Absolutely," I say, abandoning the bacon and egg bagel that Donald made for me that morning. "This is portable breakfast food," I tell her, and I flip the top of the bagel over onto the bottom half and pick it up. "Let's go."

She looks at me like I've lost my mind, and to be honest, I kind of feel like I have. Princes don't eat their breakfast on the go.

Then Tally says, "All right, let's go." She leads the way outside, while I detour over to the counter to get a paper towel. Donald ever so subtly positions himself next to the door, so that I have to pass by him to leave.

"Your Highness, you do not have to eat that on the go." He holds out his hand, as if to spare me the humiliation, but I actually wince away from him and pull the bagel closer to my body.

"I want to," I say. "This is what they do in America."

Donald looks at me like I've lost my mind, and maybe I have.

"Tally is driving," I say. "Will you please give us five minutes?"

"Ten," Titan says, joining him at the door, the jangle of keys already in his hand. "Tahlia asked us for ten," he says. "So we'll be ten minutes behind you, Your Highness."

I gape at him, sure that *my* security detail has not started taking orders from *Tahlia*. Not only that, but I've asked them for plenty of things over the years that they have ignored, and they've known Tally for five weeks, and she gets whatever she wants?

In that split second of time, I decide I can be angry about this or grateful for it, and I say, "Thank you. Ten minutes would be great."

Then I rush out the door to follow Tally, not wanting to waste a single second of my alone-time with her.

CHAPTER SEVENTEEN

TAHLIA

Cal, will you grab it for me?" I point to the next row over at
the nursery, where a huge flat of the more fuchsia-colored
purple petunias sits.

"Yes," Cal says, and he moves down to the end of the
row to go around.

I've noticed how he doesn't say *yep* or *yeah*, but always
yes. I duck my head and smile as I look at the bottle of
plant food in my hand.

"One or two, Tally?" he calls, and I look up to see the
Prince of Notavella holding a six-pack of petunias in each
palm, the blooms overflowing and making him look like he
has flower hands.

"Both," I say, though I already have too many flowers
for my aunt's wheelbarrow. I've cleared an entire flower
bed in the front yard where her fountain used to sit, and I
figure I can plant the extras there.

He comes back with the flowers, and I put the bottle of

plant food in the cart. "I think that's it," I say, and we head for the checkout.

"Oh, hey, Miss Tomlinson."

I turn at my teacher name and find one of my former students in line behind me.

"Hey, Jake," I say. "What have you been up to this summer?"

"We're just back in town for a few days," he says. "To check on the house, get a few things, and then we're going back out to the lake."

"Oh, which lake?" Cal asks, and Jake's eyes fly to his.

"Lake Moultrie," he says. "It's so great. They don't allow any motorized vehicles on the lake, so it's clean and calm all the time."

"Jake is a professional fisherman," I say, plenty of pride in my voice. "And he's really good at sketching and painting the fish that he's caught."

"Oh, I ain't no professional, Miss Tomlinson," he says.

"Can you *be* a professional fisherman?" Cal asks, and he pulls the cart forward as the line inches closer to the register.

"Yeah, you sure can," Jake says. "But you gotta have a lot of equipment for that, and I just like throwing my line in from the dock or a little rowboat."

"How far away is the lake house?" Cal asks.

I can see the interest in Jake's eyes, and I want to tell him that Cal is my brother, while also simultaneously claiming the prince as my boyfriend.

"This is Cal," I say, touching his elbow and bringing him back to my side. "Remember how I told you all my roommates got married and moved out?"

"Yeah," Jake says.

"Well, he's my new housemate."

"It's great to meet you." Jake sticks out his hand, and Cal shakes it.

"You too, Jake. I definitely want to hear more about this lake." He gives me a look and then goes back to loading my flowers and supplies onto the belt.

Jake's mother gets in line, and she says, "Oh, hi, Miss Tomlinson."

"You can call me Tahlia," I say. "We're not at school."

She just gives me that parent smile that says *I can't do that*, and I know she won't call me by my first name. "Did you ask her?" she asks, and I look at Jake at the same time she does.

"No, I hadn't gotten to it yet." He shifts uncomfortably, and I'm vaguely aware of Cal talking to the cashier behind me.

"I was just wondering if you needed a TA next year," Jake says. "I got an opening in my schedule, and the guidance counselor said I could ask individual teachers."

Jake's going into ninth grade, and he's never given me any problems. So I grin at him and say, "Absolutely. It'd be best if you helped out with a seventh-grade class, as they're the most chaotic."

He chuckles. "Yeah, I remember."

"Tally," Cal says from behind me, his hand landing lightly on my hip in a way that feels casual and intimate at the same time. "So sorry to interrupt. She wants to know if you have a phone number."

"No," I tell him, and then I watch in horror as *he*

swipes his card to pay for all of the petunias and flower-planting supplies *I've* wanted at the nursery.

"Great," Jake says, and I whip my attention back to him. "I'll go in in August and let the guidance counselor know. We'll figure out when your seventh-grade classes are."

"That would be great," I say.

His mother nods behind me. "It looks like your boyfriend's waiting."

"Yes," I say, mimicking Cal. "It was so great to see you guys. Have a good rest of your summer."

"You too," she says.

When I turn, I find that Cal is not only waiting at the end of the checkstand, but he's moved out of the way completely so other customers can go by him. He's pulled out his phone, and he frowns at it.

I nod to the woman who just checked us out, and she gives me a big grin before turning her attention to Jake and his mother behind me.

"Sorry," I say as I step over to him.

"It's fine," he says, though he's definitely not as jovial as he was on the way here.

"What's going on?" I ask, putting my hands on the shopping cart now and pushing it toward the door.

"It's just something going on back home," he says.

He's put me off about what's going on in Notavella since the Fourth, when his mother called at five a.m. his country's time.

It's only been four or five days, and we've worked in the garage every day and even ran to get burgers last night. But he's delusional if he doesn't know I've realized he's spending way more time in meetings with Don and the German Shepherds.

He texts all the way back to my car, where I load the flowers into the back of my SUV. Then I pluck his device from his fingers and watch as shock spills across his face.

"You're either going to tell me what's going on in Notavella, or I'm going to throw this phone as far as I can and then run over it with my car." I raise my eyebrows and cock my hip, daring him to contradict me.

His frown returns and deepens, and he stalks to the passenger side of the car.

I look at his phone, but the screen has gone dark, and I mimic him by heaving a great sigh before getting behind the wheel.

"I'm dealing with it," he says.

I turn on the car to get the AC blowing. How he even sat in here for three seconds without that is a mystery to me.

"Or you could just tell me," I say, flicking a glance over to him. "Is it classified information or something?"

"No," he says.

I could put the car in reverse and head home, plant my flowers, and escape with a good book into my bedroom. That's what I've done in summers past, but Cal has changed everything.

I enjoy being with him, holding his hand, listening to him talk about his country and his family, and all the security details he's had over the years. I don't want to retreat to my bedroom unless I have a very good reason.

"Listen," I say. "I get that you're royalty and all that. I

know you have princely things to do, and you might not be able to tell me everything at certain times."

I reach over and take his hand in mine, glad when he brings his other one on top and caresses the side of my thumb with the pad of his.

"But you have to tell me stuff that you can," I say. "If we want this to be a long-term thing." I duck my head, not quite brave enough to look at him. "And that's what I want, Cal."

I look out the windshield, and I can practically see the heat shimmering in the air. "I don't know what I'm going to do about my job or the Big House or any of my friends and everything I've built here, but I think you should know that I'm thinking beyond January."

"I am too," he says, his voice back to the mild, yet powerful bass that I've grown to love.

I look at him. "Are you?"

"Yes, of course."

"Then if this is not classified information, why can't you tell me?"

He rolls one shoulder and looks out the windshield himself. "It seems that the press in Notavella have realized that I'm not there," he says. "And they're trying to figure out where I am."

My heart drops to my stomach and then down to my feet. "That's not good."

"No." He shakes his head. "It's not."

"Do they know you're here?"

"Mother thinks they're very close," he says. "Because they know the private jet left Washington, D.C., and flew to South Carolina." He sighs again and looks at me with those oceanic eyes I swear I drown in every time they're pointed in my direction.

"But I landed in Columbia, if you'll remember," he says. "And they've been scouring there before expanding their reach."

I swallow. "Charleston isn't that far from Columbia."

"No, it's not," he says.

"What does this mean?" I ask. "Are there going to be reporters on the front lawn of the Big House?"

He drops his chin and traces the tip of his pointer finger around each of mine, as if memorizing the shape and size of my hand. "It's possible, Tally," he says. "I hate that it's possible, but it is."

He looks at me. "Don and the German Shepherds are doing what they can to lead them somewhere else. But it's only mid-July, and either I'm going to have to make an appearance in Notavella, or I'm going to have to announce where I am and request privacy."

My heart races, zipping along each rib and then settling in my stomach like a hive of angry bees. "Where will you make that announcement?"

"My father has suggested City Hall here in Charleston," he says. "It's an iconic building, and I can tell the public that I'm revisiting my youth and enjoying a season away from Notavella."

"I mean, you guys have summer homes, right?" I ask.

He gives me a soft smile and nods. "Yes. My parents are in the country home right now."

"Oh, *country* home," I say. "Maybe that's what the Big House is then—it's your country home."

He looks at me, pure hope in his eyes. "Do you think it

could be?" he asks quietly, his voice barely above a whisper.

I search his face, trying to find the answer he wants.

"We could spend part of the year in Notavella," he continues. "And part of it right here in Cider Cove."

I can't quite make sense of what he's saying, and I pull my hand away from his and flip the car into reverse.

"Something to think about, at least," he says.

I nod, because Cal has already given me a lot to think about, and this is just more.

We return to the Big House, with him texting his mother and me trying to stew through what it could mean to live part-time in Notavella in a castle, and still be able to return to the Big House.

I park as close to the front flower bed as I can get and start to unload the flowers and supplies. I've already filled three-quarters of the wheelbarrow with soil from the flower bed, and I add the grains of plant food and some topsoil to it. Then I reach for one of the six-packs of petunias, this one the beautiful pale pinks called Lip Gloss Sunset.

"You're not going to wear gloves?" Cal asks.

I scan him from his pristine button-up shirt down to the hem of his slacks. I'm wearing a pair of cutoff jeans and a rainbow-striped tank top.

"No," I say. "Aunt Fern never wore gloves. She said it was always good to feel the earth in your hands and on your skin. It grounds you."

I grin at him and nod to the bright purple petunias I had him get. "So come on, my prince, let's do this."

He chuckles and bends to get the flowers I've indicated.

"What do you like to do for hobbies?" I ask him. "Surely there's more to your life than being a prince."

"Yes, of course," he says. "I do enjoy cooking, and I'm expected to read and keep up with things."

"That's not a hobby though," I say. "A hobby is something you do that you don't get paid for, that's not expected of you. Something you do just because you like it."

He looks at me. "I like going out on the water in Notavella. We have ponds on the property, but they're pretty big, and I had my first personal assistant make me a sort of bed that I could lay across from the front seat in the boat to the back. Then I could lay down and watch the clouds move through the sky, making patterns and shapes."

I smile at him, at how quaint and slow and wonderful that life sounds.

"Is that a hobby?" he asks.

"Sure," I say. "Cooking counts. I'll give you that one."

"I like to go to downtown Century City," he says. "It's the oldest town in Notavella, and it's about an hour from the castle in the capital city of Chyme."

"Okay," I say.

"They have a street full of quaint shops that are centuries old that I adore—watches, an art supply store, a bookstore, and a bakery. I can spend a whole day there, perusing things and talking to shop owners."

"That sounds nice," I say. "What would you do in the evening?"

"Have a really great dinner," he says. "Preferably outside in the cooler air. And then sit down with my brother with a drink and talk about anything that doesn't have to do with the royal family or business."

I nod and pat the dirt around the last petunia. "I think that's all this is going to hold," I say. I kneel down and start to plant the extra flowers around the wheelbarrow. "That sounds like a really nice day, Cal."

He kneels down next to me, seemingly without a care that his pristine pants might get dirty. "Maybe I could show it to you one day," he says.

I nod, because today feels like the day when we're admitting this is going to last longer than the few months he's going to rent the Big House.

He hands me another petunia and says, "This is the last one, Tally."

I look at him, because of the tenderness with which he says my name, and he's right there, right at my shoulder, right at my side, willing to be *next* to me.

I drop the flower and lean into him, hoping he'll close the distance between us and kiss me. He does, his earthy hand sliding up the side of my face, twirling his fingers through my ponytail.

"You are hazardous to my health," he whispers against my lips, and then he kisses me again.

I'm falling down, down, down in love with Cal Irwin. And I've never experienced anything half as amazing as this.

CHAPTER EIGHTEEN

CAL

"Sorry I'm late," I say as I enter the second bedroom on the third floor of the Big House. This is our war room, where I've been meeting with Don, Ajax, and Titan since moving here to Cider Cove.

Both my mother and father fill the fifty-five-inch TV screen that Don hooks to his computer for meetings like this. I take my seat at the head of the table and smile at my parents. "Hello. It's good to see you guys."

"Oh, it's so good to see you, dear," Mother says, and she genuinely means it. "What have you been doing this morning?"

Don catches my eye, and I'm not quite sure what he's fed her. I find that it's always best to go with the truth when it comes to the Queen, and I fold my arms in front of me on the table.

"I've been restoring an old canoe here," I say. "I've almost got it done."

"A canoe?" Father leans forward, clearly interested. "That's great, son. Send us some pictures."

"It was Tally's uncle's," I tell them. "I haven't quite convinced her to go out on the lake with me yet." I chuckle at her stubbornness. "But I'll get there."

"Yes, let's talk personal things first," Mother says, because then she'll want to get down to business. "How are things with Tally?"

"They're going really well," I say, but I don't tell them much more. I never have, and it is not a requirement of my stay here that they know every detail of my relationship with Tally.

"Callan," Mother says in a voice she reserves for when she is most disappointed in me.

I sigh and roll my eyes. "Mother, I do not owe you a weekly report."

"No, but I would *like* one," she says. "We want to know how it's going. This woman could be a *princess* in our country."

"No, she'll never be a princess," I say. "You'll give her some other title and whisk us off to some other palace."

"Yes, but the people will want to love her." Mother watches me with those all-seeing eyes. "She sounds lovely," she adds. "I do wish you'd bring her here, so we could meet her too. Don has nothing but good things to say about her, and even Ajax and Titan's reports have been extremely complimentary."

I look at the German Shepherds, as Tally calls them. "You've been making reports about Tahlia?"

"Sir, with all due respect," Titan says, "I work for your mother, not you, and if she wants to know my opinion on your girlfriend, I'm going to give it to her."

"He has said *beautiful* things," Mother says, drawing

my attention back to the screen. "She sounds wonderful. Why can't you bring her?"

"Because it's the middle of July, Mother," I say. "She'll be starting school in another month."

"He wants her all to himself," Father says.

"Yes." I gesture to him. "Is that so wrong?"

"Of course it is," Mother says. "You are not a normal man, Cal."

"I know who I am, Mother." I sigh. "If this is the personal talk, I would like to end it."

I could tell her that I'm a hair's width away from being completely in love with Tally. That we've started talking about what life could be like if we were together past January. That I've started to imagine the Big House as our country home—our *another*-country-home.

"Cal." Mother whips my name out, and I blink to bring myself back to focus.

"Sorry." I look down at the paper that was placed in my spot. "Yes, I'm going to make the announcement this Friday at four p.m. Notavella time, which I have to say, is very early here."

"Yes, but it gives Hamilton a chance to get a press release out to all the news channels before they start broadcasting their evening news," she says. "The last thing we want is them breaking into their broadcast to go *live* from Charleston."

"There's no way they'll have TV crews here to do that," I say.

Mother cocks both eyebrows and tilts her head in a very feline way of saying, *Are you serious right now?*

"Dear," she says. "They have found you. They know

you're in the Charleston area, and I'll be shocked if they don't know you're at the Big House on Cherry Lane before Friday." She glances to my father. "Perhaps by tonight."

Panic strikes through me, as if I'm being hit with a powerful venom and then a whip—there and gone, but with a lasting effect spreading through me and making me numb.

"Mother, they absolutely cannot come to the Big House."

"Maybe we should put out the press release now," Dad says.

"It's Wednesday," I say, certain that I had more time than this. "It has taken a bit of extra time to get things situated here."

"Ma'am," Donald says, and he's always been able to placate Mother when I could not. "We do have things all lined up for Friday morning, and it would be very upsetting to Miss Tomlinson to have the press here at her personal home."

"I agree," Ajax says, and surprise bolts through me as I look at him. "Your Majesty, these are not gated communities. She lives on a lane in a quiet neighborhood, and she's friends with everyone around her. It would be quite disruptive."

"Perhaps we can move it to tomorrow afternoon," Mother says.

I glance at Dad.

"Let's just keep it on Friday," he says. "We can have Hamilton and Donald distribute privacy requests and notice of the press conference on Friday."

"If you do that," I say, "They'll have time to get here."

"So what if they do?" Mother asks.

"It will be chaos," I say. "Did you not just hear what Ajax and Donald said? I *do—not* want them here. We're going to release our own stream, on our own channel. Titan has the equipment, and we've contacted the mayor. That's all we needed to do. He's out of town, Mother, and the earliest we can do it is Friday. Please."

"Perhaps," Donald says. "We could issue an immediate privacy request," he says, speaking slowly. "And a notice that there will be a press conference in the coming days, and that we will notify them by Friday morning, Notavella time, of when and where it will be."

He looks at me, eyebrows raised. "With the time difference, Cal, they would not be able to get here in time." He looks back to Mother. "And it would satisfy them, knowing there is more news coming. And if it's attached to a privacy request..." He lets the words hang there.

Mother considers for several long moments and finally looks at Dad.

"It gives everyone what they want," he says. "And I think it's our best chance of avoiding a circus on Tahlia's front lawn."

She nods, and relief paints through me in thick strokes. "Thank you, Mother," I say.

"You have told her though, haven't you?" she asks.

"Yes," I say. "Though she does not know how close they are."

"You should tell her," Dad says. "This life, Cal..." He trails off and reaches for Mother's hand. "It is not for everyone."

"Yes, she needs more information, Dad, but not six

weeks in," I say. "I wanted six *months*. Maybe we were foolish to think that no one would care where I was."

"I told you, you're more important than you know," Mother says.

I shake my head. "I don't want to argue about this either."

She nods and lets it go.

I look back at the agenda and slide the bottom paper to the top. "It looks like Donald has sent you the speech I'm going to say on Friday."

"Yes," Mother says. "I've made a few modifications."

She lifts a paper and starts to go over them. Donald and Ajax both take notes while I simply acquiesce to the word choices she would like to use.

With the speech finally done, I deliver it, and Mother corrects me on certain inflections in my voice.

"Less than six and a half minutes," Dad says. "That's perfect, Cal."

Six and a half minutes will change everything, but I keep that to myself.

Finally, Mother says, "Are you going to have Tally with you?"

I blink at the screen, sure I have not heard the question correctly. "What do you mean? Of course she's not going to be there."

"We think she should be," Mother says. "All of us, Donald and Ajax and Titan included."

I look at my detail, a keen sense of betrayal singing through me. "You do? Why?"

"Sir," Donald says. "While you do not come right out and say that you came back to Charleston to reconcile with

Tally, everyone is going to know that's why you're here. They'll know where you're renting, they will see who owns it, and they *will* connect the dots."

Ajax slides his laptop in front of me, and I blink at the horribly grainy photos on the screen. "Are those me?" I ask, peering closer.

"With Tahlia," he growls. "In high school. Sire, I think you're an amazing prince, and I have loved being assigned to you. But you're *delusional* if you think the reporters and our people don't want to know about her."

"She's beautiful," Titan says. "And poised. And Donald would love to take her shopping to make sure she has what she needs to be at your side."

I shake my head instantly. "Absolutely not. No. You will *not* change Tally. She will wear what she wants to wear." I push to my feet and lean into my knuckles on the table. "If I can even get her there. What makes you think she'll want to be there?"

My father wears the most sympathetic face I've ever seen. "Son, this might be the first test for her."

"Sometimes we have to do things we don't want to do," Mother says in a much crisper tone.

"This is *unbelievable.*" I glare at them, then at Donald. "And you should have warned me of this before I walked in here."

"Yes, sir," he says.

I turn, jacket flap flying, and march out of the war room. I want to leave the Big House, get in a car, and drive as far and as fast as I can.

But I have no such escape here, so I move into my assigned bedroom, shed my suit coat, rip off my tie, and change out of my long-sleeved white shirt and into a dark gray polo.

When I march past the war room, the door is still open, and echoes of my mother's and father's voices follow me downstairs and into the garage.

I've made steady progress on the canoe in the past few weeks, and I just gave her a third coat of a beautiful burnt orange paint that almost looks rusty red in the bright sunlight. I'm working on the inner bench seats now, and I pick up from where I left off an hour ago, letting the easy, rhythmic motions of my hands sanding wood soothe my hurt feelings and ego.

I need to talk to Tally if I'm expecting her to stand in front of the world in less than forty-eight hours.

She went to lunch with a coworker today and then had a hair appointment, but I pull out my phone and text her: *Will you come find me in the garage when you get home? I have something very important to talk to you about.*

She doesn't answer right away, and I ignore the texts from my parents and Donald.

I turn to fitting together the pieces to make a bench seat in the canoe. I test it out and saw off another quarter inch. When I can hammer it perfectly into place, I pull it out and start to paint it white. The same motion, over and over, frees my mind to think through how I can ask Tally to stand at my side and expose herself to the world in a way not very many people have to do.

I'm aware when Titan arrives, though I ignore him too. It's hot in the garage, and I move over to the fan and flip it on. I work steadily through the afternoon on the second bench seat—the one near the back in this canoe-built-for-two—and I imagine Tally and me there together, rowing and fishing, talking and laughing, and maybe even diving off the side if the lake isn't too cold.

When Titan says, "Hello, ma'am," I lift my head and look toward the open doors of the garage.

Tally smiles at him, her golden hair even more vibrant and stunning now. "Good afternoon, Titan," she says. "I really like this tie." She reaches out and drops her fingers down the front of it. "I don't think I've ever seen you wear this much color. Is this Queen-approved?"

He smiles at her, though she still hasn't cracked Ajax, and says, "Yes, ma'am."

"Good," she says. "I don't want anyone breaking rules on my watch." She switches her gaze to me and takes a few steps into the garage before cocking her hip and gesturing to her hair. "So, tell me how amazing it is."

I abandon my tools and painting supplies and have to coach myself not to rush at her. "It's *gorgeous*," I tell her. "I mean, I didn't think it could get any better, but *wo-o-o-ow*."

She giggles and grabs onto my collar as I lean down to kiss her. "Something very important," she whispers against my lips.

"Yes," I say. "But first I want to show you the canoe." I lead her over to it. "It's painted inside and out now, and I'm working on the bench seats."

"Wow, Cal," she says. "This looks amazing."

Pride fills my chest. "I've done every bit of work on it," I say. "Just like I promised."

"Mm, yes, you have." She runs her hand along the side of the canoe.

"I'm ordering brand new life jackets," I say. "And oars.

And I've been reading up on Lake Moultrie. I want to go next weekend."

I can tell she doesn't want to go, but she doesn't dismiss me immediately. "I want to hear what we have to talk about first," she says.

I groan and turn away from her. "No, because then you'll never go out with me again."

"It's that bad?"

"Yes."

"Well then, just keep facing the back of the garage and spit it out."

At the tool bench, I keep a container of wet wipes, and I pull one out and start wiping my hands. "The press knows where I am," I say. "And to keep them from showing up on the front lawn of the Big House, I have to make an announcement."

I turn back to her and lean against the workbench. Her eyes are wide, and she's blinking fast.

"Friday morning," I say. "Seven a.m. at City Hall in Charleston. And, it is the opinion of everyone except me that you should be there with me."

One hand comes up to her mouth, while the other presses against her heart. "Me?" she asks between her fingers. "Why?"

"*That* is a great question," I say, sarcasm dripping. "Maybe you should ask Titan."

The German Shepherd standing at the corner of the garage just out of sight says nothing at all.

Tally glances toward him and then looks back at me. "Are you going to tell everyone that we're dating?"

"It's not specifically in the speech," I say. "But

everyone believes that it will be implied. Ajax has some old yearbook photos of us, Tally, and reporters know how to dig everything up."

Her shoulders fall as she exhales. "Yeah, it seems that they do."

"You can wear whatever you want," I say, gesturing to her clothes. "That would be fine."

She looks down at herself—today she's wearing loose parachute pants and a white ribbed tank top with a pink Care Bear splashed in the middle. She returns her gaze to me, pure horror in her eyes.

"You have got to be kidding," she says. "I can't wear this."

I take a step toward her, then another one. "I told them they cannot dress you up like a doll," I say fiercely. "You get to do and be whoever you want, and that includes what you wear."

"I have dresses, Cal." She smiles at me and runs her hand up my chest. "But I like this protective side of you."

I slide my hand along her waist and around her back, pulling her flush against me. "I do *not* want you to have to do this at all. I'm really sorry, Tally."

She threads her other hand through the hair at the nape of my neck. "I know you don't," she says. "But this is who you are, Cal."

"No," I bark at her. "This is what I *do*. It is not who I *am*."

Can't she see the difference?

"Who I am, who I want to be, is who I am when I'm with you—when we're eating too much popcorn, when I'm showing you the canoe, when we're planting petunias."

She nods and sweeps her hand across my forehead, pushing my hair out of the way. "Yeah, I see him too," she says. Then her teasing smile returns. "Will I have to get my dress approved by your mother?"

"Absolutely not," I growl at her.

"Unless you want to," Titan says.

I throw the corner of the garage where he's still not showing himself a dirty look. There are so many more things to tell Tally, and I don't want to do any of them within earshot of my German Shepherd, especially now that I know he's making reports to my mother.

I lean closer until my mouth is right in her ear. "My parents would like to meet you," I murmur. "But that's something we can talk about after we get through Friday. Will you really come do the press conference with me?"

"Of course," she whispers back. "But I'm assuming we can't go out tonight."

I pull away and search her face. "I've kind of forgotten about it," I say.

She smiles and touches her lips to mine in a perfectly sweet, electrifying, chaste kiss. "I figured," she says. "It's fine. We can order in and eat on the roof here. Liam and Hillary have done it."

I smile and wrap her up in my arms again. "Thank you, Tally. I'm sorry I've invaded your life like this."

"Stop it," she says. "Because I'm not."

I nod as Ajax clears his throat. I step away from her and look at him. "What is it now?" I ask, pure weariness in my tone.

He cuts a glance to Tally. "There's someone at the door for you, sir. I didn't realize Miss Tomlinson was here." He cuts a look over to Titan, clearly annoyed that he wasn't warned.

"Someone at the door?" Tally asks, moving toward him. "Who is it?"

Ajax looks at me with wide eyes, filled with apprehension. "It's Liam, sir. Shall I send him back?"

I lunge toward Tally and grab her hand. "It's just Liam. I asked him…"

I trail off because I don't quite know what to say. Tally looks at me, her eyebrows getting higher and higher with every heartbeat that ticks by. "You asked him what?" she asks.

"Tell him I'm busy," I tell Ajax. "I'll call him later."

"Yes, sir," he says, and he scampers away.

Tally pulls her arm away and settles her weight on one foot. She cocks her hip and folds her arms. "What's going on with you and Liam?"

"Nothing," I say. "I asked him for a favor, is all."

"What kind of—?"

"Tally," I cut her off. "This is confidential, okay? When I can tell you, I will."

She scoffs and blinks rapidly. "Nothing can be confidential with you and *Liam*."

Titan starts to chuckle, and that makes me smile too. "Please, just let this one go for now," I say.

She glares at me. "Fine. But only because I now have to make a *six-way* video call and figure out what I'm going to wear at a *press conference* that my *prince boyfriend* is going to have for his whole country on *Friday* morning."

She throws me a death glare and stomps away.

I sigh as I move out of the garage and stand next to Titan. "Well, she said yes," I say.

"Yes, she did, sir." Titan chuckles again, smiling as he watches Tally march up the back steps, across the porch, and into the house. "I really like her."

And it's my turn to scoff, though I really like her too. I can only hope that this press conference doesn't break us completely.

CHAPTER NINETEEN

TAHLIA

"I can't believe I'm wearing black," I mutter to myself. After all, this is an official press conference for Cal's country, not a funeral. But the nicest dress I have in my closet is the blue scuba that I've already worn on a date with Cal.

Ry pointed out that the whole nation of Notavella hasn't seen it, and it would be fine for this too, and she's right. But Claudia owns a great many beautiful dresses, and she'd come over on Wednesday after work and brought an array of them.

This black one with the scoop neck doesn't show any cleavage and the sensible sleeves make up for the way the dress hugs my every curve and glitters with crystals.

The black wedges are far too casual for this dress, and Hillary brought over a pair of black heels that she wore on the runway in Hollywood.

I feel glamorous and gorgeous and so unlike myself.

It's five-thirty in the morning, and I quickly finish my makeup and make sure my hair lays right.

"Thank goodness I had that hair appointment on Wednesday," I say, though my life seems to have exploded since then—first with this press conference this morning, and then with some sort of confidential secret between Liam and Cal I haven't been able to figure out. Both Liam and Hillary have refused to tell me as well.

It's fine, I tell myself for probably the tenth time in the past two days.

No, I don't particularly want to be standing on the steps of City Hall this morning, and I don't want Titan's camera on me, and I don't want any of the Notavellan eyes to be judging me. But I absolutely can't have people with cameras and questions come to Cherry Lane and ruin the sanctuary I've built here.

Cal knows that, and he has worked incredibly hard to preserve it. That alone endears me to him, and as I've told my friends, I've always wanted a man who knows how to take care of me.

And Cal does. In fact, he's exceptionally good at it, doing everything from brewing the coffee the exact way I like, to picking me up in my master suite for dates, to ordering the food I want and making sure it arrives precisely when I'm hungry.

Cal knows how to attend to details, and though I worry that he'll resent me soon enough, I do enjoy being taken care of by him.

I've just stepped into my second shoe when a light knock sounds on my bedroom door. "Coming." I take a big breath, press both my hands against my stomach while I hold it, then exhale slowly as I move to open my bedroom door.

Cal stands there, wearing the Queen-approved midnight black suit.

"Holy chipotle shrimp and grits," I say. "You look amazing."

His gaze drips down my body to my heeled toes and back. "So do you," he says, a clear hunger in his eyes. No smile appears, but he offers me his arm. "I'm going to tell Donald to put out a press release that I'm the luckiest man in the world to have you on my arm."

I grin, because there he goes again, saying such perfect things.

"I thought you said I wasn't in the speech," I say.

"That's why I need to instruct Donald to put it in a press release." He leads me out the front door, where all three of his detail stand next to the black town car—Titan next to the driver's seat, Don right behind him, and Ajax on the passenger side.

"You don't have to say anything," Cal says. "The speech is six minutes and twelve seconds, and that's after the mayor introduces me. Donald assured me he would not speak for more than two minutes. So that's ten minutes you have to stand there in front of the cameras."

"No Q and A?" I ask.

"Yes," he bites out. "I agreed to a Q and A. But if there's something I don't want to answer, I told my mother I'm going to say, 'Pass. Next question.'"

I giggle. "I'd like to see you do that."

"Hey, I can do it." He gives me a glare and leads me to where Donald stands on the driver's side rear door.

"Good morning, Miss Tomlinson," Don says. "My, don't you look lovely?"

I lean in and kiss both of his cheeks. "Thank you, Don."

"You're on this side," he says. "As we'll be pulling up to the curb on the passenger side, and that is where His Highness will get out."

"Great blue herons," Cal says, stomping around the car while I slide into the backseat. I'm sure his objective is to open the door himself and get in, but Ajax is already over there, and Cal glares at him as he sinks into the backseat and the door closes.

"Why are you so mean to them?" I ask. "They're doing their job."

He blinks at me, the pure grumpiness on his face melting away after a moment. "You're right. I'm sorry."

He reaches for me. "Can you slide over in that thing?" he asks, eyeing my skirt.

"Yes," I say, and hold it down at my knee as I move over next to him.

"I'm sorry I'm so upset," he says, lifting his arm around me and holding me against his chest. "Public appearances are my least favorite part of the job."

"We all have parts of our jobs we dislike," I say. "We just get through them."

"You're right," he says.

"And as much as you may hate it, Titan and Ajax and Donald are part of the job, and they deserve your kindness and respect."

"Yes," he murmurs. "I know. I'm sorry."

"You don't have to tell me," I say. "But you should tell *them*. They do every single thing you ask."

He hums, which is his way of agreeing with me.

"Yeah, I know I'm right," I say. "Because they're not in the car right now, which means you asked them to give us a few minutes. Tell me I'm wrong."

"You're not wrong," he says.

"And they're up at six o'clock in the morning, doing everything that's been asked of them, including leaving their home country and coming here so that you can—"

"I know, Tally," he says, glaring at me. "All right? I hear you. *I hear you.*"

I nod, because I believe he has heard me. I reach across him and knock on the window. In less than one second, Ajax opens the passenger door and gets in the front seat, and only a beat behind him are Donald and Titan.

They settle into the car, and the silence feels as thick as gelatin, making it hard to breathe.

Finally, Cal sighs and says, "I'm really sorry, you guys. Please forgive me for how beastly I've been the past few days."

"It's fine, sir," Ajax barks from the front seat.

Titan says nothing, and I watch Don as he blinks and looks at Cal, probably to make sure he hasn't morphed into someone else.

"Apology accepted, sir," he says.

"I know we're just all doing our best," Cal says. "And I don't mean to treat you unkindly."

I smile up at him, and he leans down so that I can kiss his cheek.

"Are you happy now?" he asks.

"Yes," I say. "But I'll be happier when this press conference is over and we're eating pancakes and bacon at Aunt Sue's."

He blinks at me. "I don't think that's part of today's agenda, sweetheart."

"Donald?" I look at him.

Donald reaches across me with a paper. Cal stares at it and then whips it out of his hand.

"Holy hawks and finches. You got Don to change the agenda."

I laugh right out loud and snuggle deeper into his side. "No, I didn't," I say. "He told me there wasn't anything *on* the agenda after this, so I figured, since we have to be up so early, the five of us could get breakfast."

"The five of us?" Cal sounds like he's inhaled helium, and that only makes me laugh again.

"Yes," I say. "This is a big sacrifice for all of us to be up and looking our best so early, is it not? I mean, look at Titan. He didn't even wear a tie with any color today."

"Huge sacrifice," Titan says in a deadpan, and that gets Don to break a smile.

The drive downtown happens in mostly silence after that, with Cal on his phone most of the time, talking with his mom and dad.

I've told all of my roommates about this morning's press conference and that they'll be able to watch it on the Royal Family of Notavella YouTube channel. I don't think anyone else in South Carolina cares one whit, so a shock of surprise moves through me when we approach City Hall and there's so much traffic that we can't get through.

Titan rolls down his window no more than five inches and shows credentials that get us to the back of the build-ing, down a ramp, and into a parking lot.

A half dozen security guards wait for us, and Donald says, "Wait here, sir," and gets out with Ajax to greet them.

They speak for probably sixty seconds, each one making my heart beat a little bit faster, and then faster, and then faster, until finally Titan says, "Ma'am, you're going to want to be right behind me."

"Oh, shoot, yes." I quickly scoot over, adjusting my dress and running my fingers through my hair one last time.

Then someone opens my door and Cal's at the exact same time, and Don is standing there, his hand outstretched to help me to my feet. I appreciate him more than ever in that moment, and I put my hand in his and feel like a phoenix rising out of the ashes as I stand from the town car.

The weight of every eye lands on me, though these are just security guards. Ajax escorts Cal around the back of the car to my side, where I link my arm through his once again.

"The mayor's wife is going to take you," he says. "Don will go with you as well."

"Okay," I say, and I simply let myself get swept up in whatever they tell me to do.

I go with Ava, the mayor's wife, and I watch longingly as Cal moves away with Ajax and Titan. He shakes the hand of every security guard and thanks them for being there that morning. Then he meets the mayor. He shakes his hand too, and I watch as he leans in and says something, and then both of them laugh.

He is *so good* with people, though I know he doesn't know it.

"Come on, dear," Ava says. She's probably my mother's age and reminds me a lot of Aunt Fern as she wears a sharp crimson pantsuit with a pair of silver heels.

"I love your shoes," I tell her.

"Thank you," she says. "Sherman got these for our fortieth anniversary. But don't worry, they're fake diamonds."

I smile at her and let her lead me into the basement of the building. She knows her way around, and she's easy to talk to. When it's time to go out onto the front steps, Don takes my arm and together the three of us walk outside.

Cal is already there, with Ajax doing a mic test and various security guards fanned out around us. The sidewalk in front of the building has been closed, and four police vehicles have parked in front of it, lights flashing but no sirens. That's one way to tell people there's definitely something going on.

In fact, a small crowd has gathered, and Titan raises his arm with a thumbs-up to signal that the camera is ready.

I feel like I'm going to be sick, but I clasp my hands in front of my body the way Ava does and focus on Cal. When I just focus on him, the world falls away.

Finally, he moves to the side and catches my eye. I give him a quick smile, and he returns it before we both focus on the mayor, who's getting one last instruction from Ajax at the podium.

Then he falls back to Cal's side, and the mayor raises his head. He looks directly at the camera and says, "It is my great honor to be speaking to you today from the steps of the glorious City Hall building in Charleston, South Carolina, United States of America.

"My name is Sherman Calvern, and I am the mayor of this great city. I want to personally welcome, on behalf of myself and my wife, as well as the great people of Charleston and the citizens of South Carolina, to our great state, the Special Envoy to the Crown—Prince Callan Irwin Kingsley."

He pauses there, and though I'm standing behind him and to the side, I can still see his glorious smile.

"He will be staying in our city for a few months, and he and the royal family of Notavella have asked for privacy. So while we encourage our great people to show their Southern hospitality, we'll also be releasing a privacy request from the royal family of Notavella.

"Prince Cal has a message from the crown that he would like to share with you, so I'm going to turn the time over to him." He steps back and gestures to the mic, his face made of eight rainbows and unicorns.

Cal transforms instantly as he steps into the line of sight of the camera. He moves next to the mayor and shakes his hand, both of them holding there in a pose clearly orchestrated for the press. Then he continues to the mic while Mayor Calvern moves to his wife's side.

I once again focus on Cal, because he said his speech is only six minutes and twelve seconds, but he hasn't actually performed it for me yet.

"Good morning," he says, and then chuckles. "Well, it's morning in the United States—quite early, in fact."

His accent becomes a little thicker as he speaks, and I realize that he understands who he's talking to, and that it's his people.

"I wish to address the rumors and speculation that I am

not in my beloved country of Notavella." He spreads his arms wide. "As you can see, they are true.

"I am in the United States, where I spent several years in my youth as an exchange student, learning more about other countries and cultures. This has been invaluable experience for my role as Special Envoy to the Crown.

"And I arrived in the United States at the beginning of June, approximately twelve days before the International Summit in Washington, D.C., which I also attended.

"I have not traveled overseas alone, and I have three of the most amazing assistants and security detail with me. We have rented a house in a suburb here in Charleston, and as part of our privacy request, I am personally asking any and all reporters, press, and anyone else interested to stay away from that property.

"It is a private residence where I have rented a couple of rooms for a few months, as I wish to return to where some of my most formative years were spent. I am reconnecting with old friends, discovering new hobbies, and enjoying the American culture while still attending to all the duties that the crown requires.

"I look forward to returning to Notavella in the New Year, or at any time that I am called home, and I can assure you that I am not abdicating nor running away."

He looks down at the podium and clears his throat. "I will not be granting any press requests while I am in the United States. There is still much to be done, and I am meeting daily and doing the work required.

"It is my wish that everyone will consider this my country home this year, and know that I am still dedicated to you, the people of Notavella, and to growing our country and prosperity in any way that I can.

"Queen Sophia and King Charles have approved this travel, and I meet with them at least twice each week. They too will be issuing their own press release through a written statement within the next hour, so please watch your inboxes for that.

"At this time, I am also pursuing personal interests, which include gardening, cooking, watching a movie from beginning to end, and yes, dating.

"Our privacy request encompasses all of those things, though I am always happy to speak to people when I am out in public. I do hope you'll remember that I am a person, and anyone that I am with is as well, and that we may be busy, or in a hurry to get to another appointment, or simply unable to talk for very long.

"I love Notavella and the people who live there, and I cannot wait to return—hopefully as a more well-rounded, better educated, happier Special Envoy to the Crown."

He places one hand in his pocket, and from my angle, he looks calm and cool and collected—the epitome of power and princedom.

"Now, we have this streaming on the Royal Family of Notavella YouTube channel, where we have opened comments and questions, and I will be taking a few of those at this time."

He lifts his phone and chuckles. "Yes, it is very good to be with all of you, too. Thank you for joining us on this broadcast."

A pause while he scans his phone, and I wonder who's manning the comment section on YouTube.

"I see here we have a question from Frederick Gustoval, at *Notavella City Hall Press*. He wants to know if I will be missing our annual duck hunt this year."

Cal looks up from his phone, while a sense of dumbfoundedness moves through me. *That's* what someone's worried about? The duck hunt?

"Unfortunately," Cal says. "I will be missing it, though I also almost have a canoe here restored, and I hope to be out on the lake birdwatching and hunting right here in South Carolina."

He glances down at his phone. "Carmel Surmisse from the *Notavellan Sunday Times* wants to know what my favorite Southern food is."

He chuckles. "I'm living in a house owned by a Southern woman who loves to cook, and let me tell you, I have eaten a lot of really tasty things. I think the best thing that I've eaten here is the pimento cheese. There's nothing like it in Notavella, and perhaps I will have her teach me how to make it so that I can share it with all of you when I return home."

He glances at his phone again. "I think I have time for one more question. Ah, yes. Genoese Trivial from *The Daily Notavella* wants to know if I am seeing anyone here in the States."

Cal looks up, and I watch his shoulders raise as well. "The answer is yes. I *am* seeing someone special here in the States, and I am hoping that it will turn into a relationship strong enough and deep enough for me to bring her home and introduce her to all of you."

He sets down his phone. "Thank you for tuning in today. That's all the time that I have. Please continue to leave your comments and questions on our video, and I will read through them and answer what I can."

He raises his hand in a final farewell, and he stays in that position awkwardly until Titan raises his thumb again. Then Cal turns abruptly away from the camera, and everything about him droops again.

I rush toward him. "Wow, that was incredible."

There's so much energy in the air, and I breathe it in, feeling it wash through my lungs and every cell of my body.

"Was it?" he asks.

"Yes," I say. "Absolutely *incredible*."

"Your Highness, this way," Donald says, and Cal puts his hand on the small of my back and guides me to turn around and go back into City Hall. We're whisked along the hallways and back down to the basement, where our car waits in the same position in the parking garage.

We crowd into the car again, where I pluck my phone out of the pocket on the back seat of the passenger side. It has positively *blown up* with texts from my friends, and as I watch, my principal and coworkers start to message as well.

"Wow, word travels fast," I say, and then I take my phone and tuck it under my leg.

Cal is typing furiously with his thumbs on his phone too, and when he finishes, I hold out my hand for the phone. He gives it to me, and I hand it to Don, who tucks it away out of sight.

"All right," I say. "Who thought that was amazing?"

"Just you, ma'am," Ajax says dryly.

I fill the car with my laughter. "Fine, just me. But we're still getting pancakes and bacon, right?"

"I have the address for Aunt Sue's programmed in as we speak," Titan says.

I beam at Cal, who finally gives me the smile I've been waiting for, leans down, and kisses me sweetly. He really was amazing, and I hope his family's privacy requests will be honored by the people in Charleston, as well as by the press in Notavella.

CHAPTER TWENTY

ELLIOTT

I'M AWAKENED FROM A DEAD SLEEP BY ONE VERY LOUD bark. Luna never barks unless it's really important, so my eyes fly open and I sit up at the same time, reaching out to see if Ryanne is still beside me in bed. She's been struggling the last couple of weeks, and I often wake up in the middle of the night and find her gone.

She's not there right now either, and my eyes immediately move to the corner of our bedroom where we finally put the recliner after I found her sleeping in it for the fourth night in a row.

Luna barks again before I can tell if Ry is in the recliner or not. She jumps up on the bed, pants in my face, and then jumps back down. I throw the covers off and go with her.

Our bedroom door stands open, which in and of itself is strange, and Luna points toward the bathroom around the corner.

I didn't grab my glasses, but I don't need them to see and hear Ry crying.

"Hey, hey, what's wrong?" I ask, crowding into the small bathroom with her.

"My water broke," she says, and pure panic fills me. I don't exactly know what time it is, but it's still really dark, which means it's the depth of night.

"All right," I say, trying not to let my heartbeat push my panic higher. "I'm going to get the baby bag and I'll be right back for you."

She nods and presses both hands to the sides of her belly. I dash back into the bedroom and grab my glasses from the nightstand, throw on some clothes, then pick up the cute teal suitcase Ryanne packed for the hospital.

Ry groans as I join her in the bathroom again, and through some miracle, I get her to her feet. "Luna," I say. "To the car."

I usually hold on to a leash attached to Luna's harness, but I haven't had time to do that yet. I get Ry in the car and toss the baby bag into the backseat unceremoniously before dashing up the few steps to the back door and grabbing Luna's leash. I put it on her, settle her in the backseat as well, and then I get behind the wheel.

My beast of a car roars to life, sounding so much louder than normal. I use the gearshift arm to put it in reverse and praise all the stars in the heavens as I glance up into the rearview mirror just as I ease my foot off the brake.

I jam it back down, sending Ry, Luna, and me all rocking forward.

"Elliott," she says, as if I did it on purpose.

"I forgot to put the garage door up," I say, quickly pressing the button on the visor above my head.

Ry stares at me. "You *forgot* to put the garage door up?"

"It's fine," I tell her. "I'm fine. I'm going to get us there."

My eyesight hasn't deteriorated so much that they've taken away my driver's license. Yes, I usually have Ry drive for us, and if I'm particularly tired or it's really late at night, my mother will drive me. But I've been asleep for four hours now, and I feel more alert than ever.

"Oh, here comes another contraction," Ry says, lowering her seat while I watch helplessly. "Oh, this is not better," she groans. "Nope, this is *not* better."

I focus on driving and let her deal with the seat however she wants. Life feels like it's being lived in fast-forward.

When we get to the hospital, I run inside and say, "My wife is in labor," and someone comes out with a wheel-chair. We put Ry in it, and I hold Luna's leash in one hand and tow the teal suitcase with the other, doing my best to keep up with the long-legged nurse who probably spends every shift on her feet.

We're checked in, and Ry is given a room. Her doctor is called, and I help her out of her clothes and into the hospital gown.

Then it's a whole lot of hurry up and wait.

I can't believe I'm going to be a father.

After the attending doctor comes in and tells Ry that she's ready to get her epidural, I look at her. "It's time," I say. "We need a final name."

She nods. "I really like Corduroy."

I smile, because I do too. "His middle name doesn't have to be after me."

"Yes, it does," Ry says in her usual grumpy fashion.

"Corduroy Elliott Hutson. It's perfect. We can call him Cord or Roy."

I grin at her and press a kiss to her forehead. "You're doing great. Thank you so much for already being such a good mom."

She smiles at me, and someone hits that fast-forward button again. She gets an epidural, and just as the sun starts to paint the hospital room with golden morning light, my baby's cries fill the air.

"It's a boy," the doctor says.

I can't look away from the tiny infant, and Ry's fingers release mine as the nurses turn their backs and take him two steps to a table.

"Go with him," she says, and I do, watching as the nurses wipe him clean, take his blood, and wrap him up tight.

"Here you go, Daddy," one of them says, and they pass the helpless human being into my arms as if I know what to do, as if I'll be able to take care of him.

"Go introduce him to his mother."

So much love fills me as I gaze down into the face of my son. Then I turn to Ry and go back to her side. She reaches for Corduroy, and I slide him easily into her arms.

"Oh, he's so beautiful," she says.

His eyes seem a little swollen shut, but he's pink all over, with the faintest of lines for eyebrows and absolutely no hair on his head at all.

"He has all ten toes and all ten fingers," I whisper, committing the sight of my son to memory. I lean over and press a kiss to his forehead. Then I climb into bed with Ry and hold both of them, hoping I'll always be able to see the three of us like this.

————

THEY'VE JUST TAKEN the lunch trays when someone knocks softly on the door. Corduroy sleeps in his little plastic bin labeled with his name and his handprint and footprint. Ry and I were just talking about taking a nap.

"It's probably Tahlia," she says.

I take the few steps to the door and open it. It's not only Tahlia, but also Claudia and Lizzie.

"Is it a good time?" Tahlia whispers, her eyes already roaming the room behind me. "Em and Hillary are going to come after work, if that's okay."

"Yeah, it's fine," I say, stepping back to let them in. "He's just asleep right there."

"Oh, look at him," Lizzie says, and she beats the other two women to Corduroy. She picks him up and cradles him against her chest, pure wonder on her face.

"Ry, he's so beautiful," she says.

Ry smiles as Tahlia and Claudia crowd in around her. Claudia pulls a bag of almond M&M's out of her pocket and slides it under the blanket at Ry's hip. "Contraband snacks," she says. "It'll be good for milk production."

I've learned to stay out of the way when Ry is with her friends, but it's beautiful to me that they love her so much and yet were willing to let me have her.

"So tell us everything," Tahlia says as she sits in the chair closest to Ry's bed. "Elliott made it sound like the labor was pretty easy."

"It wasn't bad," Ry says. "The hardest part was getting him to wake up." She looks over at me and laughs. "I finally told Luna, 'Bark, Luna. Wake him up. Bark!' And she did."

As if on cue, Luna barks right then. While she's a beautiful golden lab, she does have a very deep, manly voice. It echoes through the room, and Corduroy fills the silence that follows with a scream.

Lizzie does her best to shush him, but after only a few seconds, she hands the baby to me. "Sorry, I don't know what to do."

I certainly don't either, but I hold my son tight and cradle him as I bounce and rock him. "It was just Luna," I tell him. "Look, it's just Luna."

I crouch down and let Luna come over and sniff the baby. He settles back to sleep in my arms, and when I rise, I find Ry and all her friends watching me.

"What?" I ask. "He didn't hurt him."

"Stand right there," Tahlia says. "I want to take your picture."

While I'm exhausted and only got four hours of sleep last night, I lift Corduroy up a little so she can see his face, and I smile for all I'm worth.

"Perfect," she says. "I think he has your nose, Ell."

"Let's just hope he doesn't have my sight," I say, and I pass the baby to Tahlia. She wipes her eyes and sniffles as she gazes down at him.

"Oh, he's just so perfect," she says. "I love him so much already."

I sit on the edge of the bed with Ry, and we watch as the other roommates of the Big House love our son.

When they've all held him, Claudia passes him back to Ryanne and says, "We should go. You guys need to rest."

"It's fine," I tell them, but I get up to walk them out, hugging Lizzie, then Claudia, and finally Tahlia. She holds me for an extra beat, and when she steps back, she slides her hands to my elbows and hangs on.

"Would you and Ry ever want to live in the Big House?" she asks.

I tilt my head, confusion running rampant through me. "What do you mean?"

She glances over at Ry, and I do too. Ry wears a look of open confusion. Tahlia glances over her shoulder and down the hall before coming back into the room and closing the door.

"It's just something I want you to start thinking about," she says. "This is what me and Cal do—we say these things we're thinking about so the other can think about it. And that's what I want you guys to do."

"I don't know what you're talking about," Ry says.

"Cal's a prince," Tahlia says. "He has castles in a foreign country in Europe. If I'm with him..." She lets the words hang there, and I connect all the dots.

"You won't be in the Big House," I say.

"But I don't want to get rid of it," she says. "And you've got your mom living with you, and now you have a baby... Your house isn't that big. I mean, I know it's great, but I just want you to think about maybe living in the Big House. It's a lot, I know. There are a lot of rooms, and it needs a lot of maintenance, and the yard is huge, and maybe you won't want to, and that's fine. It really is. I don't even want you to tell me now. But Cal and I are getting pretty serious, and I really, *really* like him, and I know that if he's my future, I'll have to leave the Big House for at least part of the year."

Ry nods, her expression solemn, but I offer Tahlia a smile.

"We'll think about it," I say. "And Tahlia, we're really happy that you and Cal are getting along so well. That's very exciting."

She grins and turns back to the door. "I think so too. Don't say anything to anyone else, okay? I wanted to offer it to you first, and again, I don't even know what will happen. I just wanted you to think about it."

She nods and smiles, waves both hands in a clearly nervous gesture, and then ducks out of the room. I close the door behind her and stay there while I look back at Ry. She stares at me with equal wonder in her expression.

Then Corduroy cries again, and Ry turns her attention to him. She tends to his every need with all the care and love of a good mother. When he's dry and fed and happy, I put him back in his little bin and climb back into bed with my beautiful wife.

"I love you, Ry," I say.

She turns into my side and wraps her arm around my waist and says the best words in the world: "I love you too, Elliott."

CHAPTER TWENTY-ONE

CAL

"There she is," I practically yell when Tally finally comes into the kitchen. You'd think she was the one with morning meetings that seem to go on and on and on.

"Oh, you're a morning person," she says, already reaching for the coffee pot. "That's a strike against you, you know." She gives me a glare out of the corner of her eye and turns to put sugar in her mug.

I chuckle and wait for her to turn back to the peninsula. "Shellvador is fed," I say when she does. "And look—I packed lunch."

She steps to my side and takes in the charcuterie boxes Helena told me to make for our day on the lake. "This is not my real life," Tally says.

I pick up the disposable container that came in a package of twenty, thank you very much. So I have sixteen more than I need sitting upstairs in my bedroom. "It's a charcuterie box." I pop the clear lid off the top and tilt it toward her. "See? Cheese, meat, crackers."

Tally peers into the box, and then tips her head back to

take a sip of coffee. "Fruit and veggies too. I don't even know what to think."

"I got the idea from my sister-in-law," I say. "So don't be impressed." I fit the lid back over the veggies and dip, the grapes and strawberries, and the hummus that comes in the neatest little cups. "I had no idea you could get things like this in single servings."

"Did you hunt all of this down at the grocery store?" she asks.

"Yes," I say in a quick breath of air. "I mean, Donald had to drive me there, but I pushed the cart around and everything." And I had to spend an extra twenty minutes signing people's receipts before I could escape the store with my storage containers and small cups of hummus.

"Do I have time to shower?"

"Honey, you won't want to shower before we go out on the lake." I grin at her and pick up the four charcuterie boxes I've made. "You shower *after*."

"I didn't know there were rules for canoeing."

"Well, there are. So no, don't shower right now. Get your beach bag and meet me outside." I tuck our lunches into the cooler I bought at the store too, pick it up, and head for the back door.

I'm almost all the way outside when she calls, "Just so you know, this bossy side of you is strike two."

"You didn't come out of your room until eight-thirty," I call back. I also know she has her beach bag packed already, complete with a waterproof card game, sunscreen, bug spray, two hats—because what if one gets blown away in the wind?—and two brightly colored towels.

I put the cooler in the back of the truck I've rented,

where I've got the oars, the life jackets, and my own beach backpack. Now, I just need to get the canoe.

Easy, I tell myself as I stride toward the garage with great confidence. Thankfully, Titan and Ajax wait for me there, and the three of us heft the watercraft easily. Fine, it's mostly the German Shepherds doing the heavy lifting.

Titan lifts it up and over the tailgate, and the bottom of the canoe scrapes in a loud, grating way.

"Hummingbirds," I say. "Be careful." The last thing I need is this thing sinking with Tally in it, not after I've assured her and reassured her that the canoe is water tight and lake-ready.

"Yes, Sire," Titan says, though it's certainly not his fault that we drug the canoe a little bit. Once it's in, I move around and start tying it down for the hour-long drive to Lake Moultrie.

Tally comes out in a pair of her skin-tight shorts and a tied tank top the color of eggshells. It has three unicorns prancing across the front of it, bright pink manes flowing behind them, and the words *Gallop Toward Magic* done in violet glitter.

I abandon the tie-downs and go to sweep her into my arms. "Look at you, my unicorn."

She's had her first cup of coffee, because she smiles now. "You rented a truck."

"Yes," I say. "I was hoping you'd drive it, but if you can't, it's fine. I've been watching videos online."

Tally scoffs and steps back. "Videos online? Cal, no." She giggles that little laugh that's burrowed its way down deep into my heart. "You can't learn to drive from videos."

"Tally, I know how to drive." I take her beach bag from

her and move to put it into the bed of the truck. "I've decided—I'm driving."

"Cal—"

"I got insurance, and I have a phone, and you know the German Shepherds are going to be minutes behind us." I grin at her. "Will you please let me do this? I don't want you to drive us to our lake date."

"Oh, it's a lake *date*?"

"Of course." I take her hand and round the front of the truck to open her door. "And I know we haven't been out since the press conference, buu-ut..." I let the words hang there and indicate she should get in the truck.

"But what?"

"Get in."

Tally gives me a glare, and then climbs into the truck. "This feels like blackmail."

I laugh, close the door, and go to get behind the wheel. Once I'm in the driver's seat, I push the button to start the truck. It roars to life with a satisfying sound, and I take a moment to adjust the seat, since Don went to pick up this rental for me, and he's shorter than me.

I move the steering wheel up, and fiddle with the air ducts.

"For the love of the Lowcountry," Tally finally says. "You're making me even more nervous with all this adjusting."

I put my hands on the wheel and grip it tightly. "Sorry. I really can do this."

She nods, and I appreciate the vote of confidence. "But what?"

"I had called Elevated, remember? And they didn't have any reservations until September."

"But once they found out you're a prince, they found a spot," she says.

"No," I say, finally moving the truck into reverse. "I had put my name on the cancellation list, and they called late last night and said something has opened up next week."

I successfully back the truck onto the quiet street behind the house and get it going in the right direction. "So it had nothing to do with me being a prince."

"Okay," Tally says, and then she starts fiddling with the radio.

I manage to get us to Lake Moultrie without incident, and then I encounter my next obstacle: getting the canoe out of the truck and into the water without help.

"Could you—do you think we can do this ourselves?" I ask.

Tally looks from me to the canoe, and then that maniacal smile I've seen a few times graces her face. "Let's at least try. I don't want to have to rely on the Shepherds for everything."

I don't want to rely on them for anything, but I can admit that I don't really know how normal people live. Surely others have gotten their own canoes in the water, right?

I pull the canoe out of the truck until only the pointed front end is clinging to the tailgate by a few inches. Tally lifts it and balances it on her shoulder, a soft grunt coming out of her mouth.

"Wow," I say, totally impressed. "I think we can do this."

I lift the boat onto my shoulder too, and I take slow steps down the sidewalk to the lake. We've both taken a couple of trips, and all of our stuff waits on the shore. Just when I think I've done the most amazing thing ever, my foot catches on something, and I go toppling forward.

My whole body tenses as I flop forward into the shallow water of Lake Moultrie. I yelp as the canoe lands on my back, as Tally cries out, as more splashing happens around me.

The bottom of the boat scrapes along my back, and "Condors and crows," comes out of my mouth. "That hurts."

As soon as I can, I roll over onto my back and stare up into the sky, contemplating all the things that have brought me to this point in my life. Beside me, Tally starts to laugh, and I turn my head to look at her.

But the canoe is in the way...and drifting out onto the lake. Even as I realize it, the watercraft moves enough for me to see Tally. She's also lying down in the lake, and when our eyes meet, we both start laughing again.

"The canoe," she says.

It takes every ounce of willpower I have to get off my back and go running through the shallow water to catch the canoe before we lose it. I drag it back up onto the sand and avoid the gazes of the other beachgoers who surely saw me take that header into the lake.

Tally joins me, and we load the canoe with our bags, the cooler, and the oars. I hand her a lifejacket, and she puts it on without complaint. I do the same, and then I hold the canoe and say, "All right, sweetheart. Get in."

"I'm still a little unsure about this." She fiddles with the knot on her tied tank top while she studies the canoe.

"It's floating just fine," I say.

"It's not that."

I suddenly realize what the issue is, and I move to stand beside her. "Hey, if you don't want to go…"

"I do want to go." She takes a deep breath and reaches out to touch the canoe. "It's just—I haven't done this for a long time, and it brings back a lot of memories."

"Good memories, right?"

"Yeah." She exhales and laces her fingers through mine. "And you know what? I let go of those things in the garage, and you've remade this canoe into something new." She smiles up to me, and all I see is a brave, brave woman. "So we need to make new memories in it, right?"

I nod, not quite sure what to say. So I simply move to the back of the canoe and hold it while Tally gets in. She takes the seat in the front, and a burst of pride moves through me.

I made this canoe what it is, and I push it out onto the water, and when it feels buoyant, I push off one last time and hop, hop, hop, step into the boat. Hey, at least I don't fall face-first into the water again.

Tally's already picked up an oar, and I reach for mine too. "What should I do?" she asks. "This rocks so much."

"You just stroke whenever and however you want," I tell her, switching my oar to the other side. "I'll balance us from back here."

To do that, I have to watch Tally's every move, and shift to my right when she starts to move her oar over to the left. I watch the muscles in her back as they tense and loosen, and marvel at the way she swings her head to the right when a bird calls.

"Did you hear that?" she asks.

"Yes," I say with a chuckle. "I think it was a Blue Jay."

"How could you possibly know that?"

"I've spent a lot of time on water," I say. "Birdwatching was one of my classes, believe it or not."

"Oh, I believe it."

She slathers on sunscreen, we eat our charcuterie boxes, and I take a dip in the lake. Tally declines, saying the lake doesn't look as clean as she'd like, and I give her a pass.

The sun is setting when the truck tires finally crunch over the gravel behind the Big House. "Let's just leave everything until morning," I say.

Tally leans back against the headrest and smiles at me. "That was a great day."

"Was it?"

"Yes," she says in a crisp Notavellan accent.

I grin at her. "You sound so much like me."

"You realize you never say anything but *yes*, right?"

"It's a curse," I say. "I'll work on it." After all, Just-Cal doesn't have to be so proper all the time.

My phone rings, and *Bohemian Rhapsody* blares through the cab of the truck. "It's my mother," I say, suddenly tired.

"I'll let you talk to her." Tally gets out of the truck just as the town car pulls into the gravel drive too.

I swipe on the call as the German Shepherds and Don

spill from the car. I barely look at them, because I'd rather watch Tally walk into the Big House. "Hello, Mother," I say.

"Oh, thank the stars, you picked up."

I frown and blink just as Don pulls open my door. "You only called once, didn't you?"

"No, three times," she says. "Don says you were driving and maybe didn't have service."

I meet his eyes and see astronomical concern. My pulse spikes through my body. "What's going on?"

"Your father is in hospital," Mother says. "I know you're on sabbatical, and the things happening there are very important to you, but—"

I don't make her request that I return to Notavella. I cut her off with, "I'll be there as soon as I can." Then I get out of the truck and head inside the Big House with my detail hot on my heels. After all, we have some major travel arrangements to make—and I need to talk to Tally too.

CHAPTER TWENTY-TWO

TAHLIA

I stay in my bedroom for as long as I can, putting off the inevitable. Just like I told all my friends last night, it's not Cal's fault that his father isn't doing well.

And who should I blame that I have to be back to school in two weeks?

Or that I've had the best summer ever?

Or that Cal's offered to send a private jet for me anytime I want to come to Notavella?

"He also made it very clear," I tell myself as I look in the mirror. "That he's coming back."

Yes, Donald and the German Shepherds are going with him, and the Big House will be empty for an undetermined amount of time, but he's *coming back.*

I turn away from my reflection because I told myself that exact same thing eighteen years ago.

I leave my bedroom and cross through the foyer into the living room, where I encounter Titan wrestling with an oversized suitcase.

"Wow, you're taking a lot," I say, the sight of that suitcase making my chest pinch. "Surely you have black suits in Notavella."

He smiles at me and abandons his quest to get the suitcase through the narrow doorway and into the kitchen. He comes over to me and wraps me up in the best German Shepherd hug of my life.

My emotions waver, no matter how much I tell myself that this isn't goodbye for good, it's just goodbye for now. He doesn't even say anything, but I can feel that he'll miss me and my constant teasing about his clothes.

"I heard there will be cinnamon rolls this morning," he says.

And in that moment, I can smell them. "Yes," I say, and I bustle past him and into the kitchen, only to find Cal pulling out the tray of cinnamon rolls that I put in the oven forty minutes ago.

I still at the sight of him in his Notavellan black suit, with his hair combed just-so and his movements so precise and easy. He looks toward the door where I'm standing and freezes when he sees me.

He wears only somberness in his expression this morning, and then he turns back to the stovetop and starts to stir the frosting. My legs feel like water-filled logs as I cross the kitchen to him.

"I can do it," I say.

"So can I." He won't look at me, and it feels like he's robbed me of one last dive into his beautiful eyes.

He smears the frosting all over the warm cinnamon rolls, where it starts to melt, and I watch it go down into every crack and crevice.

"I wish I could stay to take these to Mister Beasley with you," he says.

"Oh, I'm not going this morning."

That gets him to look at me, and I put on the bravest smile I can muster. "These are all for you. You guys have a long journey ahead of you, and I figured since I can't go, this would be a way for you to introduce me to your parents."

Cal abandons the rubber spatula and pulls me into his chest.

"I miss you already," he says. "Are you sure you can't come? You don't even need a bag."

I wrap my arms around him as tight as they will go, so that he knows I don't want him to leave and I would come with him if I could.

I step back and wipe my eyes, and then shake my head.

"I can't go," I say. "I have to have my classroom ready in two weeks and school starts in three."

"Yes," he murmurs, his voice filled with resignation.

"And Claudia says it's not smart to travel on my passport when it's so close to expiring." I manage to lift my eyes to meet his, and oh, there are those beautiful blue depths that I love so much. I reach out and cradle his face in my palm. He presses into my touch, his eyes drifting closed, and I wonder if that's what love looks like.

Tenderness fills the moment, and it stretches on, as Cal's detail is exceptionally good at not interrupting us.

"Tomorrow I'm going to go renew my passport," I say. "So I'll be able to come to Notavella next time."

"Next time," he whispers, his eyes fluttering open as he leans down to kiss me. I meet him halfway, and though we're standing in my kitchen on a slow Sunday morning and there's nothing special about it, this kiss feels like it defines my life.

"I just want you to think about something." He rests his forehead against mine, and I keep my eyes closed, because Cal is always making me think about something.

"I've never been in love before," he says. "And I'm not entirely sure if that's what I feel now, but I want to say it, and I want you to just think about it."

"Okay," I whisper.

I've never had a man tell me he loves me, and my heart-beat thunders through my chest, rolling on and on the way summer storms do through the South Carolina sky.

"I love you, Tahlia Tomlinson," he says, his voice filled with emotion and kindness. "And I'm going to miss you so much." He touches his mouth to mine again in a beauti-fully sweet kiss, then he straightens and looks toward the back door.

"I'm coming," he says, and I wonder how long Don has been standing there.

"I'll get the cinnamon rolls for you," I say. "You go see what they need."

Cal moves away from me, his fingers lingering on my arm until the very last moment.

I clear my throat and pull out a plastic container that fits twelve cinnamon rolls perfectly. Using two spatulas, I transfer them from the sheet pan to the container and press the light pink lid on top.

When I turn toward the back door to follow everyone outside, I find Ajax sitting at the peninsula and holding out a piece of lettuce for Shellvador. The sight of the tall, muscular security guard doing something so mundane and simple brings tears to my eyes and a laugh out of my mouth.

"What are you doing?"

"What?" Ajax asks. "I'm going to miss this tortoise."

I move over to him and extend the container of cinnamon rolls. "I think you're going to miss me. Admit it." I grin at him while he stares first at the cinnamon rolls and then at me.

"I am gonna miss this house." As he gets to his feet, he takes the cinnamon rolls from me and reaches out to pat Shellvador one more time. "And this turtle, and how happy Cal is." His eyes finally come to mine, and in a miraculous move, he smiles, ducks his chin, and shakes his head.

"But out of all of them, Tally, I'm going to miss you the most."

Tears slither out of the corner of my right eye, and I throw myself into his arms. "Please take good care of yourself," I say. "And Cal and Titan and Don—you guys hurry up and come back, okay?"

"Yes, ma'am." His beefy hand presses on my back like a ten-pound weight. He releases me, and I step back and nod.

I'm so wrung out from all the goodbyes, but I still haven't seen Don yet. I go out onto the back porch with Ajax behind me and continue down the steps and to the town car. Titan's already behind the wheel, and Ajax goes to his place on the passenger side.

Don turns toward me, and his face lights up with a handsome smile. "We'll keep you updated," he says. "And we expect to be back within a week."

I know he can't guarantee that, but it's nice to hear. I grin at him, hug him tightly, and say, "I will miss you. Thank you for all you've done to bring Cal back to the States."

"Oh, it was all him, ma'am," he says. "I just hope we can survive his surly mood until we return." He chuckles and gets in the car, leaving me to face Cal one more time.

"I'm going to be nice to them," he says.

"See that you do," I say. "I'll send you pictures of my classroom and my passport application." I grin at him and giggle. "Because that's as exciting as my life gets."

"It's the exact excitement that I want," he says, and he takes both of my hands in his and leans down and kisses me. "I'll talk to you soon, okay?"

"Yes," I say, mimicking him and making him smile.

He turns to get in the car, but I clutch his hand tighter. He looks back at me, and I say, "I want you to think about what you would do and feel if I said I love you right now."

My composure crumbles and my chin shakes, and I return to spelling complex words to try to gain control of my emotions. *Mississippi. Lieutenant.*

"I'm not going to say it, because like you, I'm not one hundred percent sure yet."

He smiles in a very princely way and says, "I really like that word—*yet*—and I promise I'm not going to let you down this time. I *will* come back."

I nod and release his hand. "Go on then, and tell your mother and father hello from me." I nod, and he nods, and then he gets in the car and slams the door behind him. It echoes through my chest, and I back up to where the gravel kisses the lawn. I wave as Titan backs them onto the road, and then...they drive away.

I stand there for several more seconds, wondering what I'm supposed to do with myself now that the Big House is truly empty, and Cal has taken my heart with him to Notavella.

CHAPTER TWENTY-THREE

CAL

"This way, Your Majesty."

I follow my father's detail from the narrow hallway and onto an elevator. Donald is still at my side, but Ajax and Titan have been put on vacation. I only have one security detail here in Notavella—Carlo. He gets on the elevator with me, Donald, and Griffin.

All I can think about is Tally—how she would tease us for all wearing the exact same clothes. How her hand would feel anchored in mine after this long day of travel, the most stressful twenty-four hours of my life.

I know my father will not be around forever. He's always been in good health, and the news of him becoming short of breath on his usual walk around the estate makes no sense to me.

The elevator takes us to the fourth floor of the hospital. I hang back so the others can lead the way, and I nod politely to everyone who looks our way. We finally arrive in my father's room in the corner, which has two black-suited men standing outside. Donald and Carlo enter first, and I note two more men already inside.

When I see my mother, I realize why there are so many security guards. Having the king and queen together in a public space is usually avoided at all costs. Mother sits at my father's side, one of his hands clasped in both of hers.

"Cal's here." She jumps to her feet and bustles over to me.

"Hey, Mom." I wrap her up tightly, feeling her shoulders shake for only a moment. She's tough, my mother, but it's nice to be reminded that she's also human. She wipes at her eyes quickly and kisses both of my cheeks. I do the same to her, and then she links her arm through mine, so we can face Dad together.

"He's doing a little bit better today," she says.

"What have they found?" I ask, because my father's been in the hospital for twenty-four hours, and surely they've run a few tests and gotten the results back by now.

"His blood sugar is far too high," she says. "He's been diagnosed with type two diabetes. That is not pairing well with his scleroderma. They're starting him on a medication to try to get the blood sugar down."

My father smiles at me and says, "It's just a little fibrosis in my lungs."

"Sure, a little fibrosis," I repeat, the words dripping with sarcasm. I move over to him and lean down and hug him tightly. "How do they treat fibrosis, Dad?"

"There are a few pills I can take to slow the progression," he says. "That's what they want to start with. It will open up the blood vessels in the lungs and should help with some of the lightheadedness and shortness of breath I've been experiencing."

Mother retakes her chair, leaving me to loom above them both.

"How long have you been feeling like that?" I ask.

"Not long," he says.

"A year," Mother barks over the top of him. "We've known he's had some trouble for a little while."

"Why didn't you tell me?" I ask, frustration moving through me.

"There was nothing to tell at the time," Mother says. "We didn't want to worry you."

I sigh as I sit on the edge of Dad's bed. "What am I good for if not to worry over you? John and Helena worry about the whole country. It's okay if I worry about you."

Dad gives me a bright smile, but Mother only shakes her head.

"They're sending me home with oxygen too," he says. "I'm to use that if I ever feel like I'm not getting enough air."

"The lower elevation helps too," Mother says. "Once he's released from here, we're going to go to the Amalfi Coast."

I adore the Amalfi Coast with everything inside me. This is a trip I would normally take with my parents, and my mind flies to Tally in South Carolina. If I could somehow get her to come too...

I twist and extend my arm behind me, and Don moves forward without an explicit instruction. "Tally sent some cinnamon rolls," I say. "She says it's the best way to introduce you to her."

I smile as I take the container from Don and turn back toward my parents. "Through her baking; she really is an extraordinary cook."

Mother's face lights up as I pop the top on the container of baked goods. "Your father cannot have that," she says, though she eagerly reaches for one.

"I'll have to have Tally make you her collard greens," I tell Dad. "Though I think there's a bit of sugar in those too."

He chuckles. "I'm sure there is. They've got to put *something* in those to make them taste good."

"I think it's the bacon," I say, and we chuckle together. I realize that I've *missed* my parents, despite the things about them—and the situations in my life—that frustrate and irritate me.

"You couldn't get her to come?" Mother asks. Then she takes the most dainty bite of cinnamon roll I've ever seen a human take.

"No," I say. "Her contract at the junior high starts in only two weeks, with school beginning a week after that."

"I see," Dad says.

"I'm hoping to be back before then," I say, glancing between them. "But I'm willing to stay as long as you need me."

Mother swallows and looks from Dad to me. "I think you should do a few things while you're here."

"Like what?" I ask, my bones already feeling like they've been filled with cement.

"There's a new school opening, and it would be wonderful if you did the ribbon cutting," she says. "And your father usually welcomes all the university students back to classes. But I think you should do that this year."

My mind races with the timeline. "When would those be happening?"

"University doesn't start for another month," she says.

"Mom, I'm not staying here for a month." I speak quietly, yet with that princely power Tally says I have. Instead of getting angry and arguing over things across my father's sickbed, I take a breath. "We can discuss it later. Perhaps I can go back and forth."

Because I want to give my mother what she desires, so that she'll continue to let me have a long leash. Hopefully one long enough to reach across the ocean to Tally.

As my mother finishes her cinnamon roll, I say, "I'm surprised you're here. It's the middle of the night."

"It's the best time to visit," she says. "There are fewer people here, and it's far easier to get around." She glances over at the multiple security guards crowded near the door. "I should probably get going. I'll leave you to sit with your dad."

Her personal assistant steps forward, a woman named Willow. "Yes, ma'am. We can leave at any time."

"What time is it?" I ask.

"Almost four a.m., sir," she says.

I take my phone from my pocket. "Do you guys want me to video call Tally?"

Mother gasps and claps her hands together. "Yes, call her right now."

"What time is it in the States?" Dad asks.

"It's about seven," I say. "And she'll be home."

It's been seventeen hours since I left Tally. But for her, I've only been gone for ten.

I tap in my passcode and then over to the video call app she uses with her friends. "She helped me get this set up," I say, frowning at my phone. Then I see she's my only contact. All I have to do is drop my thumb on her beautiful face and the phone starts to ring.

My pulse bounces through my body, pinging from one side to the other, then Tally says, "Hey there, my prince," in her beautiful, flirty voice.

"You're on a group call," I say, my smile instant and filling my whole face. "With my mother and father in the hospital, at least eight security detail members, and Donald —we're all here together."

I lift the phone and point it over my shoulder. "Say hi to Don."

Tally waves, and Donald waves back, though none of the other security guards do. "Wait—where's Titan and Ajax?" she asks.

"They're on vacation while I'm here," I say. "I have someone new."

"Mm, I don't like *that*," Tally says.

I hold her in front of me and grin at her. "It's *so* good to see you."

"Yes—and we're on a group call," she reminds me.

I chuckle and get up, moving to go behind my father's bed. I position myself between him and Mother, lean forward, and hold the phone out. "Can you see us?"

"Yes," she says. "Hello, everyone."

"Mom, Dad, this is Tahlia Tomlinson—the woman I've told you about."

"It's so wonderful to meet you," Mother says, and I don't doubt her for a moment. She speaks with a genuine quality, and she seems to glow, even though I can only see her in a tiny square at the bottom of my phone.

"You too," Tally says. "Cal has told me so much about you. How are you feeling, Your Majesty?"

"I'm doing a lot better," Dad says. "I promise we won't keep Cal from you for very long."

Dad has always been my advocate, and if he can get me out of Notavella soon, he will.

"I just ate one of your cinnamon rolls," Mother says. "It was the most delicious thing I've ever had."

Tally giggles. Everything about her is so bright and wonderful. "I'm glad," she says. "Though I think you're lucky to get one, because Ajax and Titan can eat a dozen of those by themselves."

"I don't doubt it," Mother says. "Those men.

"I've really enjoyed having them in the Big House. They've been nothing but helpful," Tally says. "Fixing a cabinet door here and there, making sure my screen door hangs straight, cleaning out my garage."

Mother looks at me, her eyes wide, probably because she doesn't belive me, Don, Titan, and Ajax capable of such domestic, household things.

I simply chuckle. "I haven't had time to show them the pictures of canoeing yet," I say. "Dad will love them. I get my love of the water from him."

Dad nods. "I can't wait to get back out on the lake."

"I hope it will happen for you soon," Tally says. "Once I get my passport renewed, I might be able to come visit your beautiful country."

"We would love that so much," Mother says.

While there's a lot more I would like to say to Tally, I don't want to do it in front of ten people—especially my mother and father. I haven't been able to stop thinking about how I would feel and what I would do if Tally ever told me she loves me.

I did say it to her because I felt it—and now, even here, I swear a keen sense of love moves through me, simply from the way she's so easy to talk to, so bright, and so good.

"I'll let you go," she says. "It's got to be, what, five o'clock in the morning there?"

"It's only four," I say.

"Cal, you've got to get to bed," she says.

"Yes," I say. "I'll be heading back to my house after this."

"I'm going to go right now," Mother says. She gets to her feet and sweeps a kiss across my cheek. "So lovely to meet you, Tally."

"You too," she says.

I straighten and back myself into the corner so Mother can say goodbye to Dad. "I'll let you go," I say. "I'll call you later, okay?"

"Yes," she says. "Call me later."

I nod, say, "All right," and end the call.

Mother leaves, and most of the security goes with her. Only Griffin, Don, and Carlo remain, with two positioned outside for my father. Don catches my eye, and I go to see what he needs.

"We're going to leave a couple of people outside the door," he says. "But we'll go down to the cafeteria and get breakfast. Is that okay?"

"Yes," I say. "Will you bring me something?"

"I know what to get you, Your Majesty." He gives me a smile and a nod, then turns and leads the way out, leaving me in the hospital room with my father alone.

I turn back to him and take the chair Mother has been in. I sigh and lean my head back, closing my eyes. "I'm tired," I say.

"It is a long trip," Dad says. "You don't need to stay here, son."

"I know," I say. "But I'll let them go take a break and get breakfast. Then I'll go home."

Dad reaches over and pats my leg. "I know you cannot stay for a month or more," he says. "But having you here is amazing. I really appreciate you coming."

I curl my fingers around his. "Of course I would come, Dad."

He smiles at me. "You're in love with Tahlia."

Hearing him say it so concretely, without a hint of questioning in his tone, sends it streaming through me too. "Yes, I am." I smile just thinking about her. "What's crazy? I think she loves me too." I smile, unable to shake it from my face. "I just need more time with her, Dad."

"I know," he says. "Indulge your mother in a few things. The school ribbon-cutting ceremony is on Wednesday. That's only a few days."

I nod. "I can come back and do the university welcome."

"Perhaps," Dad says. "Now that I have a diagnosis, I should be able to get the medication I need."

I press my lips together, because I don't know what else to say.

"No matter what," Dad says. "We're going to get you back to her."

"Thank you," I say. The conversation ends, and Dad closes his eyes too. I let mine drift shut again. As I do, the sweetest dreams of being reunited with Tally stream through my mind. I know I'll get there, and now I can only hope I can convince my mother to let me go sooner rather than later.

CHAPTER TWENTY-FOUR

TAHLIA

Another Sunday finds me lying in bed with my tablet propped up on a pillow in front of me. I don't even know what I'm watching anymore, since this has been my reality for the past several hours.

I did get up and make cinnamon rolls today. I took them to Mister Beasley and visited with him for a while, but I've been in bed ever since. Though I have plans to bake sourdough tomorrow for all of my friends, my principal, and everyone in the art department, a sigh fills my chest. I reach for another handful of popcorn just as my doorbell rings.

My phone buzzes with a notification from the security system camera on that door. I swipe down from the top of my device and tap on it. After all, I'm not getting out of bed for just anyone.

It's Hillary. She's bent close to the camera, a huge smile on her face. She pulls back a little bit and waves, then holds up a huge drink cup from the gas station.

I throw my blanket off my legs and heave myself out of bed. She's retreated to the edge of the steps by the time I open the door, but she spins back to me.

"Hey, we got you a drink," she says. "Because I know Cal's gone, and you're in your end-of-summer slump."

I can't deny that both of those things are true. Cal being in Notavella for a week without a return date has only collided with the anxiety and depression I always feel over starting a new school year. I love teaching. I do. But sometimes I wonder how I'm going to fit it into my summer life.

"It's Doctor Pepper with cherry slush," she says, handing me the drink.

"It's happiness in a cup," I tell her, and then take a long pull on the straw.

"I know we'll see you tomorrow," she says. "When you bring the bread around. But Liam was finishing up one of his projects and he needed a drink."

I smile. "I really appreciate it. If he's still working in the shed—"

"No, he finished," she says with a wink. "In fact, he wants you to come see it."

"Me?" I ask.

"Yeah."

I figure I can either go hang out with my friends or go back to bed. I take another sip of my drink, really enjoying the slushiness of it and the carbonation as it burns my throat. "All right," I say. "Let's go."

We start across the lawn, but Hillary turns at the corner of the Big House as if she's going to go behind it.

"Where are you going?" I ask.

"It's in your garage," she says.

"Liam's project is in my garage?"

"Yes. Now tell me about Cal. When is he coming back?"

"I don't know," I say. "He did a ribbon-cutting ceremony on Wednesday. I believe his dad has a doctor's appointment on Monday—so tomorrow, which is really today for them. I think he was waiting to see the results of that before deciding. They discharged him really fast, so hopefully he's doing a lot better. Cal says he is."

Hillary leads me around to the front of the garage, where she quickly dances away from me and over to Liam's side. Together, the two of them gesture toward the garage and say, "Surprise!"

I look in that direction and freeze completely at the sight of my old bright blue bicycle. It's not old anymore but gleams with glossy paint the color of the brightest, most beautiful summer-sky day. It has new tires with white rims and a rack to put something on behind the seat. A brand-new white basket adorns the front handlebars, along with tassels made of white, blue, and yellow streamers.

The seat is a beautiful beige leather—a wide saddle that will be far more comfortable than a normal bicycle seat.

I suck in a breath. "Holy fried dill pickles." I can't look away from the bike as I take a careful step toward it. "Is this real or a mirage?"

Liam laughs. "It's real."

"How did you—?" I reach out and touch the leather, and it somehow makes my voice go mute.

Liam has found some cheap birthday flags to hang

from one side of the garage to the bicycle's handlebars and then to the other side, as if this is a showpiece. To me, it is. In every way, it is.

I turn back to them. "I can't believe this," I say. With everything they've had going on, Liam fixed up my bike?

"How did you even do this? How much did it cost? I'll pay you back."

Hillary looks at Liam, and then together they both look over at me. I can't tell what they're thinking by their expressions, but they seem a little bit surprised.

"Honey, you don't have to pay us back," she says. "Cal asked Liam to do it."

"Cal?" His name falls out of my mouth, and nothing makes sense.

"Yeah," Liam says. "He paid for everything. I told him I didn't know how fast I'd be able to do it, but everything came together really quick, actually, and I love working on bikes."

"Plus, he's waiting for that new contract to come through," Hillary says. "So he had lots of time this week."

"Yep." Liam joins me at the bike. "You want me to walk you through it?"

I nod, and so much promise and freedom moves through me as he takes me through how he got as many original items as he could.

"Claudia says the paint is Neon Sign Blue," Liam says. "It seemed close enough, so I ran with it."

"I love it." My emotions spiral up and up until I'm crying. "I can't believe—how did this...?"

"Honey, he loves you," Hillary says. "I have a feeling

that man will do anything for you." She links her arm through mine and beams at the bright blue bicycle.

I look at the bike and then over to her and Liam, noticing the concern in their expressions. "I need to go to Notavella," I say.

The words sound crazy inside my own head, and every practical, responsible cell in my body vetoes the idea.

"I have to go," I say again. "I have to see him. I have to tell him thank you, right to his face."

"You have to tell him you love him," Hillary says.

"Yes," I say. "I have to tell him that. I can't believe I didn't go with him last week." I grab on to both of them in a group hug. "Thank you so much. Really. Not just for the bike either—but for being..."

I trail off, because I don't know what to say. "...for being the most amazing friends ever."

Hillary grabs me in another hug. "You go. We'll take care of everything here at the Big House."

I feel a bump between us, and I back up, a gasp flying from my mouth. "Hillary—are you pregnant?"

Her face fills with joy and light and she nods. "Yes, and I'm planning a party to tell everyone." She shoots a look over to Liam. "So don't say anything."

"I'm *so* good at secrets," I promise. "But I'm gonna go pack a bag and buy an airplane ticket."

Liam cheers and applauds. "You go get him, Tahlia!"

I take a couple of steps around the garage and then turn right around and go back. "Wait. What about my passport? Claudia says it's not very wise to travel within thirty days of it expiring."

"When does it expire?" Hillary asks.

"August twentieth," I say. "I've already applied for a new one. I did expedite it, and it should be here in the next couple of weeks."

I pace in front of the garage, throwing the blue bicycle a death glare. "What should I do? Can I really go?" Before either of them can answer, I pause and take a deep breath.

"I'm going to go," I say. "I'm sick of living my life in the wings and waiting for something to happen to me." I look at them, my eyes wide, drinking in more than they have before. "I have to take this chance. It's time for me to take a risk."

I think of my classroom, and my students, and the sourdough bread I was going to bake tomorrow. Questions fill my mind and peck at me from inside my skull.

Can I really quit my job two weeks before school starts?

How will I pay my bills?

Do I even have enough money for a ticket to Notavella?

How will I even find Cal? They won't just let me into the castle...will they?

"Tahlia." Hillary takes me by the shoulders, and I blink my way back to her. "You need to go," she says. "I can see you're getting deep inside your mind, and you need to *stop*. Go pack a bag. We'll drive you to the airport."

"Yeah, we will," Liam says. "I'll put the bike in here and lock up." He starts to do that while I employ every ounce of bravery I have.

I head for the master suite and pull out a piece of luggage I haven't used in far too long. I barely know what I'm doing as I throw some clothes and pajamas, socks, shoes, and underwear into the bag. I zip it closed, grab my phone charger, and leave my tablet right where it is, still playing on the pillow in my bedroom.

I'm not going to be here to watch it, because I'm going to find Cal and tell him I love him.

CHAPTER TWENTY-FIVE

CAL

"I NEED TO GO."

"That's hardly a greeting for your mother." The queen sits at her writing desk, either reviewing something or writing something, I'm not sure which. My patience is at an all-time low, as I've been back in Notavella now for eleven days with no end in sight. The moment I agree to another duty, a new one crops up.

My mother is a master at waiting until only a day or two before an event to say, *If you could just...*

"I have to go back to Cider Cove," I tell her. "I'm having Donald prepare the jet."

Mother looks up, her eyes widening. *"You're* having *Donald* prepare the jet?"

"Yes." I clasp my hands in front of me and stand at attention. "And I've asked the foreign relations chairman to do this weekend's fundraiser."

Mother slaps her pen on the table. "Callan, you have no authority to do that."

"Actually, I do," I say. "I used to make all kinds of

special assignments for events—anything that the Special Envoy to the Crown could not attend, and I cannot attend this weekend."

Mother gets to her feet and crosses over to me, her gown swishing around her legs. I remain stoic, though I swear everything inside of me is a crumbling mess.

"Talk to me, Cal," she says.

"What do you want me to say?" I ask. "That I don't like who I am without her? That I don't like being someone who doesn't see her every day? That I don't like thinking of her alone in Cider Cove, wondering if I'm going to return?"

I finally move my eyes to hers and hook into them as sharply as I know how. "I've played this game before, Mother, and I let you win. I can't do it again."

"Are you in love with her?" she asks.

"Yes," I say, thinking of how Tally would tease me for how formal I am, my accent on such a simple word. "I'm in love with her, Mother. I don't want to be the Special Envoy to the Crown. Or rather—I don't *only* want to be the Special Envoy. I want to be *Cal* too, and I want to be Tally's."

I take a shuddering breath and use it to steel my nerves. "I'm leaving as soon as the jet is ready. I'm going to beg her to forgive me for being gone for so long, and I'm not coming back here without her."

"Come sit down," she says.

"Mom," I say in an overly tired voice. "You won't be able to convince me not to go."

"I'm not going to convince you not to go," she says. "The plane isn't ready yet. You can come sit with me for a minute." She moves over to the set of sofas in her suite, and I go with her.

"I'm sure you have a plan for the future," she says. "You're far too smart not to."

"Yes," I say.

"It's something you've been thinking about and talking through?" she asks.

"Yes, Mother. Tally and I have been talking about a lot of things." I fold my hands in my lap and look at them. "She doesn't want to give up the Big House, and I can't ask her to do that anyway. I've been roughing out a timeline of when we'll be here in Notavella. I'm thinking probably September or October through March, because of our Founder's Celebration, then we'll return to the country home."

I smile at my own cleverness. "I'm actually calling it another-country-home—just like you and Dad go to your second estate for a few months each year. Tally and I will do the same. The trip will simply be much longer."

When Mother says nothing, I look at her and oddly find approval in her smile. "That is not a bad plan, son."

"No?" I ask.

"You've been able to keep up with all of your duties while you've been in the States. Maybe I've been testing you a little too harshly."

I cock my head. "You've been testing me?"

"I wanted to make sure your feelings for Tally were not just a whim. Not just something from when you were seventeen years old. Not just a fantasy you conjured up in your own mind."

She puts her hand on my arm. "You do tend to be a dreamer, Cal. Admit it."

"I can admit it," I say. "But it's okay to have dreams beyond the life you've been given."

I lean forward and press my cheek against hers. "You know how grateful I am for the life you've given me, Mother, right? I've tried very hard not to be ungrateful about it."

"I know," she says. "There's just another path to happiness for you. While I had hoped you would meet a fine Notavellan girl and fall in love, I see now that is not going to be the case."

I shake my head sadly. "I've tried to be the son you wanted me to be."

"Oh, Cal," she says. "You don't have to be anyone but who you are."

I nod. "Thank you, Mother."

That's the freedom Tally gives me too, and it's glorious.

"I have to be more than the Special Envoy. You understand that, don't you?"

"Yes," she says softly. "I'm starting to understand it."

My phone buzzes. We both look at it to see the jet is ready. I get to my feet and pull my mother to hers too, so that I can hug her goodbye.

"Tally has been working on getting her passport renewed," I say. "I've committed to opening the duck hunt in September. I'm hopeful that I'll be able to bring her with me, so you can meet her then."

"That would be wonderful," Mother says. She grips me tight, and then I leave her suite in favor of the jet.

Donald meets me downstairs with our luggage, where we load into a vehicle to head to the airport.

"You managed to convince her," he says.

"I tried to leave as little room for negotiation as possible," I say.

"I'm glad, sir." Donald looks out the window and lets a few moments go by. "Titan and Ajax have been called up, and they'll meet us at the airport."

"I do hope they've enjoyed their vacation," I say sincerely.

"I'm sure they have," Donald says.

"What about you?" I ask him. "You didn't get a vacation."

He smiles over at me. "Number one—I love the work. Number two—being in South Carolina was my vacation. I've really only worked for the past eleven days."

He chuckles, and I join him. "Life is slower there, isn't it?"

"It sure is," he says.

"I miss it so much," I say. "I don't mean to sound so miserable, but I am. Nothing is the same without her."

"We're returning now," Donald assures me. "Have you let her know?"

I shake my head. "Not yet. I'm planning to call her when we touch down in Columbia, because it's after eleven and she'll be in bed already."

Donald hums, and we finish the ride to the airport in companionable silence. The airport in Notavella is not nearly as large as some of the international behemoths, but I still have the privacy and security fit for the royal family.

Finally, I climb the steps to the plane. When I enter, I

see the German Shepherds, and I start to laugh. I rush them, grabbing them both in a one-armed hug.

Titan grunts as Ajax scowls and says, "Sir—what—are —you—doing?"

"It's so good to see you guys," I say. "Are you excited to be going back to the States?"

"I don't know, sir," Titan says. "It's starting to cool off here. I looked at the weather in Cider Cove, and it's actually worse than July."

I chuckle. "Well, it's a good thing we don't go for the weather then, isn't it?"

"Yes, sir," Ajax says.

We settle into our seats. The flight attendants bring snacks and drinks, but still we don't take off. I finally look over to Don. "Can you find out what we're waiting for?"

"Yes, sir." He gets up and goes toward the cockpit. He speaks with the flight attendant for a moment. She knocks on the door and speaks with the captain.

Apprehension builds in my stomach as I watch. I force myself to look out the window just to double-check that there's no unsavory weather keeping us grounded. The flight attendant speaks to Don, who returns to me.

"Because of the weather in London, there were several arrivals that came in at unassigned times. We're waiting for the skies to clear and a runway to become available. He thinks another twenty minutes."

"Fine," I say, trying not to be grumpy about it. Twenty minutes isn't going to make a difference one way or the other. We're on the plane, and I'm still leaving the country.

I can't help checking my phone and mentally calculating what time it is in Cider Cove. I watch as the minutes tick closer and closer to midnight. Tally will definitely be asleep now, and I definitely can't tell her I'm on the way.

I'll land eight hours from now, which will be five o'clock p.m. here in Notavella—but just about the time Tally should be waking up in Cider Cove.

Only two more weekends until school starts, I tell myself. I pray with everything I have that Tally and I will be able to spend them in the canoe, or in each other's arms, or doing anything at all—as long as we're together.

Twenty minutes tick by and still the jet does not move. My phone rings and *Bohemian Rhapsody* fills the jet.

"She's probably wondering why I haven't taken off yet," I mutter. I swipe to answer the call. "Hello, Mom. We're waiting on some delayed planes, apparently."

"Okay, so you haven't taken off yet?" she asks.

"No," I say. "Unfortunately."

"I need you back at the palace immediately."

"Mother," I say, "I am *not* coming back."

She giggles—a sound that alone clues me in that something major is happening, for my mother, the queen, does *not* giggle.

"You'll want to come back," she says. "As fast as possible."

"Why is that?" I ask, my chest squeezing tightly. Then I tell myself that Mother wouldn't giggle if something had happened to Dad.

"Because you have a visitor," she says. "Go ahead and say hello, dear."

"Hey, Cal."

I swear I'm hallucinating, because that sounds like Tally's voice...on my mother's phone.

"So, Liam brought the bike over," she says. "And I love it so much, and I couldn't stand not being with you. I'm standing in the foyer of the most amazing house in the world, but you're not here."

I jump to my feet and frantically look around. I snap my fingers at the German Shepherds and Don. "We're on the way."

"Okay," Tally says. "That's great, because your mom says I get to eat breakfast with her. Isn't that great?"

I laugh at the shrill anxiety in Tally's voice, though my heart withers that I'm not there to introduce her properly and be the buffer between her and my parents.

I leave the jet without waiting for the German Shepherds to clear the area. Then I'm jogging down the steps and toward the tunnel that will get me back to the car. "We'll be there in twenty minutes. Don't worry, Tally—my mother already loves you, so just try to enjoy breakfast."

CHAPTER TWENTY-SIX

TAHLIA

"Mᴏʀᴇ ᴛᴇᴀ, ᴅᴇᴀʀ?" ᴛʜᴇ ǫᴜᴇᴇɴ ᴀsᴋs.

I don't tell her that I've only taken two sips, because hot tea isn't really my thing. "Oh, no, thank you," I say, reaching for my cup. I take another tiny micro sip and immediately want to spit out the medicinal pomegranate tea the moment it touches my tongue.

"This is lovely china," I say. "Should I assume it's a family heirloom?"

I look over to the king, who has also joined us. The queen introduced him as Charles, and he called her Sophia, though neither of them have used their names again. In my sleep-deprived state, I can't remember if Cal had ever told me their names or not.

Once again, I throw a look toward the entrance to the dining hall. We've been sitting for at least a half an hour, but it feels like thirty years, and Cal is still not here.

I've eaten two soft-boiled eggs and a whole wheat English muffin, along with a bowl of fruit, and now, a set of kitchen workers brings out trays of pastries.

"I know you're an excellent baker," the queen says. "So these probably won't be up to your standards, but they are quite delicious."

She gets served first, and she uses her hand to pluck an immaculately browned croissant from the tray. "These are almond," she says. "We grow almonds here in Notavella. Did Cal tell you that?"

"Yes," I say. "And olives, I've heard."

"Yes, our olive crop is quite amazing," the queen says, her bright blue eyes beaming with pride.

I keep my smile painted on my face because I don't quite know what else to do. I sent Cal a few texts from London, ruining the surprise of me showing up at the castle gates, but he hadn't responded. By the way he acted on the phone, I don't think he got those texts. Not only that, but he was on the jet, leaving to go to the U.S. Why would he be doing that if he knew I was coming?

Hardly anything makes sense, and my inner well of resiliency feels empty. I need to sleep, and I need to get everything I want to say out of my mouth. Then, everything between Cal and I will be out in the open, and I can start to make sense of it.

I managed to book an overnight flight from Columbia, to New York, to London. I'd arrived there on Tuesday around noon. My next flight was supposed to leave that evening, but apparently, it's a very stormy time in the U.K., and it had rained and rained and rained.

I was stranded in the London airport for twenty-four hours. The airline finally did get us a hotel around midnight, and I have learned there's a reason my luggage doesn't get used very often: because I don't enjoy traveling.

We finally took off from Heathrow for the three-hour flight to Notavella, only to be rerouted to Rome, as this airport was too busy for us to land. We stayed on—the—airplane for *three hours* before we took off again, with a new arrival time here in Chyme.

I finally landed around seven fifty-five this morning. And since it feels like I've spent centuries trying to get from the Big House to this Even Bigger House, I forgot that I was going to change my clothes and freshen up in the bathroom before I headed straight to the palace.

I sit at a table that could probably host twenty, wearing a pair of midnight blue leggings covered in stars and galaxies, along with a cream-colored sleeveless blouse bearing brightly colored cartoon dinosaurs.

Rawr.

Even now, the queen eyes it like these prehistoric creatures might come to life and attack her.

I'm considering taking another sip of tea when a commotion outside the doorway draws my attention. Don enters, and his eyes meet mine, which causes pure relief to saturate my every pore.

It's all I can do to get to my feet as he steps aside, and Cal enters. He's wearing his crisp black suit, of course—his travel outfit. He pauses for only a moment before flying around the table toward me.

"Pheasants and loons," he says. "You *are* here."

I rush toward the end of the table where he sweeps me into his arms and lifts me right off my feet. I laugh as I anchor my hands to his shoulders and hold on tight. My smile has never felt so genuine as when he sets me down and cradles my face in his hands. His fingers run through my hair and down over my shoulder, as if checking to make sure I'm real.

"You were at the airport?" I ask.

"Yes," he says. "We were in final preparations to leave for Columbia." He scans me down to my shoes and back. "What are you doing here?"

"Liam brought the bike over," I say. "And Cal—it's the nicest thing anyone has ever done for me."

He frowns. "He didn't tell me he was finished with it."

"He is, though, and it's *beautiful*. And I couldn't stand being half a world away from you. Not for another minute."

I grip the lapels of his coat and pull him closer. "I don't ever want you to go to Notavella without me again. It's been torture for the past week at the Big House without you."

"It's been no picnic for me here either," he whispers. "Did you get your passport?"

"No," I say. "There's so much to tell you."

Like how I quit my job in an email when I landed in London...

"It was really hard to get here. I swear, I've been in a time warp between London and here and Rome for two days."

"What?" he asks. "Rome?"

"I can tell you all about it later." I take a breath and pray the breakfast I just consumed won't make a reappearance. "I left on Sunday night."

"But you just got here today?" he asks.

"Yes," I say. "It's worth it, because you're here, and now I'm here with you. Even if I can't stay very long—

because I'll probably get thrown in jail when I get back for traveling without a passport—I had to come."

I swallow and shore up my nerve. "Because I love you, Cal. I don't want you to just *think* about it. I'm saying it, and it's true. I love you." I smile at him. "But I'm never flying commercial to Notavella again."

He tips his head back and laughs. The joyful, beautiful sound of it is the one thing I've been missing in my life for thirty-five long years. He holds me close as he gazes at me with love streaming from those gorgeous oceanic eyes that drown me with a single look.

"I love you too, Tally."

I experience a completeness I never have before. Then he kisses me, and I truly know what it means to be happy, healthy, and utterly whole—as a person, and as one half of a beautiful partnership.

———

"THAT'S IT," Cal says, his hand firm and warm in mine.

I yawn, though I try to hold it back. "It's beautiful," I say, as he's now shown me most of the house—palace— where he grew up.

"Let's get you somewhere you can rest," he says.

My hand tightens in his. "I don't want you to leave me."

He presses a kiss to my temple. "I won't, sweetheart. But I'll take you home, because you need to sleep." He chuckles and shakes his head. "I can't believe you were in London for over twenty-four hours."

I've shown him the texts; he showed me his phone, where he did not receive them—just as I suspected.

It's Thursday in Notavella, and Cal has already arranged for us to go to Century City tomorrow to tour the shops he's told me about. After that…I don't know. I need to talk to him about quitting my job and what I'm going to do to make ends meet for the next several months.

Did I act a little bit prematurely in turning in my two weeks' notice?

Probably, but Cal is right—I'm exhausted. I can't make my weary mind whirl through anything more today. I barely have the wherewithal to keep walking and talking.

I let Cal take care of me and get me across a vast expanse of well-maintained grounds to his house, which is about four times larger than the Big House.

"I'll give you a tour when you wake up." He leads me to a beautiful, bright, airy room on the second floor with the comfiest-looking bed right in the middle of it.

Don puts my tiny suitcase just inside the door and nods to me. "If you need anything at all," he says. "You simply pick up the phone. Someone will be there."

"Okay," I say.

Cal and Don retreat out of the room and close the door behind them. I kick off my shoes and collapse into bed, almost asleep before my head hits the pillow.

———

WHEN I WAKE, I recognize that I'm not alone in the room. Someone else breathes with me, and the familiar scent of sandalwood, fresh water, and pine tells me it's Cal.

I can suddenly feel him behind me—the weight of his arm across my waist, the way his fingers fit precisely between mine. I stay still, because I don't want to wake him, or move at all from this perfect embrace.

I enjoy the warmth of his body, and the way I'm not worried about anything when it comes to him. I tighten my fingers against his, and he stirs.

I turn over and snuggle into his chest and feel him start to wake up more and more.

"Sorry," he murmurs. "Did I wake you up?"

"No," I whisper back.

"Are you feeling better?" He traces small circles on my upper shoulder, which sends a stream of shivers through me.

"Yeah," I say.

"We can go home on Saturday."

I push away from him and tilt my head back to look at him. "We don't have to do that."

His eyes open, and he searches my face. "No? I thought you'd want to get back for school."

"I quit my job," I blurt out. "I don't have to get back for school."

Cal's eyes widen. "You quit...okay."

"We can't stay long, though," I say. "What with my passport issue. But we don't have to rush back or anything."

"My mother will be thrilled." He smiles softly at me and touches his lips to mine. "I feel like we have a lot to talk about."

"Yeah." I sigh and tuck myself back into his chest and close my eyes. "But do we have to do it right now?"

"I suppose not."

"I just want to listen to your heart beat," I whisper. "And breathe in the scent of your skin, and just be yours."

A soft chuckle rumbles through his chest. "Who says all the perfect things now?"

CHAPTER TWENTY-SEVEN

CLAUDIA

I toe open the front door of the Big House, admiring my cute new sneakers as I do. I push it the rest of the way open with the tray of ingredients I'm carrying for our Girls Night. "I hope Tahlia makes it through customs," I say at the familiar sight of the foyer.

I loved living here with my best friends, and a touch of sadness moves through me that those days are over.

"She'll be fine," Hillary says as she enters the house behind me and closes the door. "She's with Cal, and he's a prince. They probably have their own lanes or whatever."

"We'll see," I say. "It makes me nervous." I weave through the living room and enter the kitchen, then let out a yelp and come to a complete standstill in the doorway.

"What is that?" I ask, staring at the turtle in the middle of the floor. "When did Tahlia get a tortoise?"

"Don't stop here," Hillay gripes. "I'm right behind you." And she's carrying two trays of white-chocolate popcorn.

I skirt to the left, giving the grumpy reptile a wide berth. "I didn't know Tahlia had pets."

"It's not hers," Hillay says. "She brought him home for the summer; he belongs to one of her teacher friends."

"Oh, that makes much more sense." I slide my tray of tomatoes, avocadoes, onions, and taco seasoning onto the peninsula, and Hillary does the same a moment later.

"Whew." She wipes her auburn hair back off her forehead, and I grin at her.

"It's a good thing we're telling everyone tonight," I say. "Because you're totally showing."

She glances down at her belly, where she does have the tiniest bump pressing her T-shirt out slightly. "Give yourself another few weeks," she says. "I swear my body changes every single day."

She moves over to the fridge, where she pulls out the proteins she put there yesterday. She puts the three rotisserie chickens on the counter and gets out a bowl.

I put a pan on the stove and collect the five pounds of ground beef I'm going to brown and add seasoning to. We work in easy silence, both of us turning when Elliott says, "Hey, you two."

I abandon the beef immediately, because if Ell's here, that means Ryanne is too—and Corduroy. "Where's that baby?" I ask as I approach him.

He grins and indicates the living room. "Ry just wanted to come early to feed him, so he'll be good tonight."

I find her already sitting on the couch, breastfeeding her son. "Sorry," she says. "I can come help when I'm done with him, and Ell's going to go next door while we do our first female-only hour."

"It's fine," Hillary says. "But yes, Liam says he's going to help harvest the peaches."

Ry smiles. "Yep, that's what I heard too."

Since the baby is unavailable, I return to the kitchen to keep prepping our taco bar for tonight's festivities. Hillary and I requested a Girls-Only hour, with food and the pink sparkly mic, so we can make our own pregnancy announcements and get caught up with everyone.

Since I live the furthest out, I do often miss things—like harvesting peaches and about the summer babysitting job of a classroom tortoise.

I chop tomatoes, add the seasoning to my beef, and mash up avocadoes for guacamole. I've just set that to chill in the fridge to marry the lemon juice, salt, and onions when the back door opens and in walks Lizzie and Emma, already engaged in a conversation.

They bring ranch dressing, sour cream, and salsa with them—and a whole new level of energy—and put those on the taco bar where Hillary has also laid out a bag of tortillas and two of chips.

I grin at both of them, and once again leave my cooking duties to go give them each a hug. "Hey, you." I grab onto Emma and hold her tight. "How's the flower business?"

"Good," she says, her voice a bit breathless. "It's been so busy this summer."

"Lots of weddings," Hillary says, and I nod. Em does usually have a very busy summer season, and I once again feel like I've missed out by living a half-hour away and having my own very busy full-time job.

I toss a look to Hillary, as if she'll be able to advise me about what to do, but of course, she won't. Instead, I move over to Lizzie and give her a hug too. "What's new with you?"

"I have a big announcement for later," she says with a smile.

"Good," Hillary says. "That's why we're here." She's put all the now-shredded chicken in a pan on the stove, and she sprinkles taco seasoning over it, adds water, and stirs it together.

I add a lid just as a tall, broad-shouldered man enters the kitchen. He glances left and right, over to the doorway leading into the living room and toward the half-bath in the corner. Then he gestures for others to follow him, and two more men in identical black suits do just that.

Then Tally enters, and she takes a few steps into the kitchen and throws up one arm. "I made it back!"

Pure love for her fills me from top to bottom, and I press against the urge to weep. *Stupid hormones*, I think as the four of us break into applause for her return to the U.S. She wears exactly what I expect from Tahlia—a pair of black bicycle shorts and a pale blue tee...but this one has a hideous navy raven on the front.

"What's with the shirt?" I ask.

She glances down at it as Cal joins her, sliding his hand along her waist and completing her picture of happily-ever-after. "This is the Notavellan raven," she says. "He's on Cal's family crest and everywhere over there."

So I'll let it pass, and I go to hug her hello the way everyone else has. "Mm, it's so good to see you," I say. "Thanks for letting us use the Big House for our party."

"Of course," she says, and I swear she has a bit of an accent though she's only been in Notavella for a week.

I step back and look at the women in the room, noting that Cal and his entourage are very good at disappearing when they know they should.

"How was the flight?" Hillary asks.

"Tell me it was better than the trip there," Lizzie says.

"Yeah," I say. "How was flying on a private jet?" I grin at her, because she sent us the most beautiful pictures, and I've never seen an aircraft like what she flew on.

"How was meeting the King and Queen?" Emma asks, and my heart warms that we're all just throwing questions at Tahlia like this is normal behavior.

For us, it is.

"I missed the welcome back party," Ryanne says, and I turn toward her.

"Give me that baby," Tahlia says, and she steals Corduroy right from under my nose. "And you didn't miss anything. They've just been firing questions at me without waiting for me to answer." She beams at all of us, and she just seems so stinking happy.

Of course, that makes me happy too. A wash of pure love moves through me, and I say, "Okay, group hug, and then we're ready to eat."

I lift my arms and put them around Hillary's shoulders on my right and Emma on my left. Everyone else does the same, except for Tahlia, who can only use one arm as she holds Cord in the other, and we create a circle with the six of us connected together.

"I love you guys," I say, my emotions suddenly swelling all over again. "I'm so glad you're back, Tahlia, and that we get to be here in the Big House for taco night and a pink-mic night."

"Me too," Hillary says, and the others echo it.

Tahlia looks around at all of us and starts to giggle. That gets us all going, and we press in closer and closer, making the circle tighter and tighter, until I feel like my shoulders are going to get winched off.

"You guys are my favorite people," Lizzie says, and that only makes me remember everything we've been through together. Good times, bad, with terrible texts, and bad bets, and merry messes.

I sniffle and say, "Okay, I'm going to hurt myself." I drop my arms and step back while it seems all eyes have come to me.

"Are you okay?" Ryanne asks. "What's going on?" She's always been the bluntest of us, bless her heart.

"I'm fine." I turn away from them and quickly dab at my eyes with a kitchen towel so my black makeup doesn't run too much.

"Let's eat," Hillary says, and that diverts the attention away from me, thankfully.

People fill their plates with tacos or make a taco salad with chips, and when Tahlia sees the trays of white chocolate popcorn, she squeals.

"I'm so happy there's dessert tonight," she says before leading us into the living room to eat. Tahlia tells us about her trip to Notavella, about meeting the King and Queen, about Cal's personal palace.

I simply listen, because there will be plenty of time for me to talk later. Eventually, everyone turns their attention to Tahlia for a different reason, and she gets to her feet. She gave Cord to Emma several minutes ago, and now, she reaches behind the record player and lifts up our old pink mic.

"This thing could use some repairs," she says, flicking a piece of loose tape on the bottom of the coned paper towel. When she looks up, she wears too much sadness in her expression. "I'll start."

She takes a deep breath. "I have to move everything out of my classroom tomorrow, and I could use the help of anyone who's willing to come."

"Don't you have four strong men upstairs who can help you?" Hillary teases.

"Yes, I do," Tahlia says. "But I have a lot of art supplies, and the new teacher has been great about setting them aside, but I've got to get them out of her way. School starts on Monday."

A hint of surprise courses through me now, the same way it did when I'd heard Tahlia had quit her teaching job. I have no idea what she's going to do now.

"Becks and I can come," I say, since we both work Monday through Friday, nine-to-five, jobs.

"I can too," Hillary says. "But I think Liam is mowing all day."

"I'm sure he is," Tahlia says.

"I wish I could," Emma says. "But I have a huge order due tomorrow night for a party on Sunday." She looks at Lizzie. "And Lizzie was going to come help."

"It's okay," Tahlia says. "I'll have lots of help." She looks down at the mic. "I'm not sure what else to say, so I think I'll turn the mic over to someone else." She extends it out and sweeps it from left to right in front of us. "Who wants it?"

Hillary and I want to go last, so I stay right where I am, silent.

"For the love of Boise," Lizzie says, and she pushes herself to the edge of the couch and gets up. "I'll go."

She takes the mic from Tahlia, who takes her seat. "I don't have a ton of news. Matt and I are still settling into being married, and the Chem Cats still like me more than him." She grins, and I do too. "But...I just signed a contract for a huge modeling gig—an entire spring catalog with Allison Layne."

I gasp, my eyes going wide. "Shut the front door." I turn toward Hillary. "Half of my closet is Allison Layne." I face Lizzie again. "Tell me you get to keep the clothes."

She grins at me. "They're the largest plus-size clothing company in North America," she says. "For those of you who aren't Claudia." She grins at me. "It's a huge contract —they're paying me a lot, and yes, I negotiated a very steep discount on the clothes."

I clap my hands and bounce in my seat. "That's great, Lizzie."

"Where are you shooting?" Hillary asks.

"New York City," she says, and her demeanor falls. "That's the thing. I have to live up there for two and a half months, so...I'm going to need a babysitter for my dad and Matt."

Tahlia giggles. "What? Matt's a grown man. He doesn't need a babysitter."

Lizzie looks at Ryanne, and oh, something is up there. "He's no good alone, that man." She sighs like she's been cursed with a fun-loving, outgoing husband. "And anyway, I think we have a solution."

She holds out the mic to Ry, but she shakes her head. "No, I'm going last."

"I wanted to go last," Hillary says.

"Oh, you guys." Emma gets to her feet and takes the mic. "I've had a pretty stressful summer. In addition to all the floral needs, one of Aaron's customers sued him and the store, and he's been working on the case from dawn until dusk."

My heart drops to my feet. "What?" I ask.

"I didn't know that," Hillary says.

"I've seen him on his phone a lot," Tahlia says. "But I didn't know it was that serious."

"It's frivolous," Emma says with a wave of her hand. "But you have to fight it, or you get found at fault." She takes a breath. "Anyway, they just agreed to drop the claim, so that's good. I guess they're going to sign an agreement next week."

She exhales. "But we've also decided to have Thomas move in with us. He's been dating Courtney for a long time now, but he needs to live on his own—sort of—and we get along well with him."

"Wow," I say.

"So he's going to move in next weekend, I think." She nods to Ry. "Thanks for your help on getting that contract ready, Ry. It worked great."

"I'm glad," she says, and I suppose she does have some experience with living with family members, since she and Elliott live with his mother.

Emma lowers the mic, and she looks at me, Hillary, and then Ryanne.

"You're dead-set on going last?" I ask her.

"Yes," Ryanne says as she folds her arms.

"Fine." I get to my feet and take the mic from Emma. She returns to the couch, where Lizzie is now holding baby Cord.

Hillary joins me, and I hold the mic in front of us as if we're going to truly sing a duet. Our eyes meet, and we take a breath together. Then we grin and say, "There are going to be more babies in the Big House!"

Hillary leans forward even more. "I'm due on January fifth, and Claude..."

"...is due on January twenty-seventh!" I don't think I've ever smiled so wide.

Tahlia shrieks and jumps to her feet. "I knew it! I knew you guys were pregnant."

"Yeah, because I told you before you went to Notavella," Hillary says.

"Wait, you told her?" I ask.

"She felt my baby bump." Hillary puts her hands on her belly and flattens the fabric against her very noticeable bump.

"Congratulations!" Ryanne joins us on her feet and starts handing out hugs.

"How exciting," Lizzie says, and she passes me Cord. "I'm so happy for you."

"I can't wait to meet them," Emma says, and we once again find ourselves in a big group hug. I love these women for who they are, the support they've given me, the love, the acceptance, the advice.

Most of it happened right here in this room too, and I love the Big House and my time here.

"Okay," Ryanne says. "I'll go." She takes the mic and

waits for the rest of us to find our seats again. I pat Cord's bottom and gaze at the perfect baby as he snoozes in my arms.

"I don't want there to be any hurt feelings, so I'm going to tell you what we've had going on, and if there are any objections, you can voice them here."

I lift my head. Objections?

She glances over to Tahlia, who gives her a single encouraging nod. "Well, Tahlia and Cal are probably going to get married soon—"

"He hasn't proposed," Tahlia says, shaking her head. "And he's a prince. We might—*might*—get engaged soon, but a wedding? It'll be next spring or summer."

"Okay," Ryanne says. "Either way, she's not going to be living in Cider Cove full time anymore."

"What?" Hillary asks. "You're not?"

Acceptance streams through me, because how can she? Cal is a prince of a foreign country. Of course Tahlia can't live in the Big House permanently.

"But I don't want to sell the Big House."

"We're taking care of it," Hillary says.

"But you won't have to for much longer," Ryanne says. "Because Tahlia has offered it to me and Elliott and Joan. Our house is quite small, and we need Elliott's mother with us."

Mm, yes, they do.

"So Tahlia asked us if we'd live here. We'll take care of the house. We'll have more room for our family, and it'll still be available for Tahila and Cal when they are in town."

She nods over to Tahlia, who joins her in front of us.

"They'll pay my HELOC payment as their rent, and I'll be in charge of maintenance and repairs, as I'll technically be their landlord."

I have no idea how she's going to do that without a job, and then I remind myself that this is not my problem to solve. I can simply support Tahlia—and Ryanne and Elliott—by agreeing with them.

"I'm going to be gone for most of September and all of October. There's a duck hunt that Cal is going to open in Notavella, and we'll be there through some meetings he has in October. But don't worry." She holds up both hands as if trying to hold back the tide of questions she expects.

"We're going to be here through the holidays, and the New Year, and for the birth of all the babies." She grins at Hillary and then me. "But we have to be in Notavella by the end of February, and Cal's in charge of their Founder's Celebration this year, which is in March."

"They think they'll be here for a few months each year," Ryanne says. "Mostly summer months, right Tahlia?"

"Yes," she says, and oh, she so has a Cal-accent. It actually makes me smile in the best way possible.

"So we'll take the master suite on this level," Ryanne says. "Cord's not old enough for his own room yet anyway. And Joan will be on the second level."

"When we're here," Tally says. "We'll be upstairs on the third floor, using both of those bedrooms, and we'll put the German Shepherds in one bedroom on the second floor, and Donald in the other."

"Don't forget about Matt," Lizzie says.

"Oh, right." Ryanne extends the mic to her, but Lizzie

shakes her head. "Matt's going to stay here with the Chem Cats while Lizzie is in New York City," Ryanne says. "Which should work, because Tahlia and Cal will be gone most of that time."

"Or he'll be at my dad's," Lizzie says. "But we think it's a good time to sell the townhouse, so he's going to list it and we'll find somewhere else to live when I get back from the shoot."

"Wow, this is a lot of changes," I say, looking over to Tahlia. "And you said you didn't have much news."

"When are you guys moving in here?" Hillary asks Ryanne.

"Probably at the end of the month," she says. "Elliott is going to list our house this week." She hands the mic to Tahlia, who puts it back behind the record player.

I sit there, trying to absorb all the news, my appreciation for these women only growing stronger when I realize how much we all watch out for each other.

"Are you getting married in Notavella?" Hillary asks, and all eyes fly to Tahlia again.

"Yes," she says. "But don't worry. There are enough seats on the private jet for all of you."

CHAPTER TWENTY-EIGHT

TAHLIA

"The first thing I'm going to do when we get to the Big House is ride that bike." I smile over to Cal as he pulls his seat belt across his body.

I can admit watching him work as the Special Envoy to the Crown in his own country possesses a certain charm. And while I'd scoffed at him opening the Duck Hunt, it was a huge event where people showed up in droves to express their love for Cal. He said they just wanted to catch a glimpse of me, and maybe that was true. I don't know. No matter what—I was excited.

Halloween is almost here, and I expect the Big House to be decked out with spider webs, skeletons, and other spooky things, because Ry loves Halloween, and she and Elliott have been living in the Big House now for a little over a month.

"Are you excited to be coming back?" Donald asks from the other side of the limousine.

Yes, that's right, we've upgraded from the black town car so we don't have to all squish into the back seat.

I've learned that Titan and Ajax are only Cal's detail when he travels. At home, his main security is a man named Carlo. When he's out in public, he gets two more people assigned to him, usually a woman named Rain and a man named Foxtrot. I finally asked what was with all the strange names, and I've learned that they really are code names.

Cal says he told me that, but I don't remember. It makes so much more sense, but I'll forever have a fondness for the German Shepherds, who ride in the front of the limo, which apparently Titan knows how to drive.

"Yes," I say. "And I'm going to show you all an amazing holiday here in South Carolina."

We'll be at our another-country-home until the end of January, and once Claude has her baby, we'll return to Notavella so that Cal can attend all of these government meetings that happen in February and March, and I can experience Founders Day in Notavella for the first time. The Queen has put Cal in charge of a lot this year, as his father continues to adjust to new medications and treatments.

The King is doing well, and Cal's brother handles a lot as the future king. But I've noticed that Cal is more personable than John, and the people of Notavella seem quite smitten with him—far more than they do his older brother.

Anticipation builds inside of me as we approach the Big House on Cherry Lane, and when I see the welcome home banner and streamers dripping from every eave of the Big House, tears fill my eyes.

"Wow," I say. "Look what they've done."

Cal looks up from his phone and smiles at the house. "I

do love this place," he says. "There's something so calming about it."

Titan pulls into the gravel parking area at the back of the house and has to pull the nose of the limousine all the way up to the lawn before he puts the car in park.

My friends spill onto the back porch, with Ryanne holding Corduroy, taking the lead. Elliott follows her, along with Liam and Matt, who's living here in the Big House, while Lizzie is in New York. She won't be able to be here, but I'm not surprised to see Emma holding up her phone, so Lizzie's probably on a video call.

I try to open the door and find it locked, and Titan says, "Sorry, ma'am," and the distinct sound of the lock disengaging clicks through the car.

I jump out then and move swiftly to the front of the limo. "What are you guys doing?" I ask.

Hillary starts to clap—and wow, her baby belly has grown so much in the seven weeks that I've been in Notavella. Claudia stands next to her, and she looks bigger though she's due three weeks later.

I grin at Liam and Beckett and Aaron—these good men who love my friends so much. But I wait for Cal to come to my side, because he always, *always* does the same for me. He never leaves me alone in a crowd, and I'm not going to do that to him.

I take his hand and beam at him. He's wearing a real Cal Irwin smile, not a fake prince smile, and it makes my heart happy.

I wait for Titan and Don and Ajax to join me, and then the five of us start toward the Big House together.

"I thought you'd never get here," Hillary says as she wraps me in a hug at the top of the steps.

Cal starts shaking hands and saying hello, as do the German Shepherds and Don.

"We've been watching you for an hour and a half," Hillary says. "It seems like you got really stuck on the freeway coming out of Columbia."

"Yes," I say. "There was an accident."

"Well, you made it," Claudia says. "We have dinner going, but it won't be ready for a little bit."

I nod, and finish going around, greeting everyone.

"I know what you really want," Liam says, and he gestures for me to go with him. "Come see your bike."

"Have you been keeping her exercised?" I ask as I go with him.

The front of the garage is shady at this time of day, thanks to the big trees on the west side of my yard, and when we make it over there, I see that someone has set up a table, where my decorative drink containers brim with sweet tea and lemonade.

Tears press into my eyes. "Buttered biscuits, you guys. You have no idea how much I've missed sweet tea," I say.

"I think we have some idea," Hillary says dryly. "You text us about it every other day."

I can't deny that, so I simply laugh and move over to get a cup of my favorite drink. There are bowls of white chocolate popcorn, cheddar cheese popcorn, and caramel popcorn, and I laugh, even though the sweetness of this gesture makes me want to cry.

Liam has the garage open, and not only is my bike standing there proud and ready, but so are a couple of scooters and skateboards. The garage is completely cleaned out, and the street before us is ready to be ridden.

So after I throw back a handful of popcorn, I mount my bike and drive it onto the street. Matt joins me on a scooter, and it's Beckett, of course, who takes a skateboard.

We fly down the street together, the October air full of freedom and my sight filled with glorious oranges and reds, as the leaves have changed colors here in South Carolina. I marvel at it, because in Notavella the leaves are already gone and the trees sway with bare branches in the near winter wind.

We ride all the way around to Liam's and back, where I find Hillary and Claudia have set up their rocking chairs on the grass in front of the cement pad of the garage. Ry has joined them, and Emma holds baby Cord, who now sports the chubbiest, pinkest cheeks I've ever seen.

The German Shepherds and Don are nowhere to be found, but Cal rotates around in a circle on one of the scooters. He looks so casual and so free, and I can't help smiling at him with everything I have.

"I should probably take my stuff inside," I say.

"You don't need to do that," Cal says. "Don took it in already."

I glare at him. "I thought we agreed that Don was not going to be my servant while we're in my own home."

Cal gives me a withering look. "You think I could have stopped Don from taking your bag inside?"

"I have a lot of stuff," I say. "All the treats for every-one." I smile around at the ladies in the chairs. "I brought you guys the *best* Swiss chocolate in the world."

"Oh, I can't wait to try that," Ry says.

Being in Europe has been a totally different experience than living in South Carolina, because I can get on a train and be in another country in only an hour. And if I keep going, I can pass through *several* countries. I've now visited Italy, Switzerland, Hungary, and the very eastern tip of France.

I still don't like traveling much, but when it's not a days-long journey, it's a lot more fun.

"I'll go get them," I say, and I get off the bike completely and kick down the stand so that it will stay up.

"I'll get it," Cal says, and he jumps off the scooter while it's still rolling.

"Cal," I call after him as he runs off, but he just raises his hand and keeps going. "Something's going on with him," I say.

"Come sit down," Claudia says. "We haven't seen you in so long."

"You're the ones with all the news," I say as I move to sit in a chair someone has left open beside Ryanne. "Where did Elliott go?"

"He had to run over to the store," Ryanne says. "He's technically at work right now."

I sit down and Emma gets up and slides Cord into my arms. The three-month-old looks at me like I'm an alien and I might attack him at any moment, but I sweep a kiss across his cheek and bounce him, and that seems to satisfy him.

He's probably used to being passed around, and a flash of FOMO moves through me so strongly I almost gasp. I'm missing so much by not being here—from watching Hillary and Claudia go through their pregnancies, to Cord growing up, to Lizzie building an amazing career for herself, to Emma's flower shop taking off.

"So what are you having?" I ask, trying to push past the debilitating feelings that really make no sense.

Claudia nods to Hillary, who says, "Liam and I are going to have a little girl."

"Oh, that's so exciting," I say, and I reach across Ryanne and squeeze her hand.

"We're having a boy," Becks calls from the skateboard. "And I keep trying to get Claudia to let me pick the name."

"That is so not happening," she says.

"If you do it, he'll end up with a paint color."

"At least I'll give him something good. Everything he likes sounds like a dog," Claudia says.

"Hey, Jackson is a good human name," Beckett says, and I love their playful banter back and forth.

Cal returns with my bag of sweets from Switzerland, and I get up and start passing them out one-handed while he holds the bag for me.

"This is the milk chocolate," I say as I hand Ry my favorite chocolate bar. "And did you know they have milk-flavored M&M's in Switzerland?"

I pull out the milky white bag as Ry gasps. "Oh, my word," she says. "I did not know that. Look at these." She takes the bag from me, her eyes wide. "I thought I knew about every kind of M&M. What does a *milk* M&M taste like?"

"Open the bag and find out," I tell her. I've had them, and they're the smoothest chocolate I've ever put in my mouth. "I'll go get a garbage bag," I say.

"I got it," Cal says. He once again rushes off while I am left staring behind him.

Before I can say anything, Liam appears in front of me. "We canned a whole bunch of peaches for you," he says. "Let's ride over to the house and get them. You want to?"

It was such an odd request that I'm left looking at him and looking back to the corner of the garage where Beckett has now positioned himself. I'm familiar enough with security guards to recognize that he's acting as one, and I cock my hip and put my hand on it.

"What's going on?"

"What do you mean?" Claudia asks. She lifts up her chocolate bar. "This is the best thing I've ever put in my mouth."

I grin at her, though I know there's still something happening in the Big House. Otherwise, why won't Cal let me go inside?

Beckett jumps back on the skateboard and wheels on over. "Claude, do I need to go check on dinner?"

Claudia looks up at him, and her eyes go wide. "Oh, yes," she says. "I'll come with you."

I want to say that I'll come too, just to see what they'll all do, but at the same time, I have a suspicion that they've prepared a surprise for me inside, and everyone knows about it except me.

I look at Liam. "Do you really want to ride over and load me up with peaches before dinner?"

He looks at Matt, who nods like he's giving Liam permission, and I have no idea what's going on.

"Yeah," he says. "Let's go."

"I'll come too," Matt says. "I can fit some bottles in my basket."

We ride around the block again, and as I approach the Big House from the front, I look for anything I can to indicate that something is amiss, but nothing shows from the windows or door. So I continue on, and I let Liam load up my bike basket with as many jars of peaches as it will hold.

He puts peach jam in his basket and Matt's, despite my protests that there's no way I can eat that much. I'll make cobbler out of the preserves, and sometimes I like to eat them just straight out of the jar when they're nice and cold.

"Thank you so much, Liam," I say. "You've always taken such good care of me, and I really appreciate it."

"Of course. You've been the best neighbor I've ever had, Tahlia."

I ride back to the Big House, the wind in my hair and the scent of freedom in my nose, pure joy trailing behind me as the sun sets.

When we get back, the other girls are gone from their chairs but Beckett is still outside.

"Can we go in now?" I ask him, and it takes him a moment to realize what I'm really saying. "Yeah," he says. "I think dinner's finally ready."

I grin at him. "Good, because I'm starving."

I stay with Matt as he puts away my bike, and then, with my arms full of my peach preserves, I walk in with him, Liam, and Beckett.

"It smells good," I say about the pot-roasty smell wafting from the house, and as I go up the front steps, I get the scent of freshly baked bread too.

"What did you guys make?" I ask.

"I think it's a sandwich bar," Matt says. "Pulled pork, shredded beef, that kind of thing."

"Sounds good," I say, and they fall back and let me open the door and go in first.

I'm still wearing my traveling suit, which is made of a pair of dark blue pants and a bright purple shirt, so I don't need to kick off my shoes to go inside.

I can hear people talking, and then someone shushes them. I step into the kitchen and slide my jars onto the back counter. I'm expecting the house to be different, because it's not mine and I no longer live here, but not completely transformed the way it is.

Ryanne is much simpler than I am, and I honestly expected functionality mixed with baby toys. Instead, I'm assaulted by red roses everywhere. Vases and vases of them fill the peninsula, along with baskets of petunias hanging from the pot rack and the windowsill.

Everywhere I look I'm assaulted with flowers. Emma nudges one vase a few inches, and Aaron sets down a final offering of gorgeous, deep red roses.

I watch as Cal emerges from the middle of all of them. He's wearing his shiny black suit, of course. His hair perfect, as usual. And he wears the most perfectly-Cal smile in the world.

He gets down on both knees and holds up a black velvet ring case, which makes every cell in my body vibrate.

Finally.

"Tally," he says. "I have loved you since I was sixteen years old. No amount of time nor distance has dulled how I feel. I love the way you make me laugh. I love the way you think. I love the way you challenge me to be a better man. I love the way you love me, and my country, and my people, and the German Shepherds, and Don, and all of your friends.

"I simply love everything about you, and you would make me the luckiest and happiest man in the world if you would be my wife."

Sniffles move through the room, and while I have learned how to control a lot of my emotions in the past couple of months while being in the public spotlight in Notavella, my friends' tears spur my own.

"You're already my queen, but will you be my princess?"

"Yes," I say, using his formal speech and his Notavellan accent. "Yes, of course."

Applause fills the Big House as I take a few steps to be closer to Cal so he can put the ring onto my finger. He gets back to his feet and pulls me close just as I hear his mother say, "That was wonderful, dear. Welcome to the family, Tahlia."

Everyone in the room starts to cheer and whistle, and I hold out my hand and show it to all my friends and the phones that are recording.

"Okay, okay, okay," Ryanne says. "Dinner's ready, so now that Cal's got that out of the way, let's eat."

Everyone starts to queue up to do that, and I fall back to Don's side. He reaches out and squeezes my hand, and the German Shepherds nod over to me like they don't care at all. I know they do, though, and that they helped Emma, Aaron, and Cal set up all these flowers.

As my friends get their food and head outside to eat it, Cal thanks them for their help and says we'll be right out.

When we're almost alone, he smiles at me. "I think you've made me the happiest man in the world."

I beam up at him and say, "Ditto."

CHAPTER TWENTY-NINE

CAL
SEVEN MONTHS LATER:

I NEVER THOUGHT SEVEN MONTHS COULD CHANGE A man so completely. But when I look back, I barely recognize the person I was the day I brought Tally back to Notavella after our amazing Christmas celebration at the Big House.

That Cal Irwin still thought he could compartmentalize his life—South Carolina in one box, Notavella in another, himself somewhere in between. That Cal thought he could be the perfect Special Envoy, the obedient second son, and somehow tuck away the wild, vibrant woman who wears Care Bears and cartoon dinosaurs on her shirts.

He was a fool.

Now, standing in front of a mirror framed in carved gold, my collar starched within an inch of its life, I know better.

Seven months have taught me what matters.

Christmas at the Big House taught me what it feels like to be surrounded by laughter, babies being passed around like bread baskets, as Hillary went into labor a couple of weeks early and had been able to bring her little girl home two days before Christmas.

There had been sweet tea sloshing in Mason jars, more fried food than anyone should ever eat, and the rare appearance of Ajax singing Christmas carols—actually singing out loud.

That man will do anything to make Tally happy, just like me.

Founder's Day in Notavella taught me what it meant to see my people accept her—*our* people, I should say—when she waved from the castle balcony in a pale pink suit that so didn't meet my mother's requirements. But it came with a very Southern matching hat that resembled a bird's nest more than anything else, and it caused *weeks* of articles and news pieces from the fashion gossips.

The private jet flights taught me that nothing feels as surreal—or as right—as filling the cabin with her friends and watching them gape at crystal glassware and open baskets of snacks while she just shrugs and says, "Perks of marrying a prince."

And babies—dear owls and osprey, the babies.

Hillary and Liam's little girl arrived early, and they named her Holly. She has Hillary's red hair and Liam's nose, and everyone—including me—wrapped around her tiny pinky finger.

Claudia actually delayed our return to Notavella, because her and Beckett's pudgy baby boy nearly refused to come out. She'd finally been induced, and Stryker sure wasn't happy about being born.

I'm not sure why, because he has so many people who love him—and I do too. Tally's friends have incorporated me right into the Big House family, and I adore each of them too.

And let me tell you, watching Tally hold a baby, seeing her rock them while they both rest, observing her whisper words they don't understand in her Southern twang—I have never in my life wanted the future to come faster.

And now here I stand in the May sunshine, watching our guests get escorted into the gardens at the Royal Palace, where we're about to be married.

"Stop fidgeting, son," my father says from his chair in the corner. He's recovered more than any of us dared hope, and today he looks steady, his suit pressed, his smile proud. "The collar suits you."

I tug at it again. "It's choking me."

John chuckles beside me. "You say that like marriage itself isn't about to choke you."

"John," my mother warns. She sits like a queen ought, regal in a lavender gown with hundreds of gems embedded in the fabric, her fan tucked into her snowy white gloves. She looks serene, but her eyes sparkle. She's been waiting for this day too.

John only grins. "Don't worry, brother. You're marrying the one woman in the world who can keep you humble."

I roll my eyes, because I'm not the one who needs to be reminded that he's literally not the king of the world. John might be the future king of Notavella, but he has this attitude that he rules all.

I suppose I can't blame him. He's literally been raised to think this way.

The patio door opens, and Don enters. "It's time,

everyone." His dark hair is combed precisely right, and he wears the traditional midnight black suit. I'm dressed in a tuxedo this afternoon, and I try not to think about the half-dozen cameras that Mother approved to broadcast this wedding to the world.

The sunlight coming in through the floor-to-ceiling windows dims as more security guards in dark suits arrive, and everyone is separated.

My parents will walk down the aisle first, nice and slow to make sure the cameras can get every angle of my mother's dress, have a five-minute discussion on her hat, comment on the color of my dad's skin, and speculate about his health.

Once they take their places in the front row, John, Helena, and their children will go down the aisle. Hugs and kisses for my parents, and they'll take the seats on the other side of the aisle.

Mother has choreographed everything, right down to the fact that she'll hold Juney, my brother's youngest daughter, during the ceremony.

Now, she leaves through the doorway leading into the hallway while John goes outside with his detail. My father follows my mother, leaving me with Don.

"Is that what you're wearing?" I ask him, knowing full-well that he'll change the moment I leave with my guards.

"Yes, sir," he says anyway, because Don likes to follow the rules, and he doesn't want me to get in trouble with my mother. I've told him I can handle her, which is why Don is going to liven up this stuffy royal wedding.

My heart nearly falters at the fact that I'm going to see Tally in her dress soon. Honestly, the fact this wedding is still on is a miracle. Dealing with my mother and trying to have her own wedding has been difficult to say the least.

But Tally has taught junior high, and she's assured me and reassured me that she can deal with the Queen.

"So far, so good," I say as I blow out my breath.

"Sir," Carlo says, and I smile at Don and grab him in a hug.

"I'll see you out there."

"Yes, Your Majesty," he says.

I leave through the outside door and go with Carlo and Rain to my staging area. The grounds have been transformed into pure paradise. Blooming trees lean overhead, blossoms drifting down in strands of pink, purple, and green that makes me smile. Every bush bursts with white flowers, and the scent of roses and lilacs tangles in the air.

Rows of chairs gleam whitely beneath big tents with the flaps tied back expertly. The inside chairs have bright pink bows tied around them, and lanterns positioned near the back legs with pumpkin orange blooms on the handles.

Pink and orange—classic Tally. The only thing she didn't get in this wedding that she wanted was glitter.

Maybe.

The crowd holds every dignitary and noble in the country, plus too many men in black suits loitering along the fringes.

None of Tally's friends are in the audience yet, because they'll walk down the aisle after John and his family. I can't wait to see what they'll be wearing today— mostly her female friends. They'll be decked out in their best, I know, because she has two friends who are engaged closely in fashion, but it's the hats I can't wait to see.

We don't wear hats like that in Notavella, but every single one of Tally's friends will be sporting a hat—and the bigger the better, it seems.

A quartet plays softly near the hedge, and the music floats through the garden, seemingly landing on the leaves and petals. Flowers drip from the corners of every flap, from the poles, and an entire wall of fuchsia petunias stands behind the altar.

"I sure hope the cameras can handle that," I say with a smile

I stand in place and watch as my mother approaches the aisle from the right and my father from the left. They meet at the end of the aisle, and they hold there while everyone gets to their feet and faces them.

Heads bow to them, and my heart fills with love over and over again. They have been very, very good parents, and I know not everyone has such a thing in their lives. Tally doesn't—neither her father nor her mother are here today, and while she acts like it doesn't bother her, I know it does.

It doesn't matter, I think. She has me now, and she'll never have to feel abandoned and alone again.

My parents move slowly down the aisle, nodding and smiling to those around them. John and Helena follow, precisely according to the script.

"It's your turn, sir," Carlo says, and I move out from behind the flap of my holding area, and I feel myself slipping into my Prince-skin. I know how to smile for the cameras. I know how to shake hands with the right people. I know how to put a light in my eyes, so that every person I look at feels special.

I stand at the end of the aisle, and I wait, just as choreographed. Then I make the longest walk of my life, which is down the aisle and past thirty-two rows of chairs to an altar where I have to stand by myself for the next several minutes.

The officiant, a kindly old pastor who has prayed over Irwins for decades, greets me, and I shake his hand and lean in close. "Thank you, Pastor Genobli. I hope you're well."

He grins at me and nods. "I am, thank you, Your Majesty."

That'll look great on the video, and I take my place beside him, my pulse thundering in my ears.

Tally will show up. She will. She hasn't run away yet, and there have been plenty of opportunities.

I glance at Mother, who does have Juney on her lap, and then I focus down the aisle again. I have one camera on me that won't move, and I don't want to appear nervous or looking for approval.

The procession begins with Hillary, Liam, and Holly, with Hillary wearing a slinky, pretty pink dress with thick straps that go over her shoulders and have a scooping neckline that almost shows too much cleavage.

At the same time, she's completely covered, and she walks with her arm linked through Liam's, who carries their baby, who's wearing a dress the same color as Hillary's.

Her hat sits perched on the right side of her head, and it's a soft beige instead of a matching pink. Tally's color of pumpkin is woven through the hat with roses, and it looks like sprigs of wheat flying out to the side from behind them.

I love it, and I grin at the three of them as they come down the aisle. Liam is wearing a dark brown suit, with the same wheaty things behind an orange flower pinned to his chest. I barely have time to hug them and say, "You guys look great," before Claudia and Beckett are making their way toward me.

Claudia knows how to work a runway, and she knows how to dress herself so she always looks like a million bucks. Today, she's wearing a pink gown that sticks to her curves from shoulder to knee, where it then billows out in what Tally has told me is a mermaid skirt.

Her sleeves are puffy and bulging up and out from her shoulders, and she too walks with her arm in Beckett's while he carries Stryker. He also wears the same brown suit as Liam, with the same flower, but he's got greenery behind his.

Because Claudia is wearing a hat made of sticks, leaves, and beige flowers, and she too has an accent of orange in a ribbon.

I can't stop smiling, and I hug them both and look toward Ryanne and Elliott as they move to the side to take their seats.

Ry holds Corduroy in her arms, and Elliott has his left arm laced through hers while he holds Luna's leash with his right hand.

She's wearing a long, flowing dress in the same pink as the other ladies, and her sleeves billow like clouds getting whisked at by the wind. Luna also wears a pink dress, and she looks absolutely thrilled to be walking down the aisle.

Ryanne's smiling, and she brushes her son's hand away from her hat. It's a wide-brimmed thing that almost looks like a beach hat. She wears it tilted back and pinned on the left side of her head, with teeny flowers peeking through enough to see the wedding color.

The same wheat-like things that Hillary had on her hat spiral out from the center of the hat, and they wobble and bounce with every step she takes.

She pauses at the end of the first row, where Mother sits, and she nods to her, the way the others have done. Mother essentially gives her permission to keep going, and they come up and hug me.

Emma and Aaron come next, and I gasp right out loud. Emma's dress is made entirely of flowers—pink tulips and roses. I don't see a stitch of fabric anywhere, and she moves a bit slower than the other ladies.

Aaron beams sunshine and joy into the world as he stays at her side, and he's got the same dark brown suit, but his flower is pink instead of orange. In fact, neither of them sports any orange, and I wonder how that passed Tally's requirements.

Emma's hat is actually a crown of flowers done in alternating cream and pink, and my mother smiles at her and says something that makes Emma brighten. She nods, and then they continue toward me too.

"Wow," I say, because I can't come up with much more than that.

Lizzie and Matt start down the aisle, and I'm getting so close to Tally's appearance. Lizzie wears a dress that looks like it's made with hundreds of different pieces of pink fabric, each one glued to her body in a specific way.

They're different shades of pink, and she looks like pink sunshine glittering on water as she moves. Her hat is a fabric beehive-type of thing, with a few small orange blossoms poking out, almost representing bees.

They get my mother's approval, a hug from me, and move to take their place as the last pair on the front row to my right.

When Titan, Ajax, and Don step to the top of the aisle, the crowd audibly gasps—and then laughs. I join my voice to them, because Tally is going to *lose her mind*—and so is my mother.

I'm fairly sure Titan has never seen this color of pink, let alone draped his whole body in it. In fact, I've never seen pink pants like that on a man.

He wears the pants, a vest, and a suit coat in pink-so-pink-it-makes-my-eyes-see-spots, with a cream-colored tie and his usual black, shiny shoes.

He does not smile as he looks left and right and then directly at me. He waits for Ajax to join him, and that only causes another round of laughter to move through the crowd and fill the tent, mine included.

For Ajax is wearing a cream-colored suit with a bright orange vest, tie, and pocket square—and shoes. Surely he didn't buy those, and I suspect Tally altered them for him. Maybe Claudia, as she seems to know colors forward and backward, and his nearly-neon orange shoes match his tie and vest almost too perfectly.

They turn and look over their shoulders, then take a step apart at precisely the same time, which means they practiced that.

Don struts in between them, and he's wearing an orange so bright he could be mistaken for a walking traffic cone. He's wearing a black tie and shoes, but everything else is a bright pumpkin, pumpkin, pumpkin.

My mother, weeks ago, bestowed them with titles. *The Knights of the Shepherd.* Official guardians of the royal family. Today, they bow with absurd solemnity as they stride down the aisle, their brightly colored suits catching the sunlight and nearly blinding me.

I laugh as they stop at my mother's side. She blinks at them like she can't believe her eyes, which she probably can't.

Then she looks at me, almost asking my permission to allow my German Shepherds to dress like this. I cock my head to the side and bow to them, these amazing men who have given up so much to go to the States with me and help me make my dreams come true.

Mother finally waves them on, and I move away from the altar to greet them. "You guys are awesome. Tally is going to *love* you."

"I feel like a fool," Ajax growls, but Don grins from ear to ear, with Titan's mood somewhere in between.

The music shifts, and I quickly return to my spot at the altar and look down the aisle while my brightly colored detail lines up behind me. The breath rushes from my lungs, and I have to mentally command myself to breathe in again.

I tell myself not to fidget. The cameras are on. She's coming; she's just not here yet.

Yet.

Or yet.

I throw a glance toward Mother, and realize that Dad isn't with her anymore. Relief fills me, as I've forgotten that Tahlia asked him to walk her down the aisle.

Dad finally appears at the top of the aisle, and he has great color today and wears an amazing smile. Murmurs move through the crowd, and I sense movement happening behind that last row.

It has to be Tally, and then, there she is.

Her golden hair is twirled and pinned back, and she moves right into my father and sweeps her lips along both of his cheeks. He offers her his arm, and Tally links hers through it, and the pair of them turn to face me.

Tally's eyes meet mine, and her shoulders lift slightly as she takes a deep breath.

Then she takes that first step toward me. It's the best thing she's done to-date, and I can't wait to be this woman's husband.

Her gown is blush silk, flowing like pale pink cotton candy floating on a breeze, the lace catching the sunlight. Her veil trails long, dusted with tiny pearls that wink like stars. Her eyes—oh, her eyes. Wide, gorgeously blue, shining straight at me as if the rest of the world has ceased to exist.

Dad guides her down the aisle with dignity, and I love how much he loves her. They stop at the queen, and Mother gets to her feet and takes Tally into a hug. She kisses both of her cheeks too, and then she seems to give her a little push toward me.

When at last she reaches me, Dad bows slightly to me

and places her hand in mine. "Here you are, you two," he says.

"Thanks, Dad," I murmur to him. He only nods, and retreats, and I can't see anyone but Tally.

"Hi," she whispers.

I lean down and press my lips to her forehead. "Hi, yourself."

The pastor clears his throat and leans toward the microphone. "Though we stand in a place of history and tradition, what matters most today is not the grandeur of this garden or the legacy of this castle. It is the love between Callan and Tahlia, which has proven itself across oceans and seasons, in ordinary days and extraordinary ones.

"Marriage is built on such love—daily choices to forgive, to encourage, to share both laughter and sorrow. Today, before family, friends, the Queen and King, and the Almighty, they pledge to continue choosing one another."

He nods to Tahlia and moves the microphone a touch closer to her, dropping it down so it's closer to her mouth.

She turns to me, and I hold both of her hands as she starts to speak. "Cal Irwin, you've always been the one to turn my life upside down. You know exactly how to take care of me, and you always have."

Her voice breaks, and I squeeze her hands.

"You're my safe place, and I love that I can be exactly who I am with you, and it's who you want. I promise to try to enjoy the water the way you do, to taste-test every cinnamon roll, and to stand at your side through good times and bad. I love you as a prince, a man, my best friend, and simply for being Cal Irwin."

Tears blur my vision, and a slip of horror moves through me. I've been taught my whole life not to show much emotion, and then I push those thoughts away. This is my wedding day, and I can cry if I want to.

Fine, a slow weep. No one can blame me for a slow weep.

I take a breath, hoping my memory won't fail me now. "Tally, you've done what no duty, no title, and no kingdom could ever do. You made me whole. I love your rainbow sweaters, your glitter shoes, your ridiculous dinosaur tank tops. I love the way you make my mother laugh, the way you win over diplomats with sweet tea, the way you believe in me when I falter. I promise to never hide behind my title, to never let you stand alone in a crowd, and to love you with everything I have, for every day we're given. You are my queen. My heart. My forever."

The pastor's voice rings out: "By the authority vested in me, I now pronounce you husband and wife. You may kiss your bride."

I don't wait. I kiss her with everything in me, and the gardens explode—cheers, applause, and the glitter cannons I've authorized Don, Titan, and Ajax to use. The crowd screams, and Tally jumps back as well.

Rainbow glitter rains down on us and at least the first three rows of guests. I laugh at the horrified look on my mother's face, and I've never been happier to be a second son than in this moment.

Tally lifts both hands up, trying to catch the glitter, and when she meets my eyes, it's with pure love and joy in her expression. "You're in so much trouble," she says, giggling.

"Just don't look at her," I say, chuckling with her. "You wanted glitter, and I made sure you got it."

Tally laughs against my lips, then whispers the words that undo me completely. "I love you."

I press my forehead to hers, my heart splitting wide with joy. "I love you too."

———

Mm, yes, I'd like a prince like Cal to show up and rent my house! I hope you liked him and Tahlia - who FINALLY got her happily-ever-after!

Read on for a couple of sneak peak chapters at your new favorite book - The Relationtrip! Friends who travel together, Sloane and Logan, have a LOT going on when they arrive in Belize for their 5th annual Midwinter Trip... including that Logan has had feelings for her for years, and that there's only one room available...

You can get this book on any retailer with this QR code:

Get new free stuff every month, access to live events, special members-only deals, and more when you join the Feel-Good Fiction newsletter. You'll get instant access to the Member's Only area on my new site, where all the goodies are located, so join by scanning the QR code below.

MY MOM ONCE TOLD ME THAT TO MAKE A MARRIAGE
work, one had to compromise. "You don't get everything
you want," she'd said.

"Ooh, it has a pool," she says now, as she sits at my bar,
her plate of dinner long gone. I've washed all the dishes—
pots and pans too—and a certain level of exhaustion
invades my bones.

"What are you going to do with a pool in Pittsburgh?" I
hang up the dishtowel that hasn't seen this much action in
months and turn to face her.

She doesn't so much as glance up from my laptop. The
one I need to call my best friend and find out the situation
with our trip. He'd texted during my last showing, and my
mother ambushed me literally at my car as I'd said goodbye to my clients. If my SUV had been unlocked, she'd
have been lurking in the passenger seat.

Talking on the drive here. Me cooking something last-
minute. More talking. Her going on and on about how the
house she's shared with my father for the past twenty-five

years is too big now. It feels so empty, she'd said an hour ago. Wistfully.

Other times, she talks about Dad like he's the devil himself. I don't really blame her. I'd had no idea he wasn't happy in his marriage of thirty-three years. I've said very little about Dad since Mom took me to lunch and told me the news.

Some of the things she's said…

I can't go there right now, so I paste a tight smile on my face. "Does it have a gym?"

Mom's been looking at condos and fifty-five-plus communities, which I suppose I can't blame her for. I wouldn't want to do yard work and home improvement or maintenance—things she's literally never had to manage on her own.

"Hm." Mom's eyes glaze over, and I turn, open the fridge, slide my phone off the counter in seemingly one motion. I'm the oldest of three girls, and I'm very good friends with my mother. I don't entertain her nightly—usually—but we talk every day. Most days. I've always liked our close relationship, until this major bump in her life.

I feel thrown back in time five years, and I could say all the things she said to me then. I don't, because I know how harshly words can slice through a person's defenses. Sometimes those are as see-through as plastic wrap. Though it seems strong and can keep things fresh for longer, it can stick to itself, get twisted, and it's actually very, very easy to poke holes through when already stretched tight.

I know the plastic wrap Mom bears is the stretched-tight kind, so I mind my tongue. I have to get her out of here, and as guilty as that makes me feel, I do have other things to do tonight besides entertain her.

411, I send to Logan. The text flips to *read,* and the tension in my shoulders fades enough to make them finally go down.

"Never mind," Mom says. "It's over by Tree Line."

I turn back to her, Logan's response to me nowhere to be found. "What's over by Tree Lane?"

She doesn't answer, and I'm not sure how much more I can take. "Mom—" I start, a loud, shrill trilling cutting me off.

Praise the heavens.

"Oh." She jumps away from the computer, both hands flying up as if someone has a weapon pointed at her and she needs to show them she doesn't have one.

"That's Murph," I say, doing my best not to grab the computer and flee for my bedroom. "I do need to talk to him about our trip." To my own ears, I sound super sympathetic. My smile feels a bit too wide, but Mom slides from the barstool.

"I should go anyway." She sighs, as if leaving my house —which she's used some choice adjectives for in the past— is the worst possible outcome for her evening.

"Okay," I say. "It was so good to see you, Mom." I leave the call ringing, because a 411-distress call means I need Murph to call me, specifically on the computer, and if I don't answer, to call my cell only two minutes later.

I'm hoping I can kiss-kiss Mom good-bye and be headed to my bedroom by the time he rings my cell.

"Thanks for cooking," Mom says as she pauses at the front door to get her jacket. "The chicken was surprisingly juicy." Her compliments aren't always compliments, but I keep the smile hitched in place. It rides my face as she turns to me, steps into my embrace, and then leaves.

The moment the door closes, I feel like I've crossed the finish line of a marathon. I'd be one of those runners who put everything forth and then stumbles mere steps from that finish line. Tonight, I made it, and I spin back to the kitchen as my phone rings.

I'd managed to escape to my room for ten minutes to change my clothes and ditch my heels before making a gourmet feast for dinner—wherein the chicken *was* juicy and delicious, I'll have everyone know—so I'm able to jog back to the kitchen.

Jog is a generous term. Maybe a bouncy power walk. Whatever. I know when I swipe my phone from the countertop, it's about to go to voicemail and I shouldn't have attempted any sort of bouncing, power walking, or jogging.

"Murph," I say in a pant.

"There you are," he says, as if I've missed a meeting. "Let me guess. The Smithsonians demanded you show them yet another colonial, you haven't eaten since that gross pumpkin seed bar you have synced to a ten a.m. alarm on your phone, and you've just now made it back to your car."

I start grinning at the mention of my clients. Not so much that he heard me huffing and puffing. I tell myself it doesn't matter. He's my best friend, despite the fact that we only see each other once a year—on this upcoming midwinter tropical retreat.

I laugh, Logan Murphy's deeper chuckles mingling in

with mine. My heartbeat thrums in the vein in my neck, and I feel...happy. So, so happy, whenever I talk to Logan.

"First," I say. "I'll have you know I made dinner tonight. For my mother and I." I raise my eyebrows and turn toward the master suite. When I'd bought the house, it didn't have one. I worked with an interior designer, and now I have a fabulous master suite with a settee in my bay window, a walk-in closet any woman would die for, and more European glass than any single woman should ever own.

"Chicken or beef?" Murph asks, not even letting me get to my second point.

"Chicken." My feet meet the luxurious carpet in my bedroom, and I further relax.

"I bet it was so dry," he says.

"Totally," I deadpan. "Secondly, my clients' name is Smithson. Not Smithsonian." I can't erase the grin from my lips. Murph never gets names right. He gets close, but never dead-on. I grab my hamper of dirty clothes and continue when he doesn't reply. "Third, I still have to prep the paperwork for that closing tomorrow, I haven't started my laundry yet, and I have no idea where my passport is, so please tell me we don't need it."

He pulls in a breath. "You're gonna need it, Sloane."

I figured as much. "I'm starting my laundry. Start the story." We've been traveling together every winter for the past five years. This is our sixth trip together, all of them stemming from that fateful day I showed up at the airport for my honeymoon...alone.

"You're just now starting your laundry?"

"You said you'd keep it tropical." I heave the basket

into the laundry room, open the washing machine, and proceed to dump the entire contents of the hamper into the bowl. I don't sort. Who has time to sort their laundry? Not me.

"I did," he says.

"Then I only need swimming suits," I say. "I've got those laid out already."

"Of course you do." He sounds perfectly amused, which makes me smile.

"I still need other things," I say.

"No heels," he says. "No blouses. No skirts."

"Some of my cover-ups are skirts."

"I'll allow it." Murph knows how much I work, and how hard I put myself together. This trip is all about the opposite of that. I can fall apart. I can do nothing. I can relax and rest and reset for another year.

"So tell me where we're going. And what happened with the resort in the Keys?"

"It flooded," he says. "I went down far too many rabbit holes today, until I finally landed on...Belize!"

"Bless you." I drop the washing machine lid and start the cycle.

"It's great," he says, ignoring my tease. "Tropical rain forests with cenotes, the beach with all the snorkeling you love, and the resort is amazing. No cars. Only golf carts. Very quiet. Upscale."

I frown as I leave my laundry room. "Upscale? How much more is this than that place in Florida?"

"I mean, it's Belize," he says. "Not the US. So it's more. You said you could do more."

"I can." I re-enter my bedroom and head over to the

side of the bed where I don't sleep. If I didn't work fifteen-hour days, I might have a little white dog. Or a cat. Nope. A dog for sure.

Murph's barks in the background, and he makes me smile.

"It's not that much more," he says. "I called the airline and got our tickets switched. I booked the resort online. Apparently, Belize is pretty full in late January, thus the need for a more...less cheap place."

"Is it adults-only?" It's not that I don't like children. I do. In fact, since my thirty-first birthday last spring, I've really felt this urge to get back into the boxing ring. The dating boxing ring. It's like a match out there for me. But I should. Find someone to date, that is. Maybe someone to share my life with. Maybe we could have a couple of kids.

"Yes," Murph says, and I snap back to reality. A scoff works its way free from my throat.

I am never getting married. I don't want to do all the work it takes to find someone who can love me. It's too hard, and I don't think I have all the pieces of my heart back yet anyway.

Just when I think I do, my mom takes me to lunch and says my dad told her he's never really loved her. In thirty-three years.

How does someone live a lie for that long?

In truth, I was simultaneously sad for my mom, furious at my father, and relieved I'm not living in a *five*-year-old marriage that would've ended in the same way. Leon Burgiss didn't love me; that's why he didn't show up on our wedding day.

"It's all set," Murph says. "You like nice things, Sloany, and this is *nice*-nice."

"Thank you," I murmur as I take in my swimwear choices waiting on my bed. "Now, help me with the bathing suit options."

"Put me on video."

I tap to do that, and I aim the phone at the bed. "I've got the classic black one-piece, of course."

"Of course," Murph says, his smile in his voice.

I don't have the opportunity to wear a lot of swimming suits in Pittsburgh, so the fact that I have so many is kind of ridiculous. I reason that I only wear one pair of shoes at a time, but I own many pairs of those too. This is no different.

Plus, I was going to get a hot tub last year. I have the cement pad and everything. Then I realized how much more I needed to do—wiring for the plug, all the pH chemically stuff, and the fact that it snows in Pittsburgh for half the year, I swear.

"That bikini is hot," he says.

"It's not a bikini," I say. I have a fair amount of curves, and I prefer a tankini and some bottoms to the stringed type of swimwear.

"It's clearly two pieces," he argues. "The top is pink, and the bottoms are black."

"It's a sports bra and a pair of panties." The bra-top is cute, though. It has a subtle, cream-colored tropical leaf pattern running through the hot pink. The bottoms are almost shorts to contain my booty, with a thick waistband that makes me look sexy and feminine.

But not hot. I love my body, one-hundred percent, how

it is. I simply know how to make her feel and look good at the same time.

"Yeah." He clears his throat and hums in that way Murph has. I can't quite describe it, but he does it when he's thinking about something, when he's not sure what to say, and when he's trying to irritate me. I half-expect him to burst out laughing any second now, but he doesn't.

"There are nine," I say as I move the phone down the line without further comment from my best friend.

"Shocking." I flip the phone around and see his brilliant smile. "I'd expect you to have double digits when it comes to your beach clothes."

"Some of them are two pieces."

"Yeah." His thumb covers the camera, and then he disappears. A blip of disappointment cuts through me, but Murph hates doing video calls on his phone. He's already a little self-conscious about the size of his nose, and the close-up and angle of a phone camera doesn't help.

I don't know what he's talking about. He's rugged, with a square jaw and the perfect amount of scruff no matter what time of day it is. He's got eyes that sparkle like the Atlantic Ocean on a clear, gorgeous day, and just because I'm not dating and will never marry doesn't mean I don't know how devastatingly good-looking Murph is.

"I have at least three cover-ups too," I say as the call switches back to talking only. "Maybe four." I focus on the settee, where no less than half a dozen cover-ups lay, waiting for me to deem some of them Chosen Ones and take them to Belize with me.

I sink onto the bed. "Belize, huh?"

"I've never been," he says. "Dinner with your mom, huh?"

I try not to think about the hour's worth of paperwork that still needs to be done before I can actually go to sleep. "I'm closing my eyes," I whisper, a game Murph and I have played before. "Paint me a picture, Murph."

He starts to talk about what's happening in Superior, Wisconsin, where he lives. "The snowflakes fall down like angel kisses from heaven, lighting on the ship as it eases into the dock..."

Yes, I fall asleep to the deep, sexy, bass timbre of his voice, my head filled with dreams of my upcoming tropical vacation with my gorgeous-inside-and-out best friend.

SNEAK PEEK! THE RELATIONTRIP, CHAPTER TWO: SLOANE

I round the corner for the baggage claim in Atlanta, the first four or five carousels to my left, and the remaining ones to my right. I have no idea where my bag will be spit out, but I'm willing to bet Murph does.

I texted him the moment I got service, which admittedly was still a few feet above ground. I knew he'd be here already, as his flight had been scheduled to land an hour before mine. We still have four before our last leg to Belize too.

It's barely lunchtime, but my stomach growls. The biscoff on the plane is never enough. And what's with them only giving out the tiny cans of soda now? My mouth sticks together I'm so parched.

Someone moves, and there's Logan Murphy. All six feet, one inch of him. His blond hair needs a trim, as the ends curl slightly along the back of his neck. He's built like a swimmer, with those big shoulders that can make women's knees weak. Those narrow down his back to his waist, and he's wearing a pair of athletic shorts with his gray tee.

He runs some type of business from a home office in Wisconsin, and he has time to run with his dog every day, make homemade meals, and text me back seemingly at the drop of a hat. Everything about him makes me light up, and this time, instead of shrieking and sprinting toward him, I take another calm moment to drink him in.

Mm, yeah, he's good for a thirsty soul.

Surprised at my non-best-friend thoughts, I give myself a little shake. "You're not getting into the ring with Murph," I mutter. The very idea almost has me giggling. Number one, he's never indicated in the slightest that he's interested in me.

He's dated other women in the five years I've known him. A Lauren once, for a few months. Then someone named Christine. She was a complete disaster according to Murph.

He doesn't ask me about my love life. I don't ask him about his, but he does share if he has someone he's excited about.

Murph is the most genuine man I've ever met. If he's listening to someone, he's interested. If he texts me for my opinion, I know he wants it.

He turns, and the world narrows to only him. And in the Atlanta airport, that's something. Our eyes lock, and Murph's smile floods his face.

I can't help the little shriek as it flies up my throat, and I grab onto my backpack straps and hurry toward him. Not a jog—learned that lesson a couple of nights ago. Several feet from where he stands at carousel seven—with my bag —I break into a little dance.

He laughs, the sound happy enough and deep enough to fill my whole body with a thrum. I join him, pure joy filling me as I reach him, and he envelops me in his arms. "You made it."

"It was touch and go for a minute there," I say.

Murph holds me like a pro, and I don't want the moment to end. I'm suddenly trying to categorize the thrum in my system. Happy to be reunited with my best friend? The man who literally saved me from taking my honeymoon alone?

Or is this fluttering of wings in my veins built from attraction?

Can't be, I tell myself, but I'm not sure why it can't be. Logan Murphy is devastatingly gorgeous, a fact I note for the second time in as many days as he pulls away from me.

"The Atlanta police wouldn't care if the man in front of you was glinting light into your eyes for hours." His grin pulls very kissable lips back to show his perfectly straight, white teeth. He hasn't shaved in at least a week, and the beard is...hot.

I reach up and cradle his face in one hand. "I didn't throw the Coke can," I say, my own smile feeling fond on my face and in my heart. "Besides, it was a mini." I drop my hand, registering that Murph has gone completely still and silent.

He hums in the very next moment, jerks himself to attention, and pulls my bag forward. "I already got it. The line for the bathroom must've been long."

I take the bag, my eyes suddenly unable to meet his. They're dazzling and blue and glint the way pure sunshine does off open water. "Mm hm." I drop one shoulder out of my backpack strap and let the bag swing down to my suitcase. I unzip the top, reach inside, and look up at Murph through my eyelashes.

"And..." I yank out the box of candy I had to stop and buy. "I got you these!"

His gaze flits over to the box before his laugh fills the baggage claim area again. I shake the box of Milk Duds, as if he can't get them in Wisconsin.

Murph takes them from me, his eyes latching onto mine again. This time, I don't look away. "Thank you, Sloany." He hugs me again, the boxy edges of the candy pressing into my back. He takes a breath like he might say something, but then he doesn't.

He does his hum and steps back. "Should we go get over to the international terminal? Get some lunch over there?"

I nod, my voice lodged somewhere deep in my throat. I'm not even sure why. Something churns between us, but I honestly have no idea what. I turn and take the first step, Murph falling in beside me, and then the tension flees. Just like that. Gone.

Maybe there's nothing there. Maybe it's just because our relationship is usually through chats, texts, phone calls, and random GIFs. Now we're in the same living, breathing space together, and maybe it'll just take a few minutes to normalize.

"Did you meet your deadline?" I ask as I step outside.

A blast of icy wind hits me square in the face. "Wow. Who knew it would be so cold in Atlanta?"

"They're having a storm right now," he says. "International terminal shuttle, over here." His long legs eat up way more distance per step than mine do, but I keep up with him just fine. We join the line to get on, and with more people gathered together, it seems less chilly. "Met the deadline. Emailed everything in last night."

Murph grins at me, and I smile on back. "That's fantastic, Murph."

"You?" he asked. "Closing went through okay yesterday?"

"Done," I say proudly. "My third house this month."

"They're gonna put your picture on a plaque again," he teases.

I smile and shake my head. I did win a recognition award from my real estate agency last year, but it's a big place, and they won't pick me again for a while.

We get herded onto the shuttle like cattle, get bussed over where we need to go, and go through the whole process of checking in, tagging bags, and going through security again. A big German shepherd works the line, with a stern-looking cop, and I nudge Murph.

"Would Titan be able to do that?"

"Well, he is the best specimen of a dog my vet has ever seen." Murph grins and adds, "I sent you that site with all the excursion options. Did you get it?"

"Yeah," I say, holding up my phone. "As I landed."

"We can look over lunch," he says.

"Or the flight there."

He scoffs, those baby blues dancing a jig. "Right. Please. You'll fall asleep in five seconds on the flight."

"I will not." I hold my head up high as the security officer checks my passport. The machine beeps and I leave Murph to pass the test too.

Once we're all re-shod and re-packed, he says, "Burgers and fries?"

"I've been counting on it." I link my arm through his, and he presses his elbow to his side, cutting a look down at me. I keep my eyes down the wide halls of the airport. "I love this trip we take."

"Me too," he murmurs, and because he never says anything that isn't true, I believe him.

———

"YOU CAN HAVE THE WINDOW." Murph steps past our row to let me in first.

I duck under the overhead storage, drop my pack, and shimmy my way past the armrests. "You'll have to sit in the middle," I say needlessly. If he'll let me, of course I'm going to take the window. Then I only have to press my body up against his instead of his *and* a stranger's.

"It's fine." Murph eases into his seat with the grace of a ballerina, and I fumble around for a good several minutes, getting out my headphones, making sure I have lip stuff and my water nearby, getting my seatbelt buckled, and everything else I need for the next few hours.

Every cell in my body alights where it touches his, and I wonder if he's as acutely aware of how glued together we are.

We finally take off, and I lean my head back against the rest. A sigh moves through my body, and my cells finally stop vibrating. So it's taken five hours for the tension and attraction to seep out of me. It's fine.

It's *Murph.*

He lifts the armrest between us and murmurs, "Okay?"

"Mm, yeah," I whisper. I have my earbuds in, and music playing, and he's right. I'm going to take a much-needed nap on the flight to Belize.

I lean into his shoulder, and he lifts his arm around me. I've cuddled with him plenty of times—on our first trip together, when we were strangers, we shared a bed in a honeymoon suite.

He's my best friend. He knows me; I know him.

"Mm," I say again. "You smell great."

He does. Like leather and spiced apple cider hooked up and had a bottle of deliciously-scented cologne. I take another big breath of it and settle further, a keen sense of finally being relaxed overcoming me. I drift in and out, and at one point, Murph asks me something I don't answer.

I'm pretty sure he presses his lips to my temple and whispers something my ears hold onto and don't let into my brain to make sense of. It doesn't matter. It's Murph, and he'll tell me later.

———

Will he, though? Find out in **THE RELATIONTRIP**, a standalone, friends-to-more, vacation with one bed, romcom in Belize!

You can **get this book on any retailer with this QR code:**

Or in a **GORGEOUS** special edition here:

Just His Secretary, Book 1: She's just his secretary...until he needs someone on his arm to convince his mother that he can take over the family business. Then Callie becomes Dawson's girlfriend—but just in his text messages...but maybe she'll start to worm her way into his shriveled heart too.

Just His Boss, Book 2: She's just his boss, especially since Tara just barely hired Alec. But when things heat up in the kitchen, Tara will have to decide where Alec is needed more —on her arm or behind the stove.

Just His Assistant, Book 3: She's just his assistant, which is exactly how this Southern belle wants it. No spotlight. Not anymore. But as she struggles to learn her new role in his office—especially because Lance is the surliest boss imaginable—Jessie might just

have to open her heart to show him everyone has a past they're running from.

Just His Partner, Book 4: She's just his partner, because she's seen the number of women he parades through his life. No amount of charm and good looks is worth being played...until Sabra witnesses Jason take the blame for someone else at the law office where they both work.

———

Just His Barista, Book 5: She's just his barista...until she buys into Legacy Brew as a co-owner. Then she's Coy's business partner *and* the source of his five-year-long crush. But after they share a kiss one night, Macie's seriously considering mixing business and pleasure.

———

Bonus for newsletter subscribers! Just His Neighbor, Prequel: She's just his neighbor...until his dog—oops, his brother's dog—adopts her.

Get this book by joining my newsletter here: https://readerlinks. com/l/3887964 **or scan the QR code on the next page.**

A Very Merry Mess, Book 3: *Sometimes the holidays are messy...*

Christmas is the season of joy, mistletoe, and, unfortunately for Ryanne, the pressure of bringing home a date. When she vents to Elliott, her best friend and co-manager at the small-town office supply store, he impulsively grabs her phone and texts her mother that they're dating.

Date. Ing.

A Very Disastrous Dare, Book 4: *Sometimes a person speaks before thinking...*

She's just bought the flower shop and he's taken over the hardware store for his dad. Sounds peachy, right? Sure, until they both want an assistance grant from the city...and now Emma and Aaron are rivals *and* neighbors.

A Very Friendly Fiasco, Book 5: *Sometimes the friend zone is breached...*

Sometimes the friend zone is breached...

He's her office crush, and she's the colleague he can't stop thinking about. But with HR's no-fraternization policy breathing down their necks, Lizzie and Matt have to get creative if they want to explore what's brewing between them—starting with a "fake-friend" date to a concert in the park.

A Very Royal Roommate, Book 6: Sometimes a crown changes everything...

When her childhood best friend (and boyfriend...) shows up to rent the second and third floors of the Big House, she has no idea he's actually a prince—or that their former falling out is about to turn into something far more complicated than a simple roommate situation.

Elana Johnson is a USA Today bestselling and Kindle All-Star author of dozens of clean and wholesome contemporary romance novels. She lives in Utah, where she mothers two fur babies, works with her husband full-time, and eats a lot of veggies while writing. Find her on her website at feelgoodfictionbooks.com.